FOUND BECAUSE OF THE MOON

WOLF RIVER BOOK

BOOK SEVEN

REBEKAH R. GANIERE

ISBN: 978-1-63300-094-0
ISBN: 978-1-63300-095-7

Cover art by VWZDesigns.com

DEDICATION

For Angel.
Thank you for constantly teaching me to be proud of who I am, no matter what!
I love you!

NEWSLETTER

To claim your Two FREE Books and find out more about
Rebekah R. Ganiere and her other Upcoming Releases
You can Go Here:
www.RebekahGaniere.com/Newsletter

CHAPTER ONE

Wolfe clenched his gut as the booted kick struck his ribs like an elephant's blow. The crack echoed through his body, making him grunt. The crowd's roar deadened the pain and kept him focused on his goal- Winning.

Wolfe caught his opponent's leg as he kicked again, pulling him in and punching him in the face twice. The man's nose burst, and blood poured down his face. He yowled as Wolfe dropped his leg and went in for the final attack. Wolfe grabbed his weakened opponent by the back of the head and pulled him upright before slamming the man's face into his knee.

The man dropped to the mats in a heap, blood leaking from his nose and mouth.

His wolf howled at the prospect of the victory.

Wolfe threw his arms up, sucking in shallow breaths that burned his throat and made his broken ribs scrape against each other. All around him, people grabbed the chain link, cheering and yelling his name. His eyes lifted to the balcony above and landed on a slick man in a bright blue five-thousand-dollar suit. The man twisted the ring around his pinky finger and nodded once to Wolfe before leaning over to the Hispanic man next to him and taking a thick envelope of cash.

Wolfe turned in a circle and pressed on his bruised and bloodied nose, trying to staunch the bleeding.

The padlock on the cage door clicked open, and Wolfe stalked to the exit. Two cleaners ran in and hefted the unconscious human, dragging him out by the arms. Wolfe trailed them down the small path to the back of the building. Hands slapped him on the back. A woman pulled him to her and kissed him without permission. Wolfe passed them all without so much as a glance. As he entered the lower hallway, the noise from the crowd died down, and he breathed in. Every muscle shook from fatigue, but there'd be no rest for him.

Fifteen years in the cage. Fifteen years forbidden to run- or go anywhere alone. Fifteen years, a slave to Uncle Mo's fight club. Every night, he thought about ending it, about taking a razor and finishing what hunters started when he was nine. But he couldn't.

He walked to the holding room, scarcely aware of his path. How many times before? Three thousand? Four?

He pushed open the door, hit by the scents of body odor and blood. Three fighters waited for their matches. Donny and Leo owed his uncle money, paying it off by fighting for six months; Zaden fought voluntarily. The cage paid well-but only for volunteers like Zaden, not those in debt to Mo.

"Let me guess," said Donny. "You won again?"

Wolfe nodded once and walked to the bench, where he dropped.

"Man, you are unstoppable," said Leo. "I'm glad I don't have to battle you."

Wolfe was glad, too. He hated fighting and couldn't imagine having to hurt someone he actually knew.

"Dude, that guy paid twenty grand to take you on," said Leo.

"I wish someone would pay ten grand to fight me," replied Donny. "I'd be out of here quicker."

A sharp knock on the door rapped on the door, and it swung inward. His uncle stood in the doorway, followed by the man sitting next to him during the fight, and a svelte blonde wearing too much makeup.

"Donny, Leo, you're next."

The two nodded and headed out, glad not to garner anymore of Mo's attention.

Mo's gaze turned to Zaden. "Give us a minute."

Zaden left without a word, but glanced over his shoulder at Wolfe as he disappeared around the corner.

Wolfe unwrapped his taped knuckles. Throwing the bloody mess on the floor.

"Wolfe. I want you to meet my friend Elias. His brother is the one you destroyed. He wanted to meet you in person."

Elias strode forward and offered his hand. "Hey, Bruh. I had to shake the hand of the man who handed my brother his balls. You can't imagine how it felt to watch that."

Wolfe nodded and shook the man's hand. His wolf sniffed the man. He didn't like meeting new people. Hell, his wolf didn't like a lot of things, not the least of which was being caged.

"Ha-ha. The silent stoic kind. I like that."

"Wolfe is mute. Someone murdered his parents and tried to kill him, too. Slit his throat. Severed his vocal cords."

Elias' gaze moved to the scar. "Damn, man. You're f-in lucking lucky that didn't kill you."

Lucky my ass.

"We should go check on your brother," said Mo.

Elias nodded. "Yeah. Better make sure the dickwad didn't bite it. Though I wouldn't mind if he did."

Mo clapped Elias on the shoulder. The men walked to the door, but the woman devoured Wolfe, as if he were the most delicious piece of cake she'd ever seen.

"Oh," Elias turned around and slapped the girl on the butt. "A thank you present."

The girl giggled and kissed Elias on the cheek.

Mo looked between the girl and Wolfe. "You did good, son."

The two men left, and the girl stuck her fingertip in her mouth and smiled at him. Though his prick kicked in his shorts, she was not what he wanted. The cutesy girls with high-pitched voices and a strange case of the giggles that sat with his uncle up in his box were not at all what turned Wolfe on. He'd rather screw the hardened women who cheered on from the pit than those little girl women, but since they appealed to his uncle, they were the only ones he ever got action from.

She sauntered over to him in her Barbie-doll heels and a red sparkly dress sized for a toddler. Something was off with him, though. Where he would have usually taken her to get out his excess pent-up energy, he didn't feel it. His wolf had been pacing all evening, and it had Wolfe on edge. His wolf had not been a part of his life in close to a decade, so when he did make an appearance, it made Wolfe anxious.

The woman ran her hand over his shoulder and down his pecs to his abs. "I've never seen anyone with so many muscles that wasn't in a magazine before."

She crouched until her eyes met his, then lowered to her knees. Her hand ran down the front of his shorts, and Wolfe didn't move. She leaned in and kissed his mouth down to his neck as her hands rubbed him.

"You sure are big." She giggled. "I'm not sure being with Elias will ever satisfy me again if I'm with you."

Wolfe gripped her wrist, stopping her hand. Her eyebrows furrowed, and she sat back. "Is something wrong?"

Something? Try everything. His life- or lack thereof. The fact that he'd almost killed a man. The idea that she was his prize for doing it. How did she not think there was anything wrong with that?

The door burst open, and Zaden stood in the doorway. He looked between them, his expression nervous.

"Uh... Is everything okay in here?"

Wolfe dropped her wrist and signed to Zaden. *"I'm not into it tonight."*

Zaden nodded and smiled at the girl. "Hey..."

"Saundy."

"Saundy. Wolfe is beat. He's wondering if you guys meet up a different night."

Disappointment and anger crossed her face. "Well, he doesn't have to do anything. I-"

"Get her out of here," Wolfe signed.

Zaden nodded, walked over to Saundy, and helped her to her feet. "So, the problem is, sweetie, Wolfe probably has some broken ribs, possibly a concussion. Concussions induce vomiting, and our champ here would be embarrassed if he chucked all over your beautiful dress."

She wrinkled her nose. "Oh... poor baby."

"Yeah, so. How about I talk to Mo about you coming by tomorrow and seeing Wolfe in a more... intimate setting?"

Her smile broadened. "Discreetly, of course. Elias wouldn't find out?"

"Not a peep around Elias. I promise." Zaden opened the door and escorted her into the hall. She peeked over his shoulder at Wolfe, who managed to give her a small wave.

"Okay," she said. "I'll wait for the call."

Zaden waved and shut the door in her face, locking it, and turned to Wolfe. "You okay?"

Wolfe nodded.

Zaden crossed to the bench opposite Wolfe and sat. Zaden weighed half as much as Wolfe did, but what he lacked in weight he made up for in dexterity. The man flew around the ring so fast his challengers barely figured out where he had moved to before being punched, or kicked, or both.

Zaden pulled out his phone. Then he looked at Wolfe. Fear wafted off him.

"What's wrong?" he signed.

Zaden glanced at the door, up at the clock on the wall, and over at Wolfe again. "I... I did something."

Did something? What kind of something? *"What?"*

Zaden's muscles bunched tight, and his phone rang once. He jumped up and ran to his locker, yanked out a duffel bag, and tossed it to Wolfe.

"Put those on. Now."

Wolfe peered at the bag.

"You have two minutes, man, come on."

Wolfe unzipped the bag. Inside were clothes. Real

clothes. A T-shirt, sweat pants, a hoodie, and shoes. He ran his fingers over the sneakers. He couldn't remember the last time he'd had shoes.

"Dude!" Zaden shook his shoulder. "You have ninety seconds."

"Ninety seconds to what?"

Zaden pulled another bag from his locker, reached inside, and handed something to Wolfe. "Smell this and put it in your pocket."

Wolfe lifted it to his face. It carried the aroma of woods, trees- evergreen trees and maple trees. Of spring leaves and dewy grass. The sensations made his wolf howl with longing.

"In sixty seconds, a group of my friends will barrel down the hall, and all hell is going to break loose."

"Why?"

"Because this is bullshit. You don't belong here. I've witnessed you rot away in here, and I'm done. You have thirty seconds. I'm going to set off the fire alarm. When it goes off, you and I will go through the service entrance, and you will run. Run east and keep running until you smell those woods."

Freedom. Zaden was offering him freedom. Was it a trick? He'd known Zaden for three years. It had been Zaden who had taught him ASL in secret. Never told Mo. Zaden had taught him to read again after so many years of absence from it. Zaden had told him about the outside world and everything that had been happening in the last fifteen years. If he trusted one person on earth, it was Zaden.

Wolfe dropped the bag to the floor and stripped naked before grabbing the clothes inside and throwing them on. Zaden pulled out a flare and cracked it, igniting red sparks as Wolfe shoved the shoes on his feet. An alarm went off on his phone, and Zaden stood on the bench and held the flare up to the fire alarm. Seconds ticked by, and suddenly a red light began to blink as sirens filled Wolfe's ears and water poured down on them. Zaden jumped from the bench, tossed the flare in the trash can, setting it ablaze, and then tugged Wolfe by the arm.

"Come on!"

Together they ran for the door. Zaden threw it open, and a group of people rushed by, yelling and banging on the walls. Zaden pulled Wolfe deep into the back tunnel. All around them, voices and shouts rang out. Zaden dragged Wolfe forward, around a bend, and down another corridor. They bumped into a huge cart, and metal trays went flying.

"Keep moving," Zaden yelled above the sirens.

Together they lumbered down the tunnel, through the flashing red light and blaring alarm, until a light flashed up ahead. They ran for it and burst through double doors. Food assaulted Wolfe's nose as he peered around the kitchen. His stomach growled, but he continued pushing past the cooks as they tried to leave the kitchen. He slipped on the slick floor, but

Zaden caught him and propelled through the crowd. Someone elbowed him in the ribs, and he groaned and clutched at them.

He continued through the throng, heading toward the exit. Shouting behind him caught his attention, and Mo's voice barked orders around the room.

He had to escape.

Wolfe elbowed through the crowd, not caring who or what fell. Freedom. He needed freedom. He shoved, rammed, and fought his way through the kitchen until, finally, he burst through the outside door, and fresh air filled his lungs. People ran into his back and swore at him as he froze. The sounds, lights, and odors bombarded him as he took in the city, unable to process everything. He'd seen it from his bedroom window for years. Breathing in the air through the small crack in the window. But being behind glass and seeing something from the thirty-second floor was altogether different from having it surround you and take you in.

"Wolfe!" Zaden ran to his side. "Come on, buddy. You have to go."

Zaden pulled him forward again. Wolfe's sneakers slapped the pavement of the expansive parking lot as they weaved in between cars toward the street. He looked over his shoulder at the enormous hotel with a dozen fire engines and police cars pulling up to the front.

Zaden rushed to the corner and out into the street.

Horns honked at them as they wove in between traffic. They ran for blocks and blocks until Wolfe pulled to a stop, his entire body screaming to rest.

"Come on," said Zaden. "We have to leave the city."

Wolfe sucked in several breaths and clutched his side. His mending ribs pained him.

The reality of where he was made his entire body shake. What had he done?

He'd seen what had happened to men who had tried to escape before. What would happen to him if he ran? He should go back. He should tell Mo he got scared and panicked. Maybe if he-

"No going back," said Zaden. "I've been planning this for a year."

Wolfe shook his head. A year?

"Some friends of mine own a town called Wolf River. It's for people like us. Werewolves. Blood Born and shifters, too. If you make it, you'll be safe. It's south of us. Only a couple of days if you hurry. My friend is expecting you. His name is Caleb Reed. You can move faster on your own. Promise me you won't come back. You won't look back. You will go to Wolf River, and you will make a life for yourself and forget about Mo and the fight club. Promise me." Zaden stared into Wolfe's eyes.

Us? Blood Born?

Zaden's eyes flashed, and his teeth lengthened.

A wolf. Zaden was a wolf. Had been a wolf the

entire time. How had he not sensed it? Not smelled it? Something? Would he have even recognized the signs? He hadn't been around wolves since he left his parents' house. Wolves. A pack. People like him. That's what Zaden was offering. A place where he wouldn't have to fight anymore.

Wolfe looked down the darkened street and breathed in the city. Cars, food, garbage, people, and... freedom.

Wolfe's gaze locked with Zaden's. *"I promise."*

CHAPTER TWO

Opal sat back in her chair and rubbed her eyes. The words from the screen swam around in her brain like alphabet soup as she tried to remember what she'd read. For as much as she wanted her degree, all of the reading was enough to have her brain explode.

She'd been home for almost nine months, and as much as she loved being in the cabin, she sometimes wished she were back inside the treatment facility. The stress of going to school had her wanting to reach for a Xanax.

She blew out a breath and pushed from the small desk, trying to distract herself from the cravings which still plagued her. She walked into the kitchen and took a soda from the fridge. She took several gulps of the overly sweet liquid and then walked to the window over the sink and gazed out at the trees surrounding her.

She breathed in through her nose and out through her mouth the way she had practiced a million times. A memory threatened to surface of the horrific night that had changed her life two years prior, but she refused to let it, instead taking another swig of her soda and humming her favorite song.

With Stix and Satia now having Andre and the bar, her parents had taken to staying in Wolf River during the week to help out. They came by on weekends for a bit, but for most of the week, they left Opal to herself. For as much as they'd worried about her in the beginning, both she and her therapist had assured them she needed time acclimating to being on her own.

Opal finished her soda and pulled a frozen meal from the freezer. She popped it into the microwave, and it spun around. In her nine months out of rehab, she'd planted a vegetable garden, helped her dad fix up the cabin, replanted all the flower beds, started her online degree in medical assisting, and read almost as many books as the Wolf River library owned. She'd finally taken to buying books online and donating them to the library when she finished, so everyone had a chance at something new.

Magnus barked, startling her. She peered out the kitchen window, but the front driveway and the surrounding yard were dark.

Her almost completely black German Shepherd mix barked again and stared toward the back hallway.

"You need to go out?"

Magnus trotted toward the laundry room.

"What's wrong?" Opal rounded the kitchen counter, headed into the laundry room, and peeked out the window.

Magnus growled, and the motion detector lights flashed on in the backyard. It wasn't unusual for deer, raccoons, and other animals to wander onto the property.

Magnus whined and pawed at the door.

"What is it, boy?"

A figure stumbled out of the darkness. Opal took a step back as Magnus went crazy. The hulking figure in a black hoodie and sweat pants staggered like a drunk man, head down, barely moving as he shuffled forward. He stopped in the middle of the yard and lifted his head, but Opal couldn't make out anything under his hood. His legs gave out, and he crashed to the ground.

Magnus continued to bark, jumping on the sliding door. Opal waited, unsure of what to do. Animals wandering onto the property were one thing, but a person? But she couldn't remember anyone accidentally stumbling onto their property before. She chewed her thumbnail, and her ursa paced agitated.

Minutes ticked by, and the man didn't move. What if he was hurt? Maybe he needed help? She should call her parents, but... No. She could handle this herself. The last thing she needed was them thinking she might be in danger and insisting on coming back to live with her.

Finally, she opened the door a little. Magnus tried to nudge his way out, but she held him back.

"Hey!" she yelled.

The man didn't twitch.

"Hey. Are you okay?"

Her heart pounded. And when the microwave beeped, she jumped, and Magnus nudged past her out the door.

"Magnus! No!"

The dog bounded out to where the man lay on the ground. He ran right up to the man, barking and jumping back and forth.

"Magnus, get in here," she commanded, but the dog wouldn't listen. "Damn dog."

She opened the door wider and shimmied out, looking back in the house, like all the stupid horror movie victims she yelled at through the TV screen.

"Magnus, if I get murdered, I hope you starve to death." She grabbed his collar. "Sit."

He fixated on the man, and she pulled him back, commanding him to sit again. Finally, he calmed enough to obey. She should call Stix, and have him deal with it. But... her parents...

She squared her shoulders. *No. I got this.*

Opal moved next to the man who lay face down in

the grass and prodded him with her foot. "Hey... Hey, get up."

He didn't move.

Damn, what if he was dead? That was all she needed. One more dead person on her conscience. Opal's ursa whined and sniffed the man. He was a shifter. A wolf from his earthy scent. Okay. So maybe he was from Wolf River and got lost. But... he'd come from the north not the south...

She walked around him and crouched by his head. Pulling back his hoodie, his bright red hair and the rust colored stubble growing on his chin struck her as out of place. Definitely not someone she'd seen before. His face had been badly beaten, but the wounds appeared to be at least a day old, as they'd begun to turn a yellowish green. A waxy sheen paled his face, and sweat poured off him like rainwater.

She reached over and touched his forehead, finding it unusually warm. His bright green eyes flew open, and he grabbed her wrist, pulling her toward him. His eyes softened for a fraction of a second as he took in her face. Magnus went crazy. He lunged forward, and the guy let go of her. Opal tried to back away but slipped on the dewy grass and fell on her butt. Magnus bit the man's pant leg.

The man's mouth opened in a scream, but nothing came out.

"Magnus, drop it!" She scrambled to the dog, dragged him to his dog run, locked him inside, and rushed back to the man who lay in a ball, cradling his calf.

"I'm so sorry," she said. "Are you okay?"

He rolled in agony but didn't utter a sound. She tried to pry his fingers off his leg.

"Let me look."

He clutched his leg, his face a mask of pain.

"Please," she said. "I have a little medical training. Let me see how bad it is."

Finally, she unlaced his fingers, and he fell back on the grass, pounding it with his fist as she rolled his leg over. The sweats had been ripped open, and so had his leg. Teeth marks punctured his skin.

Crap! Please don't let him sue.

"Okay, you probably don't need stitches, but it does need to be cleaned." She peered into his handsome face as he sucked in a breath and sniffed her. His golden tan skin highlighted his jade green eyes. He had high cheekbones and pouty, kissable lips. Her ursa chuffed.

He peered at her in pain mixed with something else... wonder perhaps?

"I... I have some supplies inside. Wait... wait here, I'll be right back, okay?"

He nodded, but said nothing, his glassy eyes following her. She stood, and he reached for her hand. She stopped. He looked like he wanted to say something, but then dropped her hand when Magnus started barking again.

“I promise I’ll be right back.”

Opal ran into the house and rummaged through the hall closet for some bandages and iodine. She gathered everything she might need and raced back outside. The man hadn't moved.

She knelt next to him. "I am so sorry for my dog. He thought you were going to hurt me. He was trying to protect me... and..."

Babbling. She was babbling. Great.

His eyes were already closing again. "You don't look so great." His head lolled to the side, and his eyes opened glassier than before. "What's your name?"

His eyelids fluttered as she dabbed the iodine on his bite wound. He growled deep in his chest.

"Are you from Wolf River? I've never seen you before."

He sniffed her again, and his brows furrowed.

"Yeah, I'm not a wolf. I'm Stix's sister, Opal. I'm an ursa."

He blinked, his eyes soft and his expression passive. His size was formidable. Larger than even Caleb or Stix. His face looked like it had seen too many hard days, but his eyes... his eyes remained... kind.

"Okaaayyyy..." She pressed a bandage to his leg. "Not such a talker, are ya?"

His eyes fluttered again, and this time they didn't reopen.

She finished taping the gauze down and gathered

her supplies. She stared at him for a moment, and a memory flashed.

Bodies on the ground. Battered and beaten. Blood pooling. Sirens in the distance.

She shut her eyes and drew in a breath, trying to ground herself in reality. The breeze blew across her skin, and Magnus barked behind her, drawing her back to the present. She peered down at the handsome man again. What was she supposed to do with him?

"So I can't let you sleep on my grass," she said. "And you look like you need a shower. Smell like it too."

Her ursa paced back and forth. What did she do? In the kitchen, the microwave beeped again.

She prodded the guy. "Hey. Hey, wake up."

He didn't.

"Dude. You can't sleep in the grass." She shook his chest. He appeared peaceful but unwell, lying there. Like a gentle giant. Not that he was a gentle giant, who knew what he was? But he hadn't tried to attack her, or hurt her, or... anything. He seemed scared more than anything and in need of protection. She scanned his face again, along with the healing bruises. Maybe he was in trouble... running from something... or someone.

She bit her thumbnail, and her gaze moved to the house.

She should not do what she was thinking about doing.

. . .

OPAL STARED AT THE MASSIVE, HOT MAN TAKING UP MOST OF Stix's old bed, now turned guest bed. She wiped her forehead and face with the edge of her sweatshirt. She'd had a hell of a time dragging him into the house. Luckily for her, she was as strong as a grizzly bear. Literally.

She had no idea how much he weighed, but it had been obvious when she tried to get him to his feet that he was a hundred percent muscle. His eyes hadn't opened on the trip into the house, but his legs had at least tried to work as he'd draped over her shoulder. The steps had been the tricky part, and more than once, she'd thought they'd topple backward and both end up in the grass, but somehow, she'd managed.

Now lying in the bed, running shoes with the soles completely worn down, sitting on the floor, and his hoodie off as well, it was more than apparent he was sick.

Her ursa breathed in and prodded Opal to move closer to get a better whiff of him.

He made a noise, and his head whipped from side to side. Once again, she thought about calling her brother. But if she did, Stix would get all protective and probably kick the guy out, and from the state he was in, that might actually be a death sentence for the guy. Besides... as much as she hated to admit it... the thought of having someone in the cabin who wasn't a member of her family, someone whom she could talk to without them knowing her history, appealed to her. Maybe, for once, she wouldn't get all the sad smiles and 'how are you doing, dear?' The Wolf River pack meant well, but some days she wished they would ignore her instead of asking how she was.

She inspected the man's calf again, where Magnus had bitten him. She hoped it didn't get infected. Not that it would. He was a wolf and should heal quickly. Plus, she did everything right to make sure it was disinfected.

The microwave beeped for the millionth time, and her stomach growled. Opal took one last look at the guy and then closed the door and headed into the kitchen, much to her ursa's irritation.

What was she doing? She asked herself as she put her lukewarm food on the counter. What if the guy was a serial killer? A mafia hitman? A drug dealer? She snorted and pulled a fork from the drawer. She had to stop reading so many murder mysteries and romances.

Fifteen minutes later, Opal threw out her tray and brought Magnus inside. He bolted in the door, sniffed every surface, and followed the scent trail to the guest bedroom. He sniffed the bottom and scratched the guest bedroom door.

"Magnus, enough!" She pulled him away, taking

him to the living room with her. She plopped onto the couch with her food and turned on the television.

Magnus curled up in his bed with a toy, but his gazed fixated on the guest room door.

"Leave it," she said again.

Magnus puffed out a breath and dropped his head, chewing his stuffed pig.

She flipped through the channels and landed on Hallmark. They were already playing Christmas movies. She shook her head. Halloween wasn't for another two weeks.

CHAPTER THREE

Opal spent the entire next day getting up hourly from her schoolwork to check in on her guest. By evening, she couldn't remember a thing she'd studied all day. Her ursa prodded and huffed at her to go check on the man so much that Opal wished for the first time in a long time that she wasn't a shifter. She wondered what it would be like without her other half in her head.

She sat in her grandmother's rocking chair, watching him for the millionth time. He hadn't awoken since the yard the night before, and his fever seemed to be worsening. Whatever was wrong with him should run its course within the next twenty-four hours. Shifters ran hotter and got over stuff quick- if they got sick at all. Even though he would pull through, she mopped his brow with a cool towel.

Earlier in the day, when he'd kicked the covers off, she'd spotted dried blood on his feet, but couldn't find any cuts. His face had healed except for a thick, lingering gash under his eye.

Her ursa sniffed him as if trying to figure out what was wrong, but neither of them was totally sure.

Despite telling herself not to hope for anything more than patching him up and him going on his way, Opal was drawn to him. His angular, handsome face sported several small scars, but the deep scar across his throat intrigued her most. Her fingers twitched with wanting to touch it. She couldn't fathom how someone survived a cut that significant. She wondered if the rest of his body held other scars, and was certain if he removed his shirt, he'd be riddled with them.

One thing was for sure- he wasn't from Wolf River. If he lived in town, he would have made it into Doc's office at least once or twice. He came from the north-west, possibly Washington or even Canada.

He groaned, and his head whipped back and forth.

She stood and placed the wet rag on his forehead once more, and he stopped moving.

Magnus trotted into the room holding his bowl in his mouth.

Shuzbut! She'd forgotten to feed him... and herself.

She pulled out her phone- eight thirty.

Shoot. She had to eat and go to bed. She had work in the morning.

Her gaze landed on Mr. Hotty McHotterson again. But what would she do with her guest while she worked? If she left him, would he be okay? What if he got worse? Or died? Or burglarized her? That was dumb. She had nothing of value for him to take besides her computer, and even that was a few years old.

Magnus' bowl hit the wooden floor. She rolled her eyes.

"Fine. I'm coming." She picked up the bowl and backed out of the room. She tugged the doorknob to close the door, and the man moaned and growled. He pushed the rag from his head and looked at it through glassy eyes. His head whipped from side to side, and he bolted upright.

Opal stayed in the doorway until his eyes lit on her. He peered at her as if trying to remember what happened.

"Hi," she said.

He didn't say anything.

"I'm Opal. You fell in my backyard, remember? Then my dog bit you."

He glanced at his leg and turned it to check the gauze.

"I bandaged you up and cleaned it to make sure it didn't get infected. It should be better by morning."

She shifted from foot to foot.

"Uh... so do you have a name?"

He pointed to his throat.

"Your scar? Your name is scar?"

He shook his head.

"Oh! You can't speak?"

He nodded.

"Do you sign?" she signed.

"Yes," he signed back.

She smiled. "My nephew is deaf. We've all been learning sign language to communicate with him."

"My friend Zaden taught me."

She nodded. "Cool. What's your name?"

"W-O-L-F-E."

Wolf? Strange name for a werewolf shifter.

"They called me Killer Wolfe, but Wolfe for short."

Her ursa paced. Who would call him Killer Wolf?

His jade green eyes focused on her, making her skin flush with heat.

“Are... Are you hungry?"

"Where am I?"

"You're in my cabin. Well, my parents' cabin, but they are living in Wolf River right now."

His eyes widened. *"Wolf River? I made it to Wolf River?"*

"Right now you are about ten miles north, but yeah. Were you going there?"

He nodded.

"You aren't from there, though, are you?"

He shook his head. *"What time is it?"*

"It's about eight thirty. You've been asleep for

almost twenty-four hours. Are you hungry? You want some water or something? Advil for your fever?"

He sat as if deciding something. *"Anything you want to give me is more than appreciated."*

"Okay. Well, uh, I think you should shower if you have the energy. To help with the fever. There are clean towels in there, and I'll get some of my brother's old clothes. They might be a little tight, but they'll work. I can wash your clothes for you if you'd like."

"You don't have to-"

"I don't mind."

They stared at each other for a long minute. "So I'm gonna make you some soup. Is chicken okay, or do you want something else? Tomato? Vegetable?"

"Chicken. Thank you."

She nodded and turned to go. He grunted, and she turned back.

"I... I can't pay you."

She chuckled. "I'm not helping you because I think you are going to pay me. I'm helping you because..." Why was she helping him? "Because people helped me when I was in trouble, and if it hadn't been for them, I wouldn't be here. You need help. I'm paying it forward."

He appraised her, then his eyes softened, and he smiled. She returned his smile and headed for the kitchen. She dropped Magnus' bowl and placed her shaking hands on the countertop. Her own scars criss-crossed up her wrists toward her elbows. Memories of the lowest moment in her life flooded back. If Stix hadn't found her... if Doc hadn't helped... if the clinic hadn't taken her... she wouldn't still be standing. Every day, she thanked heaven she still drew breath, and so did her ursa.

Wolfe walked to the bathroom, leaning on the wall. She went to the cupboard and pulled out two cans of chicken noodle soup, though he could probably eat six.

MINUTES AFTER OPAL HANDED HIM SOME CLOTHING, WOLFE stripped off his stained, stinky clothing and stepped under the spray, letting the water rain down on him. The droplets hit his sensitive skin like tiny needles. He let the water prickle his skin until it no longer hurt, trying to make his mind work.

What the hell had he done? He'd run and run, and kept running. Even when his body had wanted to give out. Even after the shakes had started and the fever had taken hold. He'd forced his body to keep moving. To stop was to be caught. To be caught meant death.

Most of his run was a complete blur. He'd let his nose and his wolf pull him east until a sign had welcomed him to Idaho, and then, he'd kept moving.

A vague memory surfaced of falling in Opal's yard, being bitten by her dog, and her helping him inside. Her gentle gray eyes stared at him from behind his lids. The curve of her hips underneath her long sweater. The twist of her lush lips as she spoke. His wolf howled and sniffed, wanting to be closer to her. He couldn't remember his wolf ever being as present in his life as he had been in the last week. By day two of his run, his wolf had been so awake that it left Wolfe uncomfortable and scared he might be hallucinating. Wolfe had hoped running for close to thirty-six hours would have calmed the beast. Instead, it had riled him up more than ever. His wolf wanted out. It was a strange sensation after so many years of his wolf's absence. He wanted to run, to jump, to howl at the moon. He wanted to be set free. And the closer they'd gotten to Wolf River, the more urgent his wolf had become. Even so, Wolfe hadn't let him out, not that he remembered how. The last thing he'd wanted was to make it there and be shot in wolf form because he'd been on someone else's land.

His legs shook as he stood, so finally he sat in the tub and let the water wash over him. He'd done it. He'd done it- escaped Mo. Relief slammed into him, so fierce it made his ribs squeeze, and he shuddered. But fear trailed close behind, shadowing his hope. Tears slid down his cheeks as he gazed at his bruised, battered body, each scar a mark of survival and torment. The mix of pain and freedom exploded inside him.

He was free. Finally, free.

Wolfe turned off the water and reached for a fluffy

blue towel which hung on the rod. He ran it over his muscles and winced as he got to his ribs. He prodded the yellowing bruises from where his last opponent had kicked him with the steel-tipped boots. It wasn't the worst thing he'd endured in the cage, but it wasn't normal either.

Wolfe stepped to the small vanity. Scars marred his body, but none more than his tally marks. If he were still with Mo, he'd have gotten two new ones already. But now... Those were the most he'd ever have. The thought made him smile. He picked up his dirty clothes and found a small hamper sitting next to the vanity. Instead of putting them inside, he bent over and tossed them into the trash can. As he did, he got a whiff of a beautiful scent. Tentatively, he reached into the hamper, pulling out a small Johnny Cash T-shirt. He held it up to his nose and inhaled. Opal's wild and musky scent filled his nostrils once again, driving his wolf crazy and making his body harden. She smelled of wildflowers and sunshine mixed with her natural musk. Again, her kind gray eyes filled his view. Surrounded by long, thick lashes and prominent high cheekbones, her heart-shaped face reminded him of a Disney princess. She was the girl he'd always hoped Mo would bring him. Kind and gentle, but with a backbone of steel, no nonsense air that told him she'd fight if needed. She was probably the strongest female he'd ever met. Hell, she's carried his dead weight to bed.

She knew about Wolf River and her parents and brother lived there, but she didn't smell like a wolf. At least, his wolf didn't think so. Not that they'd been around other shifters in years. He'd not even known Zaden was a shifter. Could he recognize the difference in the scents of shifters from humans? Was there a difference? There had to be because his wolf knew she was a shifter instantly. Then why hadn't he been able to tell Zaden was a shifter?

Okay, so if she wasn't a wolf, what was she? Honestly, he'd never thought to ask Mo if there were other kinds of shifters. His uncle never talked about being a shifter, and when he'd been younger, and he'd asked about it, Mo had told him to never ask again. But Zaden had said he was a Blood Born, not a shifter. What did that mean?

Wolfe inhaled the fabric once more, then tossed it back in the hamper. What was he thinking? She was kind enough to let him stay with her and feed and clothe him. He owed her his life. She didn't deserve to have a killer like him pawing all over her laundry, no matter how tantalizing it smelled.

He looked in the mirror. He would eat, then find Caleb Reed. Opal was sweet and beautiful, but she didn't need trouble like him invading her life.

WOLFE WALKED INTO THE KITCHEN TO FIND OPAL PUTTING two bowls of soup on the table. She smiled, and he took another step, but her dog appeared out of nowhere, barking between them. Wolfe held up his hands and backed up.

"Magnus, enough." She ran forward and gripped the animal by the collar. "I'm sorry. He's not used to company."

"Do you not have people over?"

She shook her head. "I don't have friends. Which is why I got him. I'm out here alone most of the time. He's decent enough company. When he listens." She glared at the dog for a moment. "Relax your posture, but stand still."

Wolfe did as instructed.

She led Magnus over, keeping a hand on his collar. She reached up and took Wolfe's rough hand in her soft one.

"Magnus, he's a friend." She turned Wolfe's hand palm up, and when she did, her sleeve pulled up, and Wolfe caught a glimpse of long dark scars traveling up her arm.

Whoa. Where had those come from? Wolfe tried to imagine where a female like Opal would get such nasty-looking wounds.

Wolfe held his hand still as Magnus sniffed it, but from the dog's posture, Wolfe sensed the dog's trepidation.

His eyes traveled back to Opal's scar. He wanted to ask her about it, but there were some things people didn't like to talk about.

"Okay," she finally said. "Magnus, bed." She pointed, but Magnus didn't move. "Magnus, go." The dog was efficient at protecting her, but obviously thought he was in charge. She tugged on the dog's collar and led him over to his bed. She handed him a treat and told him to stay. Then she turned back to Wolfe. "I made soup."

The fever blurred his vision slightly and made his head pound. The longer he stood, the worse it became. His body shook as he dropped into a seat at the table.

She reached across the table and touched his forehead. "You're still burning up. You should take some ibuprofen." She walked to the cupboard, pulled out a bottle, then walked back and handed it to him. "You don't think your fever is from an infection, do you? An internal injury or something?"

He shook his head. *"This feels more like the flu or something. Not that I've been sick before."*

He swallowed four pills dry and lifted a spoonful of soup to his lips. The moment the liquid hit his tongue, his hunger exploded, and he couldn't eat fast enough. When he finished the soup, he tipped the bowl to get every last drop.

Opal sipped her soup and smiled. A beautiful thing that lit up her face and crinkled her eyes.

"Well, that's from a can, so it wasn't delicious, which must mean you are starving. Let me make you some more."

"No. I can't impose."

"Please. It's a few cans of soup. That's hardly imposing. But I do think you should lie back down and rest after you eat. I have to work in the morning, but you are welcome to stay as long as you need."

"I need to go. I'm supposed to meet someone."

"Sure. I can give you a ride in tomorrow if you'd like."

He wanted to tell her how much her kindness meant to him. To tell her he appreciated everything she was doing. To thank her for putting herself in danger, she wasn't aware of. He was putting her in danger. His presence put her in danger. He should go.

Wolfe stood.

"Hey." She rushed to his side as his head spun and he leaned on the table. "Hey, where ya goin'?"

"I should go," he tried to sign as his knees threatened to give out and his gut turned. The soup, which tasted amazing moments before, swirled in his gut, and he heaved.

"Oh boy. Yeah, not in the kitchen." She dragged him to the bathroom.

Embarrassingly, he threw up the soup as he hit the toilet. His body lurched a second time. Could he do anything more embarrassing? Maybe he should crap his borrowed pants to complete his mortification.

His wolf whined and paced.

Wolfe hung his head over the toilet as Opal wet a rag and brought it over. She pressed it to the back of his neck, and a wash of relief flooded him at the sensation. He sat for several minutes trying to stay conscious.

"We should put you back in bed."

What he should do is leave and let her get on with her life. He doubted, though, he would make it out of her yard before collapsing again. One more night of rest would do him some good, and then he'd go and leave her be.

Wolfe pushed to his feet, and Opal draped his arm over her shoulder. It amazed him how such a small female could carry so much weight. He vaguely remembered her telling him what kind of shifter she was, but he couldn't remember what she'd said.

He shuffled down the hallway like an old man and dropped back onto the bed. It wasn't as expansive as the one he was used to, but the mattress was softer, and the sheets and blankets didn't carry the stench of bleach. Instead, they smelled like the rest of the cabin, like a home.

Wolfe closed his eyes only to be bombarded by memories he'd long forgotten about. Memories of a small room decorated in dinosaurs and spaceships. The aroma of chicken baking in the oven. His mother playing Christian rock music in the kitchen as she made dinner. Lying in his fort, shining his flashlight up at the ceiling.

"I'm going to bring you some soda and crackers and put them on your nightstand. Eat them if you can, but mostly I think you need to rest."

Wolfe opened his eyes as her voice pulled him back to the present. His ribcage squeezed. He didn't deserve Opal's kindness. He didn't deserve the concern creasing her brow. But in that moment, she was a godsend. Without them, he had no idea where he would be.

CHAPTER FOUR

Opal woke as her alarm blared at seven a.m. She turned it off and groaned. She doubted she'd gotten more than two hours sleep the entire night. Bears loved their sleep, and she especially loved hers. But instead of sleeping, she'd found herself tossing and turning and thinking about Wolfe in the guest room. Even her ursa had refused to sleep. Which sucked because she had a full day of work at Doc's, followed by more schoolwork.

She shuffled to the bathroom and turned on the shower- fighting her ursa's urges to check on Wolfe before stripping down and stepping under the spray.

Ten minutes later, Opal turned off the water and wrapped herself in a towel. A door creaked open, and

Magnus barked. She opened the bathroom door to find Wolfe weaving back and forth in the doorway.

"Whoa! Hold on." She raced to him.

He tried to sign something, but she couldn't understand his fumbling attempt.

"You're hotter. I should take your temperature."

She backed him into the room and onto the bed as her towel started to come undone. She grabbed it and tightened it around herself. A wet towel wasn't ideal for wrestling a hallucinating wolf.

Wolfe tried to sit up again, but she pushed him down. "Stay here. I'll be right back."

She strode to the hall closet and pulled out a thermometer. He was already sitting up again, and she growled.

"Wolfe." She dropped the thermometer on the bed next to him and pulled his face into her hands. She bent over him, praying her towel didn't slip again. "Wolfe. You are sick. You need to rest. I need to take your temperature. Let me help you."

He swayed and motioned to his throat.

"Yes, you can't talk.'

He shook his head and motioned again.

"Thirsty?"

On the nightstand, the crackers sat untouched, but the soda was empty.

He nodded.

"Okay. Put this in your mouth, and I'll grab you

water." She picked up the thermometer, turned it on, and stuck it under his tongue.

She hurried to the kitchen. She'd halfway filled a glass with cold water when the thermometer beeped.

Not good.

She marched back, sloshing water everywhere to find Wolfe still sitting in his spot. She handed him the water, and he gulped it down as she checked the temperature. 105.7. Not good.

Shifters ran hot, especially wolves, but 106 was hot even for them. She needed to lower his temperature. Quick.

"Okay, Wolfe... We need to lower your temperature, and I can't trust that if I put you in the shower alone, you won't fall and split your head open, and if I put you in the bath, I'm afraid you'll drown. So we are about to get to know each other better than either of us expected."

Nudity wasn't something shifter shied away from; even so, it had been a long, long, long time since Opal had either shifted in front of other people, or had... done other things. So, modesty would be best.

She walked to her bedroom and yanked on her one-piece swimsuit before heading back to the shower and turning it on cold.

This wouldn't be fun.

She hefted Wolfe out of bed and helped him with his clothes. She couldn't help the breath she sucked in upon seeing all the scars and small intentional marks that marred his skin. Dozens upon dozens of them. Like tiny tally marks spanning his torso from shoulder to shoulder. Hundreds, maybe more. On top of those dozens of other scars. All different shapes, sizes, and stages of healing. She blushed when he lifted her hands and turned them over to inspect her scars. Her gut twisted, and she pulled away. Hypocritical, but she couldn't stand to have anyone look at them. Even herself. He stood in his boxers, and she walked him to the shower.

The moment the icy spray hit his skin, he grunted and tried to step out.

"Nope. It sucks, but we need your temperature down because if I have to take you to the human hospital, you are going to hate me. So is every other shifter in Idaho. So please don't make me."

His eyes fixed on her with more clarity as he shivered and his teeth began to chatter.

She rubbed his arms, trying to soothe his discomfort. His hands rested on her hips as she began to shiver. This was not how she'd seen her morning going. Or any day. If anyone had told her a week ago, she would be standing under freezing water with a hot, mostly naked, wolf shifter, she never would have believed it. But here they were.

Minutes passed, and her fingertips moved over various marks on his skin. Too many to count. But they did nothing to mar the beauty of his chiseled muscles. He didn't pull away as she ran her fingertips over the raised slashes on his chest. She wondered what they counted but didn't have the courage to ask.

Her gaze met his, and they stared at each other for a long moment. Questions swirled inside her. Her bear chuffed and sniffed Wolfe, wanting more. Something about his beautiful eyes framed in thick dark lashes made her think he'd seen even more pain and loss than she had.

WOLFE STARED AT OPAL THROUGH A FEVERISH HAZE. HER beautiful brown hair, light tanned skin, and gray eyes made his heart race. Even as sick as he was, her beauty and kindness struck him like a lightning strike he didn't understand. Her eyes roamed his body, and she didn't turn in disgust at the sight of his scars. She touched his tally marks so softly he almost couldn't feel her skin on his. His wolf pawed to be let out. A strange sensation since his wolf had rarely made an appearance in his life since the death of his parents. He wasn't sure about his wolf being so present. It wavered between comforting and annoyance. It had been so long that Wolfe wouldn't remember how to shift if he wanted to.

He leaned forward and set his head on hers. The

scent of her eucalyptus and mint shampoo soothed him. Though thousands of icy shards pelted his back, standing so close to her made him forget about the discomfort. His legs wobbled, and she moved closer to him, pressing her soft, curvy body against his. The sensation sent a flood of desire pulsing through him, foreign and unexpected. He'd been with women before, but always had to picture someone else to make his body respond. Someone... strangely similar to Opal, he realized.

Again, his wolf howled, and his body hardened despite the cold water. He let go of her and spun away from her. His footing slipped, and she slid her arms around him from behind to keep him on his feet.

"Be careful," she said. "If we both go down in here, we might starve to death before anyone finds us to help."

He faced the frigid spray so she didn't see his burgeoning arousal. Her fingers danced over his back and up to his neck. Her hands were much stronger than he thought possible, kneading his shoulder muscles and then his neck muscles.

Wolfe laid his forehead on the wall and groaned. Her hands on his skin made his body wake further.

Get a grip, asshole. She's being nice so you don't die in her house, nothing more.

Wolfe let out a shuddered breath. Opal was exactly the kind of girl he'd always dreamed would be waiting for him in his hotel room after the fights. Not for a one-night stand. Not someone who paid Mo to be with him. Someone of his own. Someone who cared about him. Knew him. Wanted him. Not the fighter, but him. His very own mate. But like everything else in his life which might have made him happy, Mo had kept women like her away. Not that women like Opal ever would have come to one of his brutal fights.

"Do you have any idea what might have made you sick?" Opal asked, breaking the silence.

He shook his head, and goosebumps raised all over his back. At first, he'd thought it had been exhaustion from running so far, but he doubted that would cause his symptoms. It couldn't be the flu, given all the vitamins Mo forced him to take daily.

"Is it something you ate? Food poisoning? Or if you caught your own dinner while out running, an infected squirrel, deer, or something."

He shook his head. The only thing he'd eaten in the last three days was the soup she'd given him, and it hadn't stayed down.

Opal's hands slipped away, and she stepped out of the shower. She returned with the thermometer and handed it to him. He stuck it under his tongue. When it beeped a minute later, she took it.

"Okay. You're down to almost 103. Back to bed with more liquids and medicine."

She turned off the water. She picked up a faded towel and placed it around his shoulders. Then she helped him out of the tub and rubbed him down. Her hands traveled his body again, making his flesh pebble. Down on her knees in front of him, he got a perfect view straight down her swimsuit to the tops of her curvy breasts.

Really, Wolfe? What the hell is the matter with you?

Wolfe glanced away. How could he oogle Opal like that? She'd only been kind to him. Nicer than anyone had. Anyone who hadn't been paid, anyway. Not even Zaden had ever played nursemaid or rubbed Wolfe down with a towel. He chuckled at the thought despite himself.

For the first time in days, his mind turned to his friend. He prayed Zaden had gotten away from Mo. Some place far away. He would hate for his friend to be hurt because he'd helped Wolfe escape.

A bang on the front door pulled Wolfe's attention, and he growled. Magnus barked aggressively in the front room. Opal got to her feet and stepped toward the door, but Wolfe took her hand and shook his head.

Panic laced through Wolfe. He didn't want her to be hurt.

"It's okay," she said. "I'll be right back." She sat him down on the toilet seat and smiled.

Wolfe grabbed her again, and she turned. *"Don't answer it."*

"It's fine," she said. "Probably the old lady from down the road. She comes over to complain when she thinks Magnus has been in her garden."

He shook his head, and another forceful knock sounded.

Opal's brows drew together. She opened the hamper and pulled out the Johnny Cash T-shirt and a pair of sweats.

"Stay here," she said. "Believe it or not, I can handle myself."

CHAPTER FIVE

The heavy knock rattled Opal's front door again.

She walked into the front room where Magnus barked, tail standing straight up.

"Okay, Mag," she said. "Enough."

The dog quieted to a growl but didn't back away from the door.

She peered through the glass front, tension prickling beneath her skin, and spotted the back of a tan shirt and tan pair of chinos. *Peachy*.

Opal opened the door, and the human sheriff turned to her.

"Morning, Opal."

Opal nodded. "Sheriff. What can I do for you?"

"Checking if anyone's seen anything suspicious the past few days."

“Suspicious?”

“I got a few calls a couple of nights ago about a man running through people’s properties. A couple of your neighbors said they spotted him heading this way.”

Opal’s blood rushed to her toes. *Wolfe*. “Uh... nope, haven’t seen anyone.”

“Did you hear anything unusual? Magus barking at something at night?”

She shook her head, heartbeat quickening. “No. I’m a sound sleeper, though. Out of curiosity, if you got called a few days ago, why are you here now?”

He chewed his lip. “Mind if I look around? I’d feel better knowing you’re safe here if I gave the property a quick once-over.”

Opal swallowed hard, grateful the sheriff couldn't catch the way her pulse thundered or the odor of fear that clung to her.

"Sure. My parents and Stix would appreciate it."

The sheriff tipped his hat to Opal, and she shut the door. She waited until he walked off the porch and around the side of the house before rushing back to Wolfe.

He sat with his head on the counter. She hefted him to his feet and opened the door, looking out the front windows, ensuring the sheriff was nowhere in sight. She waited a moment before bolting to Wolfe's room.

He dropped onto the bed. *“Is everything okay?”*

She forced a smile. "Everything's fine. Rest. I'll fix some broth."

He stopped her. *"If you need to be somewhere, I don't want to keep you."*

She checked her watch. Late. "I'll go in soon."

He appeared like he might protest, but she stopped him and covered him with several quilts.

"Don't leave the room, okay? I'll try to find you some dry underwear."

He nodded.

Opal took a step and considered putting a chair under the door to keep him in. But that wouldn't be right. She didn't want to scare him.

She walked to her room, picked up her cellphone, and dialed Doc's office. The phone rang, and rang, and rang.

"This is Doc."

"Doc? It's Opal."

"Are you not coming today?"

"No. I am. I just wanted to apologize. I had a..." *A what?* "A cousin came to visit, and he's sick, so I've been taking care of him."

"Deacon is back?"

"No, not Deacon."

Doc didn't speak for a moment. "Shifter?"

"Wolf." *Dammit. Why had she said that?*

"I didn't know you had wolves in your family. What's wrong with him? You need to bring him in?"

"No," she said, too fast. "He's sleeping now. Fever's been high."

“How high?”

“105.7. But I put him in an icy shower, and I have him down to 103.”

“Infection?”

“Not that we think.”

“That’s strange. I should take a look-”

“He uh...” *He what?* What did she say? “Well, he’s sleeping right now, but if he isn't better by tomorrow, I’ll bring him in.”

Doc didn’t speak for a minute. “Stay with him today. It’s gonna be slow here anyway. I’ll call in a few hours and check how he’s doing.”

“Thanks, Doc.”

“Gotta go, pregnant shifter heading in the door.” The line went dead.

Opal laid her cellphone down as another knock sounded at the front door.

Shit. Why couldn’t the sheriff go away?

She opened the front door with a huge fake smile. “All done?”

"Yup." He nodded. “I did find something suspicious in your backyard, though.”

Opal fought against the knot tightening in her gut. “Oh?”

He held out his hand. Showing her a bloodstained piece of torn fabric from Wolfe’s pants, where Magnus had attacked him.

"Recognize this?"

She swallowed hard. “It’s mine. I had been in the woods on a nature walk. I snagged my sweats on a rock and cut my leg.”

He looked at the scrap. “And it fell off in the yard?”

"Magnus licked my leg, then ripped it off and ran. You know how dogs are."

He didn't move.

Did he believe her? She couldn’t tell, and the uncertainty pressed on her heart. But she refused to break.

"I can toss it." She held out her hand.

He handed her the fabric.

"I've got a lot to do. Need to go."

“Going into town?”

Why would he ask that? “Uh... no. Did you need anything else?”

The sheriff rarely went into Wolf River. Technically, he wasn’t the sheriff there, as it was privately owned, and Alpha Jeremiah Reed and his family kept everyone in line. It was one of the reasons her parents and brother had moved there permanently. Their cabin was on state land and, therefore, subject to the sheriff’s jurisdiction. But Wolf River was off limits.

“No. I was going to have you tell your parents hello.”

The sour scent of his lie hung in the air. The sheriff didn’t know anything about Wolf River. Nor about shifters in general. Wolf River was only for the Reeds’ werewolf pack, as well as close friends and family. Opal's family had been friends with the Reeds her entire life. And Opal's sister-in-law, Satia, was a saber-tooth tiger whose pack Alpha was also friends with the Reeds. And apparently Wolfe knew the Reeds as well, though she hadn't had a chance to ask him how.

"I'd better be off," said the Sheriff. "A few more houses to check, then my report."

"I'll tell my parents you said hello when they visit tomorrow." It was a lie, but perhaps one that would keep him away. She shut the door before he replied. Her father and the sheriff had never had a bad interaction, but her father's imposing stature and aura kept him from their property unless necessary.

She moved to the window in the front room and moved the semi-sheer curtain aside as the sheriff headed to his SUV.

Magus growled.

"Yeah," she said. "I don't trust him either."

Opal watched until the Sheriff's taillights disappeared down the road, and then let the curtain fall back in place. Her heart hammered. That had been too close. Why did she feel so responsible for Wolfe? She didn't know him. She didn't even know what he ran from. Still, the compulsion to shield him burned, irrational and fierce. Magnus sniffed the crumpled, bloodied fabric. She walked to the fireplace and tossed it in, forcing her hands steady as she lit two thick logs. The fabric caught, sending the evidence up in smoke.

She pulled the screen in front of the fireplace and padded back to check on Wolfe. He slept, his breathing shallow but steady. His fever seemed to have broken somewhat- his forehead only warm when she brushed it with her fingertips.

Opal spent the rest of the morning studying, checking on her patient, and bringing him water when he stirred. The stress of the morning and her sleepless night caught up with her, and by afternoon, she curled up on the couch and peered into the dying fire.

A crash jolted Opal awake. She sat bolt upright, disoriented for a moment before another thud sent her racing toward the hall.

"Wolfe?" She flung open his door to find the bed empty, sheets tangled and half-dragged to the floor.

Wolfe bent on his hands and knees, trembling so hard his limbs shook. Sweat streamed down his face and neck. His eyes darted everywhere, wide and unfocused, as if terrified of something only he saw.

"Hey, hey, it's okay," Opal approached him.

At her words, Wolfe's head jerked up, but he gazed through her. He scrambled backward, pushing himself along the floor until his back hit the wall, his chest rose and fell in rapid, uneven gulps.

"Wolfe, it's me. Opal." She reached for his arm.

He recoiled, shoving her hand away with such force that she stumbled. His lips pulled back in a snarl, eyes glassy with fever and fear.

"You're at my cabin, remember? You're safe." She tried again, moving closer.

Wolfe's eyes widened in terror. His body went rigid, and he gaped at something behind her. Opal glanced over her shoulder.

When she turned back, Wolfe raised his arms over his face, elbows locked and forearms shielding his eyes. His mouth opened in what should have been a scream, but only a hoarse, broken wheeze escaped. He flinched, jerking and twisting his torso as if absorbing invisible blows.

"No one's hurting you," she whispered, her heart breaking at the sight. "Wolfe, please. You're hallucinating."

His eyes squeezed shut, his body curling in on itself as he slid down into the corner.

Darkness clawed at him, punctuated by flashes of stabbing light behind his eyelids. Wolfe's consciousness swam back, dragging him from blessed nothingness into a world of torment. His head pounded like a war drum, each beat sending shockwaves through his skull. Thirst burned one moment, chills overtook him the next. The contradictions mocked him.

Where was he? Everything around him felt off. The mattress beneath him, the worn sheets against his skin. The aroma of nature, not cleaning supplies. This wasn't his bed. Not his hotel room. Not Seattle.

Mo. Zaden. The escape. Running.

Wolfe jerked upright, heart hammering. This wasn't his room at the hotel. The walls were wood, not concrete. There was a window with actual curtains. Real, homey curtains, not industrial ones. A trap. It had to be a trap of some kind. Some way for Mo to mess with his head. Make him think he'd gotten away, when in reality he hadn't.

He tried to stand, but his legs betrayed him, tangling in unfamiliar sheets. The floor rushes up to meet him as he crashed down, his shoulder taking the brunt of the impact. The pain barely registered through the fever haze.

Footsteps. Someone was coming. Wolfe tried to push himself up, to prepare for whatever punishment awaited him for attempting to escape.

The door flew open. A woman. Not one of Mo's girls. Her face worried, not mocking or pandering. But he couldn't trust her. Mo used pretty faces before.

"Wolfe! Are you okay?" Her voice sounded distant, underwater.

She reached for him, and panic surged through his

veins. He lashed out, shoving her hands away. His wolf snarled, confused and terrified.

"Don't touch me," he tried to sign, but his hands shook too hard to form the words.

"It's me, Opal. Remember? You're at my cabin."

Opal? The name should mean something, but he couldn't grasp it. The room spun, walls bending inward like they might collapse. His breath came in shallow gasps.

"You're burning up again." She moved toward him once more.

The wooden floor transformed into the dirty mats the pit. The woman's face blurred, shifted, becoming Mo's- younger, from years ago when Wolfe was fourteen.

"Pathetic," Mo spits, unbuckling his belt. "I paid a lot of money for you. Made you strong. And this is how you repay me? By losing to a nobody?"

No. Not again.

The belt whistles through the air. The phantom stings across his back, his shoulders, his legs. Each lash a punishment for a missed punch, a failed block, a moment of weakness.

"Next time," Mo hisses, "you win, or I'll let them kill you."

Wolfe's mouth opened in a scream. His vocal cords strained, but produced nothing more than a ragged wheeze.

The belt comes down again and again, each strike

burning across his back like fire. Wolfe couldn't tell what was real anymore- the cabin walls or the underground training room where Mo had first broken him. His uncle's face looms before him, twisted with disgust and rage.

"Worthless mutt. I gave you everything, and you embarrass me like this?"

Wolfe's throat constricted as he tried to scream, to beg, to explain that the other fighter had been twice his size, and he'd been scared. But no sound emerged- just like that night, when his damaged vocal cords had refused to give voice to his torment.

Through the haze, gentle hands landed on his skin. Not Mo's brutal grip, but something softer. Kinder.

"Wolfe, please. You're safe. No one's going to hurt you."

Opal's voice penetrated the nightmare for a moment before the memory dragged him under again. The belt whistled through the air, and Wolfe scrambled backward until he hit the corner. He pulled his knees to his chest and crossed his arms over his head, making himself as small as possible.

"I'm sorry," he tried to say. *"I'll win next time. Please stop."*

"Wolfe." Opal's voice again, steady and calm. "Whatever you're seeing, it's not real. Not anymore."

She moved close enough that he sensed her presence, but far enough away so she didn't crowd him.

The hallucination flickered- Mo's sneering face fading in and out, replaced by Opal's concerned gray eyes.

"I don't know what you're seeing," she said softly, "but I promise you're okay. No one's going to hurt you."

Wolfe pressed himself harder against the wall, his breath coming in ragged gasps. A corner, Security- no one would come at him from behind. His wolf whined, confused by the mixed signals of danger and safety.

"I'm going to stay right here," she said. "I won't come closer unless you want me to. Just breathe."

Minutes passed. The belt stopped falling. Mo's face grew dimmer, less substantial. The cabin walls solidified around him. Wolfe's breathing slowed, his body still trembling.

Opal hadn't moved. She crouched silently, her eyes never leaving his face. No judgment, only patience and something like understanding.

"Want some water?" she asked when his eyes focused on her.

Wolfe hesitated, then nodded. She left and returned moments later. Instead of handing it to him, she set it on the floor within his reach and backed away again.

His hands shook as he reached for it. The water cooled his parched throat, and he emptied it greedily.

"Better?"

Wolfe nodded, finally able to meet her eyes. The kindness there made his gut tight with an emotion he couldn't name. When was the last time someone looked at him like he mattered?

"I'm sorry," he managed to sign, his hands steadier.

"You don't have anything to apologize for," she said. "You're sick and scared. That's not your fault." She studied his face. "Do you want to tell me what happened?"

Wolfe's jaw clenched. He couldn't tell her about Mo, about the fights, about what he was. She'd helped him because she thought he was a lost wolf who'd wandered into her yard. If she knew the truth- that he was a man and more dangerous men were looking for him- she'd throw him out. Or worse, she'd be afraid of him. He couldn't handle her looking at him with fearful eyes.

"Bad dreams."

Opal's expression suggested she knew there was more to it, but she didn't press. "Fevers make everything more real," she said. "More intense."

He scanned the overturned nightstand, the scattered contents. Damn. He'd made a huge mess.

"Think you can make it into bed?"

Wolfe pushed himself up the wall, his legs wobbling. Opal stood but kept her distance, letting him move at his own pace. He made it three steps before his knees buckled.

This time, when Opal reached for him, he didn't pull away. Her arm slipped around his waist, supporting his weight as she guided him to the bed.

"Easy." She settled him against the pillows. "I'm going to check your temperature again."

The thermometer beeped, and Opal frowned at the reading.

"Still too high. We need more fluids for you, and to keep monitoring this." She checked her watch. "I should call Doc."

"No." Panic flared again. *"No doctors."*

"Wolfe, if your fever spikes again-"

His eyes met hers. *"No doctors. I'll be fine."*

She hesitated, clearly torn. Finally, she sighed. "Okay. But only if you answer one question for me truthfully. Deal?"

Wolfe nodded, relief flooding through him.

“Did you... "Do you...?” She struggled for words.

“Ask.”

“Do you take drugs of any kind?”

“No. I mean. On occasion for pain, but that’s it.”

She chewed her lip.

“You don’t believe me?”

“I want to believe you,” she said. “But your symptoms... I’ve had them before. When I was in rehab.”

His gaze drifted to her scars again. What had she been through?

“I don’t take drugs.”

She nodded. “Okay. Well, if you aren’t better by tomorrow. I’m going to call Doc.”

He held up his hand to protest.

“Trust me. Doc has seen it all. He won’t tell anyone

you are here. You aren't in Wolf River, so he is under no obligation to tell anyone. I've known him my whole life. Whatever you are going through, you can trust Doc. He's a shifter, too."

Wolfe's eyelids grew heavy as lead weights. Before he replied, exhaustion pulled him under once again.

CHAPTER SIX

Opal dragged her body out of bed more exhausted than she had been in years. She hadn't checked on Wolfe, but every couple of hours, he'd been out of bed, either using the bathroom, the shower, or pacing. Her ursa grumbled, wanting more rest. But it wasn't to be. She had to work today. She didn't have many bills, but she liked to eat at least, and she was sure that when Wolfe was able to hold food down, a guy as massive as him would eat a truckload.

She schlepped to the kitchen and threw on a pot of coffee while she showered. Magus yowled at her, and she walked to the back door and opened it for him.

"Don't go off. I don't have the energy to find you today, got it?"

Magus trotted down the back stairs, and Opal shut

the door. She piled her hair on top of her head and wrapped a scrunchie around it while heading toward the bathroom.

The tub was always Opal's sanctuary, her one carved-out stretch of time where the world dulled to a background hum. She lingered under the stream, letting its familiar rhythm scald away the relentless edge of exhaustion. Outside the cabin creaked and settled, its old bones groaning in the cooling weather. In the tub, she pretended she was the only living creature in the world and focused solely on herself.

But as soon as she closed her eyes, Wolfe's nightmares replayed behind her eyelids. The night before, he'd cowered in the corner, knees tucked, arms shielding his head. The posture of someone expecting pain, someone who'd learned how to shrink themselves to absorb the least of a beating. He'd flinched from her touch as his fever blurred the lines between the waking world and whatever hell of a memory he lived in. She'd seen it a hundred times in the treatment center- men and women unraveling under the weight of trauma, bodies remembering what minds tried to forget. Hallucinations, night terrors, the haunted reek which clung to the air after a bad episode.

Wolfe was gigantic, nearly double her size, muscles stacked on his frame like cordwood. It should have made him invulnerable, a walking threat. But the way he'd moved- the way he flinched- said otherwise.

Someone, or something, had put every single mark on him with the intent of breaking him. And judging by the ragged, silvery scar at his throat, they'd nearly succeeded.

She tipped her chin to let the warm water drip down her spine. There'd been a time when she would have cowered in primal fear at the thought of a wounded werewolf loose in her house. But after last night, a dull ache lodged in her chest- a sort of kinship. A recognition of someone the world had specialized in chewing up and spitting out.

Wolfe refused to let her call a doctor, and she'd respected that, though it made her ursa twist with anxiety. The power dynamics in Wolf River weren't like the dynamics in city packs. Sometimes, the wrong phone call meant life or death. Whatever Wolfe was running from must be bad if he'd rather die of infection than risk being found.

The sheriff's visit yesterday bothered her, too. He'd shown up on her porch, all bland smiles and polite curiosity, pretending to check on "the lone woman out on the old road," but Sheriff Holden would never come out because of a few calls about a man in the woods. He'd been fishing for something- something about Wolfe. The encounter put every one of Opal's nerves on edge.

Groaning, she turned off the water and got out. She slapped a handprint on the foggy mirror, revealing her tired face. It had been six months since she'd started with Doc's small-town medical office, and these last three months alone had been the final test of her ability to fend for herself. So far, she hadn't died or killed anyone else, so she considered it a win. Now, she just had to keep someone else alive; that was her newest goal.

She brushed her teeth and pulled on her oldest, softest pair of scrubs. The color, once a cheery robin's egg blue, had faded to the hue of winter sky. She brushed her hair, then wrapped it in a scrunchie once again and padded to the kitchen.

The coffeemaker hummed as she retrieved a mug and reviewed her game plan for the day: keep Wolfe hydrated, keep Sheriff Holden away, and keep her own head down. If she managed all three, by the end of the week, she'd have made a positive impact on the universe.

She poured a cup of coffee, added enough sugar and creamer to turn it the color of sand, and sipped. Though delicious, she was going to need possibly ten more cups to get the caffeine boost she craved, with it being so diluted.

Through the window, Magnus nosed around the front of the property. The dog moved with a purpose, patrolling the invisible perimeter he'd established the first night Opal brought him home. She opened the door and called him with a whistle.

"You're on duty until I'm home," she told him,

ruffling the fur between his ears as he trotted inside. “Wolfe is asleep. Be nice and protect him.”

Magnus snorted as if to say he’d think about it, then plopped down on his bed. She refilled his water bowl and poured some kibble for him, then turned her attention to Wolfe’s room. Her ursa's urge to check on him warred with her instinct to give him space. She bit her thumb and listened at the door. Nothing. Not even the creak of bed springs. The silence made the back of her neck prickle.

She knocked lightly, then eased the door open a crack.

The sight that greeted her was both hilarious and mortifying. Wolfe sprawled face-down across the bed, naked. The borrowed clothes she’d left for him lay balled on the floor, and the sheets and underwear discarded in a heap, as if he’d wrestled them off. His broad back spanned half the bed, and his long feet dangled over the edge. The window stood open, letting in a rush of cold air.

Opal’s ursa rumbled in approval. He was beautiful in a primal, dangerous way- like the grizzly she carried inside, all raw potential and wounded spirit.

She averted her eyes and backed out, closing the door with exaggerated care.

She fanned herself at the kitchen table and chided herself for staring at him for so long when he's been so vulnerable.

Finally, after getting herself together, she found a piece of paper and a pen and scribbled a note:

Wolfe,

Had to go to work. I'll be back around 6.

If you're up and about, help yourself to whatever- kitchen is yours.

If you need me, use the phone on the wall to call my cell at the number below, and press 1 three times. I'll come right home.

Please try to rest. And Don't Leave.

-Opal

She added the number and stuck the note on his nightstand with more water.

Magnus tracked her as she walked back into the front room, head tilted, canine eyes sharp and knowing.

"If our guest wakes up and tries to eat the couch, please don't kill him."

Magnus yawned, stretched, and curled up next to the fireplace as if to say she worried too much. It was the best she would get.

THE DRIVE INTO TOWN WAS FIFTEEN MINUTES OF WINDING gravel roads and forest that always seemed more alive than the human towns only a few miles further away.

The trees arched overhead, lacework of orange and red leaves and the sweet rot of last year's leaf litter on the ride. Opal drove with the windows cracked, letting the frigid breeze and morning sun wake her better than caffeine. Her ursa chuffed in approval but wanted to be let out to explore.

It wasn't until she pulled into Doc's office that her ursa finally backed down.

Doc's office was half house, half office with pine siding and mismatched shingles. A hand-carved sign above the door read: "Tucker Family Practice." The parking out front was empty except for Doc's battered Subaru and a mud-caked pickup she recognized as belonging to Caleb Reed.

Inside, Doc was already at his desk, glasses perched on his nose as he scrawled in a patient's file. He didn't look up as she entered, but he sniffed the air and the corners of his mouth quirked up.

"I was beginning to think you'd decided to play hooky again," Doc called.

"Sorry, I'm late. My... cousin is still sick."

Doc peered at her over his reading glasses. "I don't recall Stix mentioning any cousins coming to visit when he had Andre in here last week."

Opal shifted. "It was... unexpected."

She headed down the hall and peeked in the first door as she passed to find one of Caleb's men sitting on a table with his arm in a sling.

He gave her a tight smile. She waved and kept

moving. She hung her jacket in the back room and returned to the front desk, and checked the appointment book- routine checkups and one prenatal visit scheduled for the day.

“Now,” said Doc to the man in the first room. “Keep ice on it today and take some Ibuprofen if you need, but you should be better by tomorrow. If it dislocates again, come back.”

Opal arranged the files on the desk for the day and didn’t bother to look as the man passed her and walked out the front door, though she felt his eyes on her.

She recognized his face but not his name. Didn’t matter, though; everyone knew about Opal, the younger sister of Stix, and murderer of humans.

Doc approached the desk, removed his glasses, and studied her face. "This mysterious cousin- he wouldn't happen to be the same 'strange man' Sheriff Holden was in town this morning asking about, would he?"

Opal's heart skipped. "The sheriff came here?"

"First thing this morning. Asked if any strangers came in for treatment. Said he was investigating suspicious activity in the area north of town." Doc's eyes narrowed. "What are you mixed up in, Opal?"

Opal leaned against the doorframe, weighing her options. Lying to Doc felt wrong- he'd been there for her during her darkest days. Had never judged her and always kept her secrets. But this wasn't her secret to tell.

"It's not what you think," she said finally. "He showed up at my door sick and injured. I couldn't turn him away."

Doc's expression softened. "You always did have a weak spot for strays."

"He's scared. He was headed here but dropped from exhaustion in my yard. As soon as he's better, I'm going to bring him to town. He's not dangerous like the sheriff says."

"The sheriff said he's been tracking someone who matches your 'cousin's' description since the state line. Said he's a wanted man." Doc folded his arms. "I'm not telling you what to do. Lord knows you've got enough people in your life doing that. But be careful. This town has enough ghosts without adding yours to the collection."

Opal nodded, grateful for his concern but eager to change the subject. "I'll be careful. And... would you mind not mentioning my cousin to anyone until I figure out what's going on?"

"Doctor-patient confidentiality," Doc said with a wink. "Though technically, he's not my patient. Yet."

“I'll bring him in, I promise. He didn't want a doctor at first, but I told him you are a shifter too, and I think that reassured him.”

“What's wrong with him?”

She shook her head. “It appears like drug withdrawal, but he said he's never taken drugs, so I'm not sure.”

“How many days?”

“About three.”

Doc nodded. “If he’s not better by tonight, bring him in first thing tomorrow.”

The bell above the door jingled. Opal straightened her scrubs and moved out of the reception area, relieved by the interruption.

Dakota Reed stood in the doorway. The young woman's dark hair was pulled back in a messy bun, and she carried a baby carrier.

"Morning, Opal," Dakota said. "Not too early, am I?"

"Right on time." Opal pulled a chart from the stack on the desk. "A checkup today?"

"Yep. My guy is getting chunky." Dakota smiled at her baby.

Opal led them to the exam room, and Dakota stopped and sniffed her. "You smell... different."

Opal avoided Dakota's eyes. "Must be the new laundry detergent."

"No," Dakota said slowly, her nose twitching. "It's something else. Something..." Her eyes widened.

"Doc will be right in. I need to grab another chart." She shut the door and banged her head on it.

Of course, other Blood Born and shifters would catch Wolfe's scent on her- his scent would be all over her cabin. She’d been alone so long she’d completely forgotten. If she bolted, Dakota would know something was up for sure. She prayed the rest of the appointments for the day weren't family friends.

THE REST OF DAKOTA'S APPOINTMENT WAS A DANCE OF avoidance. Dakota threw curious glances Opal's way, but thankfully didn't press the issue.

"He's all good," Doc announced after an eternity. "Healthy as a wolf- well, a small, loud, chubby wolf."

Dakota laughed and nuzzled her baby. "Thanks, Doc." She turned to Opal. "You should come by the house. Griff would love to see you."

"I will," Opal promised, knowing she'd avoid it as long as possible. If she went to dinner at Dakota and Griffin's place, they would invite Caleb, McKayla, and possibly Jeremiah and his mate. The house would be brimming with werewolves. Werewolves who'd smell Wolfe all over her.

Opal's ursa paced, agitated by the separation from Wolfe. It made no sense- but her bear didn't care about logic. It recognized something in Wolfe, something that called to her on a primal level.

"Settle down," she muttered, pressing a hand to her sternum where the ursa rumbled. "We'll check on him later."

Her ursa was not appeased. But that was her problem. Opal was in charge, for at least the moment, and at the moment, she had work to do.

. . .

THE REST OF THE DAY CRAWLED BY. OPAL FILED PAPERWORK, restocked supplies, and took inventory of medications- mindless tasks which left her thoughts free to wander. Was Wolfe awake? Had his fever broken? Was he rummaging through her things, or had he already disappeared into the woods?

At four o'clock, Doc emerged from his office and stopped her from organizing tongue depressors for the third time.

"Go home. You won't stop worrying by alphabetizing the supply closet."

Opal managed a small smile. "Okay. I'm sorry. I'll be back Friday, but call if things get crazy and you need me..."

Doc chuckled, the sound warm and familiar. "Right, because we're so swamped around here. Three patients is almost a stampede."

She nodded.

“Opal?”

She looked at him.

“Don't make me come out there.”

She nodded. “I won't, Doc. Promise.

Outside, the afternoon had turned golden, autumn sunlight filtering through the dried, falling leaves. Opal drove to the grocery store near town, her mind already making lists of what Wolfe might need.

Protein, definitely. Calories. Electrolytes to help with the fever. Easy stuff to digest.

She filled her cart with steaks, chicken, eggs, protein bars, sports drinks, fresh vegetables, fruit, and bread. Enough food to feed a small army- or one recovering werewolf. She added pain relievers, more bandages, and antiseptic cream.

"Opal, honey?"

Opal froze, her hand hovering over a package of noodles. Her mother stood at the end of the aisle, a small basket over her arm.

"Mom!" Opal's voice came out an octave too high. She pushed her cart forward and accepted her mother's hug.

As they embraced, her mother inhaled her and then pulled back, eyes narrowing.

Opal backed away, busying herself with arranging items in her cart.

Her mother's eyes drifted to Opal's overflowing cart. "That's... quite a haul. Planning to feed the whole forest?"

"Restocking." Opal shrugged. "I haven't been shopping in over a month. The cupboards are bare."

Her mother raised an eyebrow. "Uh-huh. And you need a four-pound steak because...?"

"I've been craving protein. My ursa's been restless." It wasn't a lie- her bear had been unusually active, though not for the reasons her mother might assume.

"Well, you look well," her mother said. "There's more color in your cheeks than I've seen in a while."

"I feel good." Opal smiled.

Her mother searched her face for a lie.

"I should go. Magnus needs to be let out, and I've got studying."

Her mother's lips quirked. "Of course. Give Magnus a pat for me."

Opal hugged her mother again, quickly this time to avoid further invasive sniffing, and hurried to the checkout.

As the cashier rang up her purchases, Opal tried to calm her racing thoughts. Her mother wasn't stupid. She knew something was up. The question was, would she let it be, or would she show up unannounced? And if she did show up, how long before the pack caught wind of her houseguest? It didn't matter. If he wasn't better by morning, she would be forced to take him to Doc, and everyone would know.

Opal loaded the groceries into her car and drove home, watching the rearview mirror for the sheriff or her mom. The weight of secrets pressed down on her, heavier than the bags she'd carried. But underneath it all, a strange excitement thrummed in her veins, her ursa practically purring with anticipation as they neared home.

Home. Wolfe. The two concepts had become inexplicably linked in her mind, in less than three days.

The attachment forming without her permission scared her. Attachment led to heartbreak.

And yet, as she turned onto the gravel drive, she couldn't deny the flutter of anticipation in her belly. Her ursa sensed it before she did- a change in the air, a shift in the atmosphere.

Wolfe was awake.

CHAPTER SEVEN

Wolfe read Opal's note. A simple message full of warmth and protectiveness that wrapped around him like a warm blanket. He still found it hard to believe he'd ended up at Opal's, cared for by someone who didn't treat him like a fighter or property, but as a person. The fever had begun to wane, leaving behind a sense of clarity he hadn't experienced in a long time.

He racked his brain, trying to piece together the fragmented memories of the past few days- the chaotic muddle of fear and adrenaline blurring into something softer, something real.

He winced as he recalled Magnus biting him. He remembered waking in Opal's cabin, light filtering through the window and falling across her face as she sat nearby, watching him with an almost reverent expression. He still felt the softness of her swimsuit against his skin, the heat that had danced around them in the shower. The memory sent warmth and comfort through him, like stepping into a dream.

Then the memory of collapsing on the bed sent a pang through him, not from the embarrassment but from the raw vulnerability. Opal had helped him, her hands warm, steady, and supporting. She hadn't recoiled from his scars, hadn't flinched at his size, as so many before. Hadn't shown an ounce of disgust as he'd puked all over her toilet. Instead, she'd regarded him with empathy, as if she found the man hidden beneath the layers of violence.

And then... the nightmarish memories followed by a long night of his skin feeling like it was crawling off him. The maddening itch had kept him awake, with the fever lapping at him like fire. He'd fought the urge to claw at his own flesh to find relief. But through it all, Opal's presence had grounded him- a voice in the dark, promising safety and sanctuary.

He had to make sure he wasn't a burden any longer. He pushed himself into a sitting position. Every muscle protested as he swung his legs over the side of the bed, the sensation of cool air against his skin disturbing him.

What the...? He was naked. Had she seen him like that? Naked and vulnerable? He shook his head. He couldn't have been more mortified if she had wiped his ass. Wait... she hadn't done that, had she? No... no... of course she not... At least he hoped not.

After a few moments of collecting himself, he stood and took shaky steps toward the door. The structure quiet except for the sound of the wind rustling outside. The aroma of damp leaves, mingling with something sweet and earthy, lingered in the air, calming him and his wolf. He wrapped the sheet around him and shuffled forward, acutely aware of every muscle as he made his way to the bathroom- his body felt lighter, as though the fever had lifted not from his skin, but from his soul.

As he opened the bedroom door, Magnus sat in the hallway right outside the bedroom door at the end of the hallway. Wolfe stopped.

Magnus watched him but didn't move.

Wolfe scooted down the hall. Magnus' gaze followed him as he closed the door, but he still didn't move.

Heart thumping, Wolfe leaned into the mirror, studying the reflection staring back at him. Days-old stubble scratched his chin. His bloodshot eyes told of his several sleepless nights. He rubbed water over his hair and face, and then he rinsed out his mouth, wishing more than anything he had a toothbrush.

He glanced around for his clothes but couldn't find them. He used the toilet and slowly reopened the door.

Magnus sat firm, muscles rippling beneath his sleek coat, a mixture of wariness and protectiveness radiating from him. Wolfe froze, remembering the chaos of their first encounter.

Wolfe waved at the dog, unsure what else to do.

Magnus's ears perked up, and he tilted his head. The wolf within him stirred.

He waited for sounds of Opal, but only silence met him.

Okay... well, he at least needed to find something to put on before she returned. A bedsheet wasn't proper attire in someone else's home.

Wolfe took a cautious step into the hall, extending a hand slowly, palm up, as he tried to convey peace to Magnus.

The dog sniffed the air, his tongue lolling out, and he stood, taking a tentative step. Wolfe held his breath, waiting for the dog to either accept him or try to rip him apart again. Tension hung thick in the air, a fragile moment teetering on the brink of trust.

Finally, Magnus moved forward, nose nudging Wolfe's hand. Wolfe exhaled a sigh. Did that mean he wasn't going to be bitten again? He sure hoped so. He'd never been around a dog before. Hell, he'd never been around any animals before.

The connection sparked something within him, a flicker of warmth in the pit of his stomach. The simple gesture felt monumental.

As he knelt to meet Magnus at eye level, the dog pushed into his touch, and the tension in his body eased.

Wolfe smiled and scratched Magnus' ear until his legs started to shake, and he forced himself to his feet, leaning on the wall for support. Magnus wagged his tail and sauntered into the living room.

So, no biting. Progress.

Wolfe's stomach growled, and he made his way back to his room. He scanned and found a stack of folded clothing on a chair. He walked to them and pulled on a pair of sweats and a sweatshirt too tight across his torso and legs. At least they covered him, so he couldn't complain.

His stomach growled again, and he walked to the kitchen. He closed his eyes and breathed in deep, letting the silence flood him. He couldn't remember the last time he'd heard... nothing. All he remembered was the hotel. The traffic, the clubs, the tourists. But here, the quiet permeated everything. Peaceful. Simple. The silence and peace tugged at an old memory, but he couldn't grasp it.

The sound of a vehicle approaching broke through his thoughts. He peeked out a small curtained window in the kitchen. A sheriff's vehicle stopped in front of the porch. Wolfe dropped to the floor, pressing into the cabinets.

Magnus peeked around the island at Wolfe. Wolfe didn't move as heavy footsteps pounded up the steps and someone knocked on the front door.

Magnus turned and barked several times. Wolfe breathed slowly as his wolf paced, wanting out. His hackles raised, and he bristled and paced. But like always, his wolf wasn't strong enough to force a shift...

but he'd gotten stronger. His pull and urgency more prevalent.

"Robert? Opal? Stix? Joyce?" the sheriff called from outside the door.

Magnus barked again.

Wolfe snapped his fingers, trying to make Magnus come, but the dog stayed by the door, growling.

The front door creaked open. "Opal?"

Magnus snarled and ran for the intruder. The door slammed, and Magnus hit it with a series of aggressive barks and jumps.

"Easy, boy," said the sheriff from outside. "Good boy. Good dog. Marvin... uh... Marcus?"

But Magnus' barks and snarls told Wolfe he was having none of it. Magnus barked and scratched at the door, jumping on it and hitting it several times. Finally, the footsteps stomped across the porch and down to the gravel below. Wolfe waited a minute and then peered through the bottom of the semi-sheer curtained window. The sheriff looked through the front door before walking around the side of the cabin. Magnus raced to the living room window and barked. Minutes later, a door handle jiggled toward the back of the house, and Magnus shot out of the room. He kept snarling as he banged into another door, barking.

Wolfe wasn't sure what to do. His wolf growled and paced, panicked from being trapped. Lightning shot through his body, and Wolfe sucked in a sharp breath and clawed his chest. What the hell was going on? Another burst of pain traversed his entire body, and he crumpled to the floor trying to breathe.

Stop, stop, stop, stop! What the hell? Stop!

As fast as the pain started, it ended, leaving him panting on the floor. Dizziness blurred his vision, and he let the cool wooden floor comfort him. *What the hell?* His heartbeat pounded through his entire body, but his wolf had gone strangely quiet.

Magnus' barking and jumping had slowed but not stopped when another vehicle crunched up the drive. Wolfe got to his knees. Opal's Jeep stopped next to the Sheriff's vehicle. A moment later, Opal hopped out. Wolfe tapped on the window, and she spotted him. He pointed to the side of the house, and her eyes narrowed. She strode around her car to the porch. Her curvy hips swished, and her dark hair bounced on her head in a messy bun. The sight stirred something inside him, making his wolf chuff.

Wolfe dropped back to the floor.

Tension crackled like electricity, and every muscle in Wolfe's body coiled in preparation for a battle. He wouldn't let Opal get in trouble because of him. No matter the cost, he would defend her in any way necessary.

"Magnus, stop!" Opal's voice rang out from somewhere behind the cabin.

The dog growled, and Wolfe held his breath.

Finally, Magnus' growls softening into whines.

“Why are you banging on my back door? Opal asked.

“I stopped by again to make sure you haven't had any more disturbances.”

Wolfe's heart thundered, and he fought the urge to bolt.

“What do you mean, more?”

“I mean, about the guy seen running the other night.”

“I told you, I didn’t see anyone.”

“Oh? Did you?”

“Yes. Then you found my bloodied pajama pants piece and asked me about it.”

“That’s true. How did you get hurt again?”

“Sheriff, I’ve had a long day at work. I have an entire truck full of groceries defrosting. If there is nothing else, I’d like to get on with my evening.”

“Of course. Do you need help with the groceries?”

“I can manage fine on my own.”

“Honestly, it’s no problem.”

Their voices faded as they rounded the house.

Wolfe crawled to his knees and peered out the edge of the window. Opal glanced his direction before heading to the back of her SUV and opening the trunk. The sheriff followed her. She hefted several reusable bags full of food and stomped toward the door. The sheriff picked up a small bag.

Lots of help he was.

Opal jogged up the steps onto the porch and

opened the front door. Magnus rushed to her, and she told him to sit as she placed the bags on the island. Her eyes connected with Wolfe's. Anger burned through her gaze like a winter storm.

Quietly, she said, "Magnus, guard."

Magnus jumped to his feet and onto the porch, barking.

"Whoa," said the sheriff.

"As I said, I can handle the groceries," Opal walked out the door. "Have a nice evening, Sheriff. And the next time you try to enter my house without a warrant or probable cause, I'll be sure to notify Jeremiah Reed and his son, Logan, my lawyer. Because of my constitutional rights and everything."

Reed? As in, Caleb Reed?

The sheriff didn't answer, but after a minute, a car door slammed, and an engine started.

The sheriff had turned his vehicle around and driven halfway down the road before Opal slammed the trunk lid and stormed back inside with the remaining bags.

Opal kicked the door shut and dropped the bags on the counter before turning to Wolfe.

"I'm sorry," he signed.

"Why? You aren't the nosey bastard trying to break into my house."

"I'm causing you problems."

She snorted. "Trust me. I've caused enough problems for myself in my life. This is nothing." Opal knelt by her dog. "You did perfect, buddy."

The tension in Wolfe's muscles dissipated, but the fear still lingered.

She stood again. "Are you okay?"

"I'm fine. The sheriff... is looking for me. And he doesn't believe you."

Opal's face hardened, and she crossed her arms. "Do you happen to know why he's looking for you?"

Wolfe wasn't sure how to answer. Mo had obviously done something to have people looking for him, but what he'd told people, Wolfe had no idea.

"I should go." Frustration bubbled up within him. *"I need to reach Wolf River."*

"Then you will," Opal insisted, her voice firm. "But not this moment."

Wolfe shook his head. *"I've caused you enough trouble."*

"Wolfe, stop!" She planted her hands on her hips and blew out a breath. "If you want to go, I won't stop you. But you are in trouble and hurt. You need help no matter what you've done. Besides, the Wolf River pack doesn't answer to the human sheriff; we answer to the Alpha. So if you've done something worthy of being arrested for, Jeremiah will make the decision on what to do. Not that pompous, bloated, self-important glorified kid park security guard."

His wolf whined. He didn't like upsetting Opal.

He nodded. *"I trust you. If that's what you think is best. But if he comes back-"*

"If he comes back, he will have to deal with my parents, my brother, the Alpha, as well as myself, and trust me, he does not want that."

Wolfe nodded. *"Whatever you think is best."*

Opal snorted. "Uh-oh. I think I let my ursa show too much. Don't tell me I scared you off so easily."

Wolfe wasn't sure how to respond.

She chuckled. "Trust me. If I ever decide to go full mama bear rage, you'll be more than scared. You'll be terrified."

Wolfe couldn't help but smile. Something inside him stirred and wanted to see that side of her very much.

CHAPTER EIGHT

Opal slammed a can of soup onto the shelf, her hands trembling with suppressed anger.

She couldn't believe the stupid man! Two times he'd been to her house and searched the property as if he owned it. But him trying to enter when she wasn't home... that was too far.

Magnus whined, sensing her distress.

There was no denying he was looking for Wolfe specifically, not some random 'suspicious person'. He wouldn’t be doing half as much work for a random person.

Wolfe stepped forward and took a can from her hands before she smashed it on the shelf as well.

She backed away. “Sorry. I just hate being watched in my own home."

He looked like he might apologize again, so she turned away and snatched up another bag of groceries.

They worked for a few minutes, Opal directing Wolfe about where things belonged. He seemed steadier- his movements more fluid, his eyes clearer. The fever had broken, leaving behind a man both stronger and somehow more vulnerable.

With the last item stored away, Opal leaned against the counter. "You seem a lot better. You're out of bed and standing on your own."

Wolfe gave a shy smile. *"It's all because of you."*

She waved him off. "I didn't do much."

"You did, and I will forever be in your debt."

She didn't doubt he meant it, but the thought made her ursa grumble. She didn't want Wolfe in her debt. She wanted... What did she want? Heat flushed Opal's skin, and she fought to make her thoughts turn somewhere else.

"So, what do you want to eat? I bought a little of everything, so you name it, and if I can cook it, I will."

To her surprise, Wolfe's hands moved in a graceful gesture. *"Let me cook for you."*

Opal raised an eyebrow. "You cook?"

He nodded, a small smile playing at the corners of his mouth.

"You shouldn't overdo it."

"You said I look a lot better."

True, she had said that, but she didn't want him to worsen.

"Cooking will help me... feel normal."

She studied him for a moment, then shrugged. "Okay, but only if you're sure. Honestly, I hate cooking, so you're doing me a favor. I've got a ton of schoolwork to catch up on."

His face brightened with the first genuine smile she'd seen. His features softening, years seeming to fall away from him in an instant.

"I'm going to clean up and change." She backed toward the hall. "The kitchen is all yours."

He waved and began taking things out of the fridge and cupboards.

She stood in the hallway for a minute. Damn, his butt looked fantastic in tight sweats.

Her skin flushed, and she turned away as her ursa chuffed in approval.

No. No. No. No.

Man, she'd been alone too long in the woods.

OPAL PULLED ON A PAIR OF FUZZY LEGGINGS AND AN oversized sweater that hung off one shoulder. She unbound her hair, letting it fall in waves around her face, and took a moment to study herself in the mirror. She chewed her lip, contemplating whether or not she should put on some makeup.

Her ursa bounced around happily at the thought.

Opal rolled her eyes and decided against it. Who was she kidding? Wolfe was going to Wolf River. In a day or two at most, she would drive to town, he would start his new life, and she would be in her cabin alone, studying and working. He would move on, and she would be staying right where she was. Besides, he'd seen her without makeup the entire week. It would be weird to start.

A pit grew in her stomach at the thought of him leaving. Was that why she kept telling him he needed more rest? Because *she* wasn't ready for him to leave?

The idea made her ursa grumble.

Crap. She hadn't realized how attached to him she'd become in a few days. Opal slid to the floor.

Not good. This was not good. How had it happened? She hadn't been looking for a connection or trying to feel something for him... So, when had it happened? When had she started enjoying his company? And why was her damn bear so keen on him?

An answer formed in Opal's mind, but she dismissed it. Nope. No way. There was no way in the world Wolfe was meant for her.

WHEN OPAL RETURNED, THE KITCHEN WAS ALREADY A HIVE of activity. The scent of sizzling meat and garlic made her stomach rumble. Wolfe moved with surprising grace for his size, gathering ingredients and working with a quiet confidence totally at odds with his earlier vulnerability. The transformation was striking-standing in borrowed clothes he looked almost... normal. Domestic.

Opal settled on the couch with her laptop, pulling up her anatomy coursework, trying to ignore the delicious aromas wafting her direction. Her computer screen filled with diagrams of the human nervous system, but her attention kept drifting to the man in her kitchen.

Wolfe deftly chopped vegetables, his massive hands handling the knife with unexpected precision. His movements fluid and purposeful, no longer hampered by fever or fatigue. The bruises on his face had faded, and the haunted shadows in his eyes had evaporated.

Her stomach growled so loudly that Wolfe looked over, a hint of amusement in his eyes.

"Sorry." Heat rose in her cheeks. "Whatever you're making smells incredible."

He smiled and winked at her, then focused on his work, adding spices to a sizzling pan.

Opal couldn't help the flop her heart did into her belly as he winked at her.

Stop. He would be gone soon.

Opal tried to focus on her reading, but the words

blurred together as her mind wandered. She couldn't help wondering about him- where he'd come from, what he ran from, why the sheriff wanted him. And beneath those questions lurked a deeper concern- what if his apparent recovery was temporary? She'd seen it before in patients going through withdrawal- brief periods of lucidity followed by crushing relapses.

Wolfe approached, gesturing toward the table he'd set. Two places, complete with actual plates, silverware, and a small wildflower in a water glass as a centerpiece that she hadn't noticed before. When had he done that?

"Oh," she said, closing her laptop. "You didn't have to go to all this trouble."

"It's no trouble." He pulled out a chair for her.

Opal sat, running her fingers over the plate. "I haven't eaten at a real, set table since my parents left. Or used real dishes and place settings, for that matter. I had no idea we owned placemats."

Wolfe tilted his head as he served a fragrant stir-fry over rice.

"Where are your parents?"

"In Wolf River. They have a restaurant my brother and his mate run. The Hungry Bear." She picked up her fork. "They moved to help out after... well, after I came back."

Opal took a bite savoring the explosion of flavors. "Oh my gosh, this is amazing. Where did you learn to cook?"

"Where I used to live. The only place I went was to the kitchen to work with the chefs."

"You lived at the restaurant?" Opal took another bite. Her taste buds sang with delight at the perfect balance of spices. "This is seriously incredible. I can't believe you made this from the random stuff in my house."

"I lived in a hotel."

Opal paused mid-chew. "A hotel?"

He nodded, his expression neutral as he took a bite of his own food.

"That's... unusual. How does that happen? I mean, hotels are expensive."

"My uncle owned it."

Opal sensed he held back. She studied his face, noting how his eyes darkened and his body tensed.

"So what did you do? At the hotel, I mean. Besides learn to cook."

Wolfe's hands remained still for several long moments. He stared at his plate, then at her with an expression which clearly said he'd rather not discuss it.

"I didn't mean to pry."

"It's okay. I just... I don't want to think about it right now."

"Of course. I'm so sorry."

She took a bite of food and moved her fork around her plate as the heat of his stare lingered on her.

Wolfe reached across the table and touched her hand.

"I want to tell you. I do. But... not tonight."

She nodded. "Trust me. I get it."

He smiled, and they both resumed eating.

They finished their meal in companionable silence. Opal found herself stealing glances at him, at the way his broad frame seemed too substantial for her kitchen chair, at how he handled the delicate fork between his scarred fingers. His powerful and gentle nature was a fascinating contradiction.

As they cleared the dishes, a thought occurred to her. "You've been cooped up for days. If you're up to it, how about we go for a short run?"

Wolfe looked at her quizzically. *"Run?"*

"Yeah."She laughed. "Shift and let our animals stretch their legs. The woods are gorgeous, especially at dusk. I bet your wolf would love it after being sick for so long. Plus, as you know, we heal faster in our animal forms."

His expression changed to something she couldn't quite read- confusion and almost shame.

"I don't think I've ever shifted before."

Opal nearly dropped the plate she held. "But you're a werewolf. A Blood Born, not a bitten werewolf. I can smell it on you."

He nodded. So that's what Blood Born meant.

"How is that possible? I thought all shifters naturally transformed during puberty at the latest."

Wolfe shrugged, his hands forming hesitant signs. *"Never learned how, I guess. Never allowed."*

"Never allowed?" Opal repeated, incredulous. "Who'd stop you from shifting? It's like... It's like breathing. It's who you are."

His jaw tightened, and he busied himself with wiping down the counter.

Opal stood frozen, her mouth open as she tried to process Wolfe's words.

"Wait- never? You've never shifted? Not once?" She couldn't keep the shock from her voice.

Wolfe's hands hesitated before signing again. *"Not that I remember."*

"But that's..." She struggled to find words. "That's like never having used your lungs to breathe."

"My uncle wouldn't allow it. Said it made us vulnerable. Weak."

Opal's ursa rose protectively. "Your uncle kept you from shifting? For how long?"

"After my parents were killed. Fifteen years, possibly longer."

"Fifteen years. You've been denied your wolf for fifteen years?"

He nodded.

"But how? The urge to shift is biological." She ran her fingers through her hair, trying to make sense of it. "During the full moon-"

"Something to keep the wolf sedated, I assume. And..." His hands faltered. *"Other methods."*

Opal remembered the myriad of scars across his body. As well as his nightmarish hell of a hallucination, she'd witnessed.

"That's why you were so sick," she said. "It wasn't simple exhaustion. You're going through withdrawal from whatever they gave you to suppress your wolf."

Wolfe stared at her.

“What else did your uncle give you?”

The wheels turned in his head as he thought.

A chilling thought popped into her head. "Were you held against your will? Did you escape?"

His eyes met hers with a plea not to ask for details he wasn't ready to give.

Her ursa growled.

Opal's mind raced with implications. A werewolf who had never shifted was unheard of. The trauma of suppressing such a fundamental part of oneself for so long...

"Wolfe," she said gently. "Would you like to try? To shift, I mean."

His head snapped up, eyes widening with something between terror and desperate hope.

"I'll help you. We’re safe here. Just you and me. To see if-"

"I don't know how."

"It's instinctual," Opal assured him. "Your body knows what to do if you don’t." She paused, considering. "But maybe not tonight. You're still recovering and-”

"No... I... I want to try."

They stared at each other for a long minute. His eyes held both fear and curiosity.

She nodded. "Okay. Let's finish the dishes, and we can go."

Wolfe nodded and wiped down the counters faster.

CHAPTER NINE

Twilight settled over the forest as Wolfe followed Opal through the trees behind her cabin. Every step deeper into the woods intensified his restlessness. His wolf paced, clawing, desperate for possible release after years of imprisonment. His heart hammered, each beat a tornado of anticipation and terror. Wolfe felt his wolf more acutely, leading him to believe Opal had to be right. Mo had done something chemical to him to keep his wolf depressed.

Where before his wolf had been a distant voice he sometimes heard, now it was almost as if his wolf lived inside his skin instead of somewhere distant. He felt what his wolf felt, heard his wolf's distress, all of which made him edgier and eager.

"Magnus wanted to come," Opal said over her

shoulder, "but I thought it might be better without an audience for your first time."

Wolfe nodded. The borrowed clothes clung like a vise, his skin crawling with a restless panic that tightened with each breath.

They walked in silence. Pine needles crunched under their feet. The forest aromas overwhelmed his heightened senses-earth, decay, animal musk, the sharp tang of sap. His wolf drank it in, growing more frantic with every breath.

After a few minutes, they reached a small clearing bathed in the fading purple hue of sunset. Ancient firs, spruces, and pines created a natural barrier around the space, their branches swaying in the evening breeze.

Opal turned to him. "So. You have options."

Wolfe raised an eyebrow.

"If you'd been raised in a pack, you'd be used to it." She shrugged. "Nudity is... normal. Practical, really. Clothes don't shift with you."

"Are you going to get naked?"

Opal laughed, the sound bright and unexpected in the quiet clearing. "Yes, because I don't have an unlimited supply of underwear and clothing. I hate ripping up the ones I have when I shift."

The tension eased at her laughter. He was not opposed to her getting naked, nor was his wolf. But... did that mean he was going to get naked in front of her as well?

That was fine. It was fine. He'd been naked in the

locker room thousands of times in front of other guys... but... those had been guys. Whenever he'd been with women, he'd insisted the lights be off.

"Do we undress here? In the open?"

"That's where you have options. It depends on what you are comfortable with. I'm gonna go behind the trees to give you some privacy. But if you want to go into the trees as well, that's fine too."

Wolfe chewed his lip, his wolf's pacing and whining blared louder than his own thoughts. A rising wave of panic clawed up his spine.

When he didn't move, Opal walked to him and took his hand. "We don't have to do this if you aren't ready. You have all the time in the world here."

Wolfe nodded and swallowed hard. He wanted to do this. He needed to. No matter how scared, the possibilities thrilled him.

"I want to."

Opal gave him a small smile and headed toward the trees.

Wolfe began to undress, struggling against his wolf as he removed his borrowed shirt and pants, laying them on a nearby rock.

The instant cold air caressed his bare skin, his wolf slammed forward- ferocious and unstoppable. Wolfe choked on a gasp, crumpling to his knees, chest racked with something savage and hungry, clawing to rip free. The intensity stole his breath, drowning him in wild, untamed need and fear.

"Easy," Opal said, back at his side. "Your wolf senses freedom."

Wolfe strained as pain ripped through his body. Opal crouched next to him and placed her palm on his back. Pine needles prickled his palms and knees. Opal knelt in front of him, close enough that he caught silver flecks in her gray eyes.

"Breathe," she said. "The first time is going to be painful, I'm not going to lie. But it will become more bearable the more you do it. You will learn, adapt."

"I'm used to pain."

A shadow crossed Opal's face. "Not like this. This is different. This is your entire body rebuilding itself."

Pain was pain. He'd endured countless beatings, broken bones, and the agony of the fights. How much worse could it be?

"The control you've used to keep your wolf in all this time, you need to let go of it. Don't fight the change. If you struggle, it hurts more."

Wolfe nodded and drew a breath. He focused inward on the barrier which had been erected years before. The wall containing his wolf. He pictured it exploding.

His wolf surged forward with such force that Wolfe gasped. The sensation immediate and overwhelming. His bones cracked, tendons stretched, muscles tore. Pain exploded through every cell of his body, white-hot and all-consuming.

Opal was right. This was unlike any he'd experienced. It wasn't localized like a broken rib or knife wound, but total and consuming, as if his entire being was unmaking and remaking itself.

Panic seized him. He instinctively pulled the reins back, desperately trying to halt the transformation.

"Wolfe!" Opal placed her hands on his back. "Breathe. You have to breathe."

He fought with his wolf, stuck in a terrible limbo. Bones broke and reformed, broke and reformed. His body couldn't choose a shape- human or wolf. His mouth opened in a silent scream.

"You have to let go," Opal urged. "Completely. Otherwise, it's going to keep going like this. It won't stop until you shift. You've held back too long. Let your wolf take over. You can learn to control him in the future. Today isn't that day."

Terror clawed through him, sharp and cold. What if he never came back? What if his wolf, wild with freedom after being caged so long, never surrendered control again? Panic narrowed his world to the point of forcing him to shift back.

"I know you're scared." Opal laid her forehead on his. "But I won't let anything happen to you. I'm right herc."

Wolfe concentrated on her eyes- calm, steady, a gray harbor in the storm of his transformation. Something about her gaze soothed him, anchored him as his body rebelled.

"I'm right here." She touched his cheek as tears

sparkled in her eyes. “You’re going to be okay. Just let go.”

Electricity scorched every nerve and crashed through him, twisting, shattering him until he broke. At last, he surrendered.

His wolf rushed through him like a tidal wave, jubilant and wild.

Convulsing, he contorted as joints popped and reformed. His spine extended with excruciating cracks. Fur erupted like thousands of pins pushing outward. His face distorted into a muzzle, teeth lengthening into fangs. The agony beyond anything he’d experienced- this was being unmade and remade through a volcano. Suddenly, the storm passed. The torture receded like a wave pulling back from shore, leaving him trembling in its wake. Wolfe collapsed onto his side, his massive form heaving with each breath. His tongue lolled from his mouth as he struggled to process the flood of new sensations- scents a thousand times sharper, sounds so crisp they seemed to have texture, colors his human eyes had never perceived.

Opal knelt beside him. "You did it." She reached out slowly to touch his fur. "Your wolf is beautiful."

Wolfe tried to lift his head but couldn't quite coordinate his body. Everything felt wrong- too many limbs, strange muscles, unfamiliar weight distribution. His wolf mind struggled to reconcile with his human consciousness, creating a disorienting blur of instinct and thought.

"Don't rush," Opal said. "Breathe. Let your wolf explore. He's been waiting a long time for this."

Wolfe's eyes fixed on her, trying to communicate his gratitude. His wolf whined, the sound strange in his own ears.

"I'm going to shift too."

Opal transformed- smooth and fluid where his had been prolonged and violent.

Her bear emerged with surprising grace, rising onto hind legs before dropping to all fours. A magnificent cinnamon-colored ursa with intelligent gray eyes that somehow still held Opal's essence.

She approached him, her massive form dwarfing his wolf despite his considerable size. She nudged him with her nose, encouraging him to stand.

Wolfe struggled to his feet, legs splaying awkwardly as he found his balance. His first strides were clumsy, more stumble than stride, but his wolf's instincts gradually took over. He padded in a small circle, getting the feel of his new body.

Opal's bear huffed, the sound almost like laughter, and bounded a few feet away before looking back at him expectantly.

His wolf understood the invitation even if his human mind was still catching up. Wolfe took a tentative step forward, then another.

"I'm not going to hurt him," Opal said. *"I hope he knows that."*

Wolfe stopped moving. He... he heard her. How was that possible? Was it a ursa thing?

"I know she won't hurt me, she's too kind. I wish I could tell her I'm not afraid."

Opal's ursa cocked her head to the side. *"Wolfe?"*

His heart hammered. *"Opal."*

Her ursa chuffed and stamped her paws. *"Oh my gosh! I can hear you,"* she said. *"I wasn't sure if I would because of your injury, but it totally makes sense because our connection is a mental one between our animals, but I didn't want to get my hopes up or your hopes up, so I didn't say anything."* Her words came out so rushed, Wolfe fought to understand.

"You can hear me?"

"I can hear you."

"You... hear my voice."

She jumped forward and shoved into his shoulder with her enormous weight. *"Wolfe, I hear you. I hear your voice. Say something. Anything."*

What? What did he say? *"Rubber duckie."*

"Rubber duckie."

His heart pounded. *"Fudge nuggets."*

"Fudge nuggets."

"Eenie meanie minie mo."

"Eenie meanie minie mo. Catch a werewolf by the toe," she answered.

He couldn't believe it. He could talk. Well, not talk but... communicate.

"I have so many questions," he said.

She snorted. *"Me too."*

His wolf propelled him forward.

"We should let the questions wait and let your wolf run."

"Can you keep up?"

She laughed. *"You try to keep up."* She tore off into the trees.

Wolfe's muscles bunched as he launched himself after Opal, his paws digging into the damp earth with each powerful stride. The sensation was unlike anything he'd ever experienced; the ground flying beneath him, wind rushing through his fur, scents painting vivid pictures of the forest around him. His wolf howled with joy, reveling in this long-denied freedom.

Opal's bear form moved with surprising agility, weaving between trees and leaping over fallen logs. Her cinnamon fur caught the moonlight as she glanced back at him, her gray eyes twinkling with challenge.

"Having trouble keeping up?" She teased.

"Just getting started." He pushed faster.

He trailed her through a shallow creek, water splashing around his paws, then up a steep embankment where needles and leaves cushioned their steps. His instincts guided him, showing him where to place each paw, how to distribute his weight, how to dig in his claws, and when to leap. With each passing minute, he became more connected to the newfound part of himself, as if puzzle pieces long separated were finally clicking into place.

After a mile or so, he caught up, running alongside her massive form. Her bear huffed.

"Not bad for a first-timer."

Wolfe's confidence surged. He pushed himself harder, muscles burning as he pulled ahead. *"Race you to the ridge!"* He darted forward.

Opal's bear roared playfully and gave chase, but Wolfe's wolf was built for speed. He reached the ridge first, skidding to a stop.

"Show-off."

He chuckled. *"You can't win every time."*

"Can't I?" She swiped at his leg with her massive paw, making him stumble before she took off again.

"So that's how it's going to be, huh?" He tore off after her, his wolf beyond ecstatic.

They continued their exploration, racing through meadows silvered by moonlight, splashing through streams, circling massive trees. Wolfe lost all track of time, lost in the pure exhilaration of running wild and free.

"This is what you were meant for."

He couldn't find words to express his agreement. A boundless, soaring happiness lifted every cell of his body.

Eventually, they crested a hill and found themselves in a small clearing. By mutual, wordless agreement, they slowed to a stop. Wolfe's lungs heaved with exertion, his tongue lolling as he panted. Beside him, Opal's bear dropped onto her side, her massive chest rising and falling rapidly.

Wolfe collapsed beside her, his legs finally giving out as the adrenaline ebbed. He rolled onto his back, paws splayed awkwardly in the air, and found himself staring up at the night sky. The vast expanse above them blazed with stars, scattered across the darkness like diamonds.

"I've never..." His thought trailed off, wonder overwhelming him. *"They're so bright. I didn't realize there were so many."*

Opal's bear shifted beside him, her massive head tilting to follow his gaze upward. *"It's because you've been in the city. Light pollution blocks most of them. Out here, nothing is between us and the universe."*

Wolfe drank in the spectacle. The stars pulsed and shimmered, some clustered in misty clouds, others standing sharp and alone against the blackness. A streak of light flashed across the sky. A shooting star.

"I used to watch from my window," he confessed, the words flowing in the strange mental connection. *"But I only ever spotted a few. Not like this. Never like this."*

They fell silent, the only sounds their slowing breaths and the whisper of wind through trees. The breeze ruffled his fur, cool and refreshing. Something unfamiliar settled inside him. A peace he couldn't remember experiencing before. His wolf, so long caged and sedated, seemed reborn by the release.

Time stretched around them. Wolfe's thoughts drifted, touching briefly on the horrors of his past before being pulled back to his first perfect moment of true freedom. The freedom, the sky, Opal beside him, knowing what his wolf needed... All of it was a dream he’d never dared to hope for.

"Why do you live alone?" The question formed before he could stop it. *"Away from town."*

Opal's bear turned, gray eyes reflecting starlight. A heavy sigh escaped her, ruffling the grass between them.

CHAPTER TEN

"*It's complicated,"* she finally answered. *"I needed space to heal."*

Wolfe didn't respond.

She might as well tell him the truth. He'd seen her scars. There was no hiding what had happened.

"Two years ago... I tried to kill myself."

The confession hung in the air between them, stark and honest. Wolfe stayed still, his eyes fixed on her.

"I had... issues. I... fell in with some humans from school. It wasn't easy being one of only two ursa in town. And even more so of being the little sister of the golden boy, Stix. He ever treated me like that. Stix is the best." She took a breath. *"Anyway, I begged my parents to let me transfer to a different school for my senior year, and they did. But even amongst the humans, I didn't fit in. I fell in with a group who partied a lot. I didn't drink or anything,*

and they liked me because I drove them around, though I didn't have a license. But... one night... one of the guys insisted on driving. I tried to stop him, but he wouldn't listen."

Her ursa whined, wanting to comfort her, but there was no comfort for what had happened.

"There was an accident. Three were killed. One was paralyzed. And the other, the guy who drove, ended up losing a leg. But their parents blamed me for the accident. They said I should have insisted on driving. I should have called someone. The online bullying was the worst. People say hurtful things when they can hide behind the anonymity of a screen name. Especially people who have no clue what really happened, they go by what other people post. I couldn't handle it. So I took a razor to my wrists and tried to end it. I nearly succeeded, but my brother found me."

"I want to hug her. She's such a kind and beautiful person. She didn't deserve that."

Opal would have blushed if possible. Wolfe had no idea she'd heard him. She would need to help him learn how to turn the connection on and off in the future.

"Okay," she said. *"You have now both seen me naked and learned my darkest secrets, so your turn. Where are you from? What are you running from? And why is your name Wolfe?"*

He sighed. *"Wow, go right for the jugular."*

"I showed you mine. Time for you to show me yours."

"Maybe I'm shy," Wolfe teased.

Opal snorted. *"Somehow I doubt it."*

He watched the sky and didn't speak for a long time.

"I don't remember much about my childhood before age seven or eight. I remember my mom and dad being attacked by someone and killed. They tried to kill me, too. Cut my throat. But it didn't go deep enough. It did cut my vocal cords, though. My uncle Mo found me, took me in, and raised me, sort of."

"The one who owns the hotel?"

"Yeah."

Wolfe stopped talking for so long Opal almost told him he didn't have to continue.

"When I was old enough, I fought for him."

"Fought?"

"He owns a fight club in his hotel. Special clientele only."

Her ribcage squeezed. *"And you fight in it?"*

"I did."

"Is that why you have so many scars?"

"Yeah."

Her heart reached for Wolfe. What would it be like to live your life in a hotel, fighting?

"Do you enjoy it?"

He paused. *"I'm an expert at it."*

"That's not what I asked."

"If I have it my way, I'll never fight again."

She nodded. *"I hope you were at least paid well."*

Wolfe flipped to his feet. *"Want to race back?"*

A pit grew in her gut. He still held back, but she didn't want to push him.

"Absolutely." Opal took off.

"Cheater," Wolfe growled.

"My brother calls it pressing the advantage."

Wolfe nipped her tail before shooting past her. *"What advantage?"*

Her ursa snorted.

"Come on, girl, we can't let him get away with that."

CHAPTER ELEVEN

By the time they got back, Wolfe's body ached, and his head fuzzed over. He'd begun to sweat, and the shakes started again. He tripped when they got to the back stairs, and Opal took his arm.

"Guess you aren't as graceful in human form." She chuckled.

He opened his mouth to talk, but remembered they were no longer in their animal forms. Sadness rooted inside him. Being able to communicate with her and then not being able to was a torture more horrible than shifting.

Worry creased her brow, and she touched his forehead.

"The sweat isn't from running, is it?"

Before he responded, he heaved and threw up, barely missing her bare feet.

"Oh man. I was afraid you might not be ready for all the exertion."

Wolfe tried to sign 'sorry,' but she focused on the door, not his hands. She'd seen him puke twice in as many days.

His wolf whined and sniffed the air as if sensing something.

Magnus met them at the door, and Opal told him ineffectively to go lie down. Instead, he raced outside, barking.

"Dumb dog."

She helped Wolfe through the laundry room and down to his room. She laid him on his bed and touched his forehead.

"I should take your temperature."

"I'll be fine."

She stopped and chewed her lip.

"What?"

"I've asked you this before, but... do you think it's possible, without your knowledge, maybe, your uncle gave you something. Drugs perhaps? Something to give you an edge in the ring?"

Wolfe wanted to say no, but every evening before a fight, Mo had had a doctor give him a shot. He'd said it was vitamin B, some herbs, and caffeine.

"It's possible," he finally signed.

She nodded. "Well... as a shifter, we have a faster metabolism, which means we go through withdrawals harder but also process the drugs out of our system faster. Where it takes humans a week or longer, you should be done by tomorrow or the next day at the latest. Let me grab you some water."

As she left, Wolfe groaned and curled into a ball on the bed. He wanted to kill Mo. After everything he'd done to Wolfe, to drug him as well? Why? Mo made money whether Wolfe won or lost... not that he had ever lost after the first few fights... but... from what other guys had said, clients paid Mo a lot of money to fight Wolfe or to have someone else fight Wolfe. Like the brother of the last guy he'd fought. And if Wolfe had started losing... people would stop paying.

Opal returned with a tall glass of ice water. She sat on his bed and held it to his lips. He sipped it, the water sliding down his throat. After several substantial gulps, he stopped, and she put the glass on the nightstand.

"You might be more comfortable if you strip down," she said.

He nodded.

"Let me help you."

He tried to concentrate on anything besides her strong fingers tracing up his sides as she slid his shirt off. She tossed it to the floor and reached for the waistband of his sweats. His wolf chuffed, and he placed his hand over hers. He didn't have words to tell her that, despite his fever and puking and the shivers and everything else he had going on in his body, his dick worked fine, and his wolf was more than happy for Opal to touch him.

"I can do it."

She nodded and stood. "I'm gonna bring Magnus in. I'll be back in a minute."

When she left, he shimmied out of the sweats. He tossed them to the ground as Magnus bounded into the room and jumped up on the bed, sniffing Wolfe all over.

"Magnus, off," Opal barked.

Magnus licked Wolfe's face and sniffed him.

Opal pulled him from the bed. "Mag, not now. I'm glad you aren't wanting to bite Wolfe, but seriously, personal space, dude."

She walked out of the room and started to close the door, but Wolfe knocked on the wall, getting her attention.

She turned. He hated looking weak, but at the same time, being with Opal comforted both him and his wolf.

"Would you... Do you mind... staying for a little while?"

She smiled. "Let me feed this monster and grab you some medicine, and I'll be back."

Wolfe nodded and shut his eyes.

CHAPTER TWELVE

Opal fed Magnus and grabbed a bottle of ibuprofen from the medicine cabinet. She hurried to her bedroom, her mind racing as she peeled off her clothes, still damp with sweat. The freedom they'd shared in the forest drifted away like a distant dream, replaced by the harsh reality of Wolfe's condition.

She slipped into a cotton camisole and her softest pajama pants, then filled a glass with water and shook four pills into her palm. When she returned, Wolfe had curled on his side, shivering despite the sweat glistening on his skin.

"Here." She handed him the water and meds.

He propped himself up on one elbow to swallow the medication. When he finished, he collapsed, exhaustion etched in every line of his face.

Opal hesitated for a moment, lifted the blankets, and slid beside him. The mattress dipped under her weight, and Wolfe's eyes fluttered open, surprise evident in their depths.

His hands moved between them. *"Sorry for all this hassle."*

"It's not a hassle. If people hadn't helped me when I was in trouble, I wouldn't be here. I'm glad I can do the same for you."

Something in his expression softened; the vulnerability made her heart ache. His eyes fluttered again, his breathing steadying as the medicine took effect.

Opal lay beside him, watching the gentle rise and fall of his chest. Her ursa stirred restlessly, concerned for this wounded wolf who had somehow found his way to their door. The bear wanted to curl around him, to share warmth and comfort the way their kind always did.

In the dim light filtering through the curtains, she studied his face. The strong line of his jaw. The dark sweep of his lashes against his cheeks. The fullness of his lips. Even in illness, he was undeniably hot- raw masculinity tempered by gentleness.

The fragments he'd shared of his past painted a grim picture. An uncle who'd exploited him, a childhood stolen, a wolf denied its nature. The tally marks carved into his skin- were they victories? Defeats? Lives taken? The thought made her gut clench.

She suspected Wolfe had been more prisoner than

anything, a weapon wielded rather than cherished. Fury blazed inside her. Why would anyone twist such gentleness into a tool for violence?

A bead of sweat rolled down Wolfe's temple, catching the moonlight. Without thinking, she brushed it, her touch feather-light against his skin.

As she began to withdraw her hand, Wolfe's eyes opened. His fingers encircled her wrist, warm and solid despite his weakened state. He guided her palm to rest over his heart. The steady rhythm pulsed against her skin, strong and reassuring.

Opal's breath caught. The simple gesture more intimate than any words they'd spoken.

She should pull away. He would be gone soon... but she couldn't bring herself to break the connection. The warmth of his skin, the steady beat of his heart under her palm... she liked it more than she should. So did her ursa.

It struck her then, with startling clarity- despite everything Wolfe was going through. Despite the fever, the nightmares, the withdrawal... she enjoyed having him there. Not just anyone, but him specifically. Where she usually couldn't wait to usher visitors out, with Wolfe, it was different. Easy. Natural. She appreciated his presence in a way that both comforted and confused her.

She had no idea what to make of the way her ursa recognized something in him that transcended their brief acquaintance. Her eyelids grew heavy as she pondered the idea, the warmth of his body and the rhythm of his breathing lulling her toward slumber.

The last thing she registered before drifting off was the pressure of his fingers around hers, anchoring her to him as surely as he had become anchored in her life.

OPAL WOKE TO THE FIRST GRAY LIGHT OF DAWN FILTERING through the curtains. The weight of an arm across her waist unfamiliar yet somehow right. She blinked, aware of the warm body against her back, the steady breath tickling her neck.

Wolfe.

She should move. She should slip out of bed and retreat to her own room before things became awkward. But his fever had broken during the night-she could tell by the dry warmth of his skin, so different from the clammy heat of the evening before. And he slept peacefully, perhaps for the first time since she'd found him.

Five more minutes, she told herself. Five more minutes, and then she would face the day and all that came with it. Including Wolfe leaving.

Opal's ursa lifted her head and groaned. Outside, a car engine rumbled, growing louder as it approached. Opal tensed, alert. It was too early for casual visitors.

The vehicle slowed, gravel crunching under tires. Magnus let out a warning bark, followed by the sound of his nails clicking across the hardwood floor toward the front door.

Wolfe stirred, his arm tightening around her waist. She rolled toward him, and his eyes opened, instantly alert despite the lingering exhaustion in his face.

"Someone's here," she whispered.

He nodded, already reaching for his discarded clothes. His movements were more fluid than the night before.

Opal slipped out of bed and moved to the hallway, looking out the front window.

Her ursa roared in anger at the sight of the familiar tan uniform.

"It's the sheriff," she said, turning back to Wolfe. "Again."

His gaze hardened.

"Let me handle this."

Before he protested further, she slipped out of the room, closing the door behind her. She smoothed her hair and straightened her camisole, then padded to the front door where Magnus stood growling, hackles raised.

The sheriff's knock came as she reached for the handle.

"Magnus, quiet." She plastered on her most convincing smile as she opened the door. "Sheriff Holden. You're making quite a habit of these early morning visits."

The sheriff's weathered face impassive as he

removed his hat. "Sorry to disturb you so early, but I've had some developments."

"Oh?" Opal leaned against the doorframe, blocking his view. "What kind of developments?"

"The man I've been looking for-" He paused, studying her face. "I have reason to believe he may be dangerous."

Opal's heart skipped, but she kept her face neutral. "That's concerning, but I still don't understand what it has to do with me."

Sheriff Holden reached into his pocket and produced a folded piece of paper. He opened it to reveal a grainy photograph of a man in a fighting cage, his face contorted in a snarl, fists raised. Despite the poor quality and the blood obscuring some of his features, there was no mistaking Wolfe.

"This man," he tapped the image, "is wanted for questioning in connection with a murder in Seattle. I have reason to believe he passed through this area a few days ago."

Opal's blood chilled. Murder? She couldn't reconcile the sweet man who had cooked dinner in her kitchen, who had held her hand to his heart as he slept, with the savage fighter in the photograph.

"I haven't seen him." The lie sat bitter on her tongue.

The sheriff's eyes narrowed. "Are you sure? Because I received an anonymous tip that someone matching his description was seen at this property."

Behind her, something crashed in the kitchen. The sheriff's hand moved to his holster as he tried to peer around her.

"What was that?"

"Magnus. He likes to jump on the counter when I'm not looking. Magnus, get down."

"Opal, if you're harboring a fugitive-"

"I'm not harboring anyone," she interrupted, forcing indignation into her voice. "And frankly, I'm getting tired of these accusations. I told you before, if you want to search my property, you're going to need a warrant."

He studied her for a long moment, his face unreadable. Finally, he tucked the photograph back into his pocket.

"I'll be back," he said simply. "With a warrant, if necessary."

"You do that." Opal fought to keep her voice steady. "And I'll call Logan Reed and make sure he's aware of the situation. Now, if you'll excuse me, I need to get ready for work."

She slammed the door before he responded, and fell against it, heart hammering as she listened to his retreating footsteps. Only when his car started did she allow herself to breathe again.

"Wolfe?" she called, turning toward the kitchen.

He stood in the hallway, dressed in the borrowed clothes, his face pale but resolute. *"I heard,"* he signed. *"I need to leave. Now."*

"Not without answers." Opal crossed her arms. "Murder, Wolfe?"

"No."

"Then why would he say it? He may be a nosey prick, but he's not smart enough to make something like that up."

Wolfe's posture slumped. He gestured toward the kitchen table, a request for them to sit.

Opal nodded, her mind racing with questions and fears. Whatever his story, it was about to get much more complicated.

WOLFE SETTLED AGAINST THE KITCHEN COUNTER, HIS HANDS hesitating before he began.

"It wasn't murder," he signed, his movements deliberate and careful. *"It was self-defense."*

Opal remained guarded as she sat at the table, watching his hands. "Tell me everything," she said. "No more half-truths."

Wolfe nodded, drawing a breath before his hands began to move again. *"Mo- my uncle- started training me to fight the day he took me in. I was just a kid, grieving my parents, and he put me in a gym with trainers four times my size."*

Opal's eyes widened, but she didn't interrupt.

"I lived in a hotel room by myself most of the time. The only person I saw regularly besides Mo was a tutor who

taught me to read, write, and do math. That lasted until I was about fourteen." His hands faltered before continuing. *"By then, I was fighting in Mo's underground club two or three nights a week."*

"Fighting... other children?" Opal asked, her voice barely above a whisper.

Wolfe shook his head. *"Adults. Always adults. Mo liked the spectacle of it- the boy against grown men."*

He walked to the table and sat across from her, his movements heavy with exhaustion. *"It's not a ring, like in boxing. It's a cage- steel mesh on all sides, open at the top so the spectators on the upper levels see everything."*

Opal's face paled, but her eyes never left his hands.

He needed her to believe he hadn't done what he was accused of. He was dangerous, but he would never do anything to hurt her.

"By fifteen, I was winning every match. That's when the tally marks started." His fingers traced the pattern of marks through his shirt. *"One for every victory. Mo's way of keeping count."*

"How many?"

"Three matches a week for the last eight years. Twelve hundred and fifty-eight, as of last week."

Opal's hand flew to her mouth, her eyes filling with tears. "Wolfe."

He turned away, unable to bear the horror in her eyes. *"It wasn't all bad,"* he signed, though they both knew it was a lie. *"After I got great, the beatings stopped, and the... perks started."*

"Perks?"

"I moved into the penthouse suite. Had more freedom to move around the hotel- to go to the kitchen, to work out, to swim. Without someone watching me every second." He paused. *"And there were... other things Mo considered perks..."*

Opal's face darkened with understanding. "Women?"

Wolfe nodded once.

"Were you ever allowed to leave the hotel?"

"Never."

"How did you get away?" Opal leaned her elbows on the table. "What changed?"

"I had a friend- Zaden. He worked security at the hotel, then became a fighter. He figured out I was a wolf. He's the one who taught me ASL." A ghost of a smile touched Wolfe's lips. *"He told me about Wolf River, said it was a place for shifters where I'd be safe."*

Wolfe's hands moved faster. *"About a week ago, Zaden arranged a diversion. Created a small fire in the locker room during fight night. In the chaos, he got me out through a service entrance and told me to run and not stop until I found Caleb Reed. But I collapsed in your yard before I reached Wolf River."*

A heavy silence followed, broken only by Magnus's whine from his spot near the door. Opal stared at Wolfe, tears streaming unchecked down her face.

"Don't look at me like that. It wasn't all bad. Really."

"Wolfe." She reached across the table to touch his

hand. "What you're describing is imprisonment. Torture. Trafficking."

He shrugged. *"It was just my life."*

"And the murder?"

"My second-to-last fight. The guy- he wasn't supposed to fight me. He was one of Mo's bodyguards who'd screwed up. Mo put him in as punishment."

"You killed him?" Opal prompted.

"No. I refused. Even when the guy came at me with a knife and sliced me before I disarmed him."

He lifted his shirt, revealing the jagged scar along his ribs.

"I wouldn't kill him, and Mo was super pissed. Shot the guy in front of everyone."

"And no one did anything?"

"You don't know the pull Mo has."

Opal sat back.

"The sheriff," she said finally. "He said he got a tip. Could that be your uncle? Could he have learned you were headed this waycoming here?"

"Mo has connections everywhere. And he won't stop looking for me. But the only way he would know I went this direction is if Zaden told him. And the only way Zaden would tell him is..."

"Is what?"

"Is... if Mo tortured it out of him." Bile rose from Wolfe's stomach. He should go back. Make sure Zaden wasn't paying for Wolfe's escape.

"Why doesn't he find another fighter?"

"Because I'm worth millions to him. And because no one leaves Mo. Ever."

Opal stood abruptly, her chair scraping against the floor. "We need to head to town. The Reeds will protect you- they protect all shifters who come seeking sanctuary."

"The sheriff-"

"Has no jurisdiction," she interrupted. "It's private property, owned by the Reeds. Human law enforcement can't enter without permission from Alpha Jeremiah."

"Why would they help me? I've done terrible things."

"You haven't done anything terrible. Your uncle did. All you did was survive," she corrected. "You did what you had to do in an impossible situation. And now you deserve a life."

She crossed to the window. "We'll leave now. I'll pack a bag."

Wolfe stood, and he waved at her to get her attention. *"Opal, I..."* He what? What did he say? *"Thank you. For everything."*

"Don't thank me yet. We still have to get you to town."

As she moved past him toward her bedroom, Wolfe touched her arm.

"I won't let anything happen to you because of me. Whatever comes, I promise you."

Something fluttered inside Wolfe at the thought, and his wolf stood and howled. In the last few days, they'd both become more than fond of Opal; something else had begun to form. Something Wolfe didn't understand.

Opal nodded once, squeezed his hand, and then jogged to her room.

CHAPTER THIRTEEN

Opal pulled up in front of Stix's house. It was still early, but he'd have to be up to prep at the restaurant anyway.

"Wait here. I'm going to go talk to my brother."

Wolfe nodded, but anxiety shone through his eyes as he took in the neighborhood.

"It's okay," she reassured him.

He gave her a curt nod.

She jumped out and marched to the front door. She rang the doorbell and knocked twice, waited a minute, and knocked again.

Heavy footsteps descended the stairs. The loose floorboard squeaked, and the door opened a crack, and her brother blinked several times.

"Opal?" Stix asked, thick with sleep. "Everything okay?"

"No. I need help, Stix. And I need you not to ask too many questions right now."

After a pause, he seemed to wake up. "I'm listening."

"I have someone who needs protection."

"Someone?" Stix repeated, fully alert now.

"A wolf shifter," she said. "He's in trouble. Serious trouble."

"What kind?"

Opal weighed how much to reveal. "The kind that has Holden showing up at the door four times in less than a week with accusations of murder."

"Jez, Opal," Stix breathed. "What have you gotten yourself into?"

"He's innocent," she insisted. "He escaped trafficking. He was being forced to fight in an underground ring. For years."

Stix looked over her shoulder at her Jeep.

“Stix, please. After everything I’ve put you through, you're probably leery, but I promise this isn’t about me; it’s about him. He needs help, and you know the Reeds better than I do.”

"You're sure about this?"

"Yes," she said without hesitation. "I'm sure. Besides, his buddy who broke him out told him to come here and find Caleb."

“Then how did he end up in contact with you?”

She didn’t want to explain on the doorstep. “It’s a long story.”

"Okay," Stix said finally. "Bring him in. I'll talk to Caleb. But Opal?"

"Yeah?"

"If what you're saying is true, whoever had him won't just let him go."

"He has no one else. And after what he's been through, he deserves a real life."

Stix nodded. “All right. Come in. He can have Deacon’s room since he’s out on tour again. I’ll have Satia make coffee.”

Opal gave her brother a tight smile. “Thank you. Oh... uh... there's one more thing.”

Stix groaned.

"I had to bring Magnus."

He sighed. "Just what we need. That monster tearing around the house."

"He'll be good, I promise. We all will. Thank you so much."

He massaged his temples before smiling. “What are older brothers for? I’m assuming mom and dad don’t know about this?”

She shook her head.

“Yeah, well, that’s gonna change quick. As soon as he leaves your car, everyone will smell a new wolf in town. So, it would be better if it came from you.”

She groaned. “Fine. But coffee first.”

Stix nodded.

Opal sat at Stix's kitchen table, her fingers tightened around a ceramic mug of coffee as her mother's eyes hardened. The warm kitchen, filled with the aroma of fresh pastries Satia had put out, was anything but comfortable. Her father sat beside her mother, his weathered face calm but concerned. Stix leaned against the counter, arms crossed, while Satia busied herself with the coffee pot.

Wolfe sat cross-legged on the floor with Andre, Stix, and Satia's three-year-old son. Her nephew stacked colorful wooden blocks while Wolfe signed something that made Andre giggle.

"So," her mother said, drawing Opal's attention back to the kitchen table, "is he the reason you bought enough groceries to feed a small army?"

Opal sighed. "Yes."

Her mother's lips pressed into a thin line. "I thought we weren't lying to each other anymore, Opal."

"Mom-"

"We had an agreement after rehab. No more secrets. No more lies."

Magnus whined at her mom's feet and looked up at her.

"I'm sorry," Opal said, setting her mug down. "I didn't know what to say. I didn't want to freak everyone out, and I worried that telling anyone might scare Wolfe away. He was sick, injured, and needed help."

"You should have called us," her mother insisted. "What if he had been dangerous? What if-"

"Joyce," her father interrupted, placing a calming hand on her mother's arm. "Let's take a breath. What's done is done. If Wolfe needs help, we help him. That's what we do."

Stix cleared his throat. "I called Caleb. He'll be here in about an hour to hear Wolfe's story before taking anything to his father."

"I want to be there," Opal said.

Stix raised an eyebrow. "I'm sure Wolfe can handle talking to Caleb himself."

"No," Opal snapped, her voice sharper than she intended. "Wolfe only signs. They will need an interpreter."

The kitchen quieted, everyone staring at her unexpected vehemence. Heat bloomed in her cheeks, embarrassment and determination mingling, but she held her ground, meeting her brother's surprised gaze without flinching.

Her father broke the tension with a cough. "Why can't Opal be present? After all, she's the one who brought Wolfe to us. Caleb will want to speak with her anyway, to understand the full situation."

"It may not be my place," Satia said from the counter, "but watching how he is with Andre..." She nodded toward the living room. "That's not a murderer. Look at him."

They all turned. Andre had climbed into Wolfe's

lap, showing him a picture book, pointing at the animals while Wolfe signed their names. The little boy copied the signs with clumsy enthusiasm.

Something warm and primal stirred in Opal. Her ursa rumbled with contentment at the sight, unbidden images flashing through her mind- Wolfe cradling a dark-haired infant, teaching their own cubs to sign, his strong hands gentle as they were with Andre.

Her cheeks heated, and she turned away, only to find her mother watching her with a knowing gaze.

"Well." Her mother's expression softened. "I suppose we should make sure the guest room is ready. He'll need a place to stay while the Reeds decide what to do."

"He can stay here with me," Opal said.

Her father chuckled. "Let's not get ahead of ourselves, sweetheart. One step at a time."

Thirty minutes later, the doorbell rang. Magnus jumped to his feet and barked. Opal caught Wolfe's eye across the room. He stiffened at the bell, his body instantly alert. He carefully put Andre down. She gave him what she hoped was a reassuring smile before taking Magnus to the back door and pushing him outside.

Stix glanced at his phone. "That's probably Caleb. He's early."

"It's okay," she mouthed to Wolfe. "Just Caleb."

Wolfe nodded, but his posture remained rigid as he watched the hallway. Andre, oblivious to the tension, stacked blocks against Wolfe's knee.

Moments later, Stix returned with Caleb Reed. The Beta of Wolf River was younger than Stix but carried himself with the same quiet authority. His dark hair messy, and his sharp eyes missed nothing as they swept the room, lingering on Wolfe before settling on Opal.

"Opal," he greeted with a smile. "It's been too long."

"Caleb."She stood to accept his brief hug.

"And you must be Wolfe."

Wolfe stood, his size obvious as he stood to his full height. Andre whined at the interruption, but Satia distracted him with the promise of a doughnut.

"I understand you've had quite a journey," Caleb said, extending his hand to Wolfe. "I'm here to listen."

Wolfe hesitated, then shook Caleb's hand. His gaze flicked to Opal, a question in his eyes.

"Let's talk in the study." Opal moved to stand beside Wolfe. "More privacy."

Caleb nodded. "Lead the way."

As they moved toward the hallway, Stix caught Opal's arm. "Be careful, your ursa is showing."

Opal pulled her arm free. "I'm fine. I just want to make sure he gets a fair hearing."

But as she led Wolfe and Caleb into the study, she couldn't deny the protectiveness surging through her veins. Her ursa had recognized something in Wolfe from the beginning- something worth fighting for, and Opal was starting to believe her bear might be right.

The study door closed behind them with a soft click, sealing them away from curious eyes and ears. Caleb took a seat in one of the leather armchairs, gesturing for them to do the same.

"So. Why don't you tell me your story, Wolfe? From the beginning."

Wolfe looked at Opal.

“Wolfe can’t speak. I can interpret for him, though.”

Caleb nodded.

WOLFE SETTLED UNEASILY INTO THE LEATHER ARMCHAIR, acutely aware of Caleb's presence across from him. There was something about the man- something beyond his physical stature or calm demeanor- that made Wolfe's wolf stir. It wasn't fear exactly, but a primal recognition of power that radiated from Caleb like heat from a furnace. His wolf, usually so eager, shrank back, making himself smaller in the presence of this unfamiliar authority.

"I appreciate you calling with me," Caleb began,

his voice measured and steady. "I understand you've been through quite an ordeal."

Wolfe nodded.

"First, tell me about your life before you were taken in by your uncle. Do you remember where you lived? Your parents' names?"

Wolfe furrowed his brow. The memories slept hazily, distorted by time and neglect. His hands faltered as he searched for answers.

"I don't remember much," Opal translated. *"We lived in a forest somewhere. There were mountains. I remember running through trees with my parents."*

"And their names?" Caleb prompted.

"My mother's name was Selena." The name brought a fleeting warmth. *"I don't remember my father's name. I only remember his face and the faces of my grandparents and a few uncles and cousins, I think."*

"But not the uncle who took you in?"

"I don't remember him from before he saved me."

"Tell me more about your uncle's operation? Where is it located? Are there other shifters involved? Anyone else being forced to fight?"

Wolfe's hands moved more confidently, describing the underground ring under Mo's downtown Seattle hotel. *"I don't think there are other shifters, besides my friend Zaden,"* he signed. *"Mo kept me... separate for the most part. The other fighters are either in his debt or fight because the money is excellent."*

Caleb nodded. "And this friend who helped you escape- Zaden-"

"Have you heard from him?" he signed urgently.

A shadow crossed Caleb's face. "Zaden lived here for a short time, a few years back. Did some construction work for me. Good guy, but restless- couldn't get used to the quiet life. He had his younger sister with him. Their parents had died. He contacted me a few weeks ago, mentioned helping a wolf who may need sanctuary."

"Anything since?"

Caleb shook his head. "Nothing."

Wolfe slumped, his hands falling into his lap. Zaden had risked everything to help him escape, and now he might be paying the price.

Opal reached over and touched Wolfe's hand. He looked up, and she gave him a smile.

"I'm concerned too." Caleb's voice softened. "Zaden can take care of himself, but Mo sounds like a dangerous man."

"He is. If he found out Zaden arranged it..."

The sentence didn't need finishing.

"Tell me more about your uncle," Caleb said after a moment. "How did he keep you from shifting all these years? That's not... normal. Not natural."

Wolfe explained about the injections, the drugs he thought probably kept his wolf sedated, and the punishment that followed any sign of his wolf emerging. Caleb's jaw clenched, his eyes darkening.

Caleb exhaled slowly, exchanging a glance with Opal. "That's enough for now. I need to discuss this with my father, but I believe we can offer you a new life here."

Relief washed over Wolfe, so fast it made him dizzy. His hands moved before he could stop them. *"Thank you."*

"Don't thank me yet," Caleb warned. "Your uncle sounds like the type who doesn't give up easily. And if the sheriff is already involved, things might get complicated."

"What should we do in the meantime?" Opal threaded her fingers with Wolfe's.

We. She'd said the word 'we'. His wolf yowled. He'd never had someone to think of as a 'we' before. But both he and his wolf liked the idea of being a 'we' with Opal.

Caleb considered for a moment. "Wolfe should stay here with your family for now. It's safer than the cabin, and we can monitor things until my father makes a decision." He turned his attention back to Wolfe. "You understand if we grant you residency, there will be conditions? Rules to follow."

Wolfe nodded without hesitation. After a lifetime of Mo's arbitrary and cruel restrictions, the prospect of living under rules designed to protect rather than exploit him seemed like a dream.

Caleb got to his feet. "I'll come back tomorrow. I

have a few things to address today. In the meantime, rest."

As Caleb moved toward the door, Wolfe stood, his hands forming one last question.

"Zaden," he signed, Opal translating. *"Will you try to find out what happened to him?"*

Caleb paused. "I have people looking. If he's out there, we'll find him."

After Caleb left, Opal turned to Wolfe, her gray eyes searching his face. "Are you okay?"

Wolfe's hands moved slowly. *"I didn't expect to be so... intimidated by him."*

"That's just Caleb." Opal gave a small smile. "He's an Alpha in waiting and currently the Beta of the pack. You're feeling his power- his wolf rank. It's natural for your wolf to respond to that, especially since you've never been around other wolves before."

"My wolf... cowered."

"That's not weakness," Opal assured him. "It's pack dynamics. It would happen to any wolf meeting Caleb. It will be stronger with Alpha Jeremiah, but you'll get used to it. It won't be as uncomfortable as it is now. As soon as you are part of the pack, you'll be able to run and bond with everyone, and it will be more like Jeremiah is the head of your family, and Caleb and his brothers are your older brothers. Your wolf will only cower if the Alpha or his Betas command you to do something. But Jeremiah rarely does. It will be like one huge family."

Wolfe considered the information. He'd spent his life battling humans, never knowing an entire world of werewolves with their own rules and hierarchies existed. The realization that he had so much to learn was both daunting and exhilarating.

A family. A real family. He had no idea what that would be like, but something inside him awakened, and a memory surfaced of his mom and dad squeezing his chest.

"Do you think they'll let me stay?"

Opal gripped his arm. "Yes. The Reeds protect their own. And now, that includes you."

Before Wolfe responded, the study door opened, and Stix poked his head in. "Everything okay?"

Opal nodded. "Caleb's gone to talk to his father. He thinks Wolfe should stay here for now."

"Already got the room set up," Stix said with a small smile. "And fair warning- Mom's in full mama bear mode in the kitchen. She's determined to fatten you up, Wolfe."

Despite the tension of the day, a smile tugged at Wolfe's lips. The concept of family- of belonging- was so foreign to him it hurt to hope. Yet he was surrounded by people genuinely concerned for his welfare, offering protection because he needed it.

As they moved toward the kitchen, the delicious aroma of home cooking filling the air, Wolfe caught Opal's hand. Surprise flickered across her face.

"Thank you. For everything."

Her smile dawned like a sunrise after the long, dark night that had been his life.

"You're welcome," she said. "Now come on. You haven't lived until you've tasted my mom's pancakes."

For the first time since his escape, Wolfe allowed himself to hope that maybe- maybe- he might have found not only safety, but a home.

CHAPTER FOURTEEN

Opal had never been as happy in her entire life as she had in the last twelve hours. Eating with her family, laughing and joking. Playing games with Wolfe and Andre. Watching the delight in Wolfe's eyes as he let his entire guard down and totally relaxed. All of it made something shift inside her. Something she couldn't place. Wolfe had crashed into her life like a bulldozer, and somehow, he'd become so important to her that she couldn't imagine him not in her life, moving forward.

Satia came up beside her, watching Wolfe struggle to have a conversation with her dad, who hadn't picked up ASL as easily as the rest of them.

"He's sweet," said Satia.

Opal looked at her sister-in-law and smiled. "He is."

She turned back to Wolfe as he tried to teach her dad a sign.

“Not bad looking either.”

Opal nodded. “He’s totally hot.” Her cheeks heated.

Satia chuckled. “The moment you stuck up for him with your mom, we all saw it.”

“Saw what?”

Satia cocked an eyebrow. “You have feelings for him. Your ursa has feelings for him.”

Opal’s cheeks heated further. “I... I...” She what? What did she say? It was the truth. Over the last few days, she’d come to feel for Wolfe in a way she wasn’t sure she'd ever feel about someone else.

“How... How did you know?” she asked. “With Stix, I mean. How did you guys...” She felt stupid asking.

Satia shook her head. “I don’t know. I thought he was hella hot from the moment I saw him, but it was more. It was the way he treated me. The way he cared. Then Andre came along, and seeing him with Stix, I just... knew. He was the one I was meant to be with.”

"He can speak when we are in our animal forms.”

“That’s super interesting.”

“I think it’s because his vocal cords may have been cut, but that doesn’t have anything to do with the mental link between shifters.”

“I’d never thought of that before, but it makes sense.”

“Has Andre ever tried when you guys shift?”

Satia shook her head. "I don't think he realizes he can or how. I'll have to talk to Stix about it. I would love for him to be able to communicate with us as well as his siblings."

"Are you pregnant?"

Satia smiled. "We haven't told anyone yet, but yes. Stix says it's twins. He can hear the heartbeats. I think he's being hopeful."

Opal hugged Satia's arm. "I am so happy for you guys."

Satia beamed. "We are too. We've been trying for a bit."

"It can be a little harder for interspecies pairings. But it happens all the time. I wonder if they will be ursa or saber. Or one of each."

Satia laughed. "That would be different."

"At least they won't be mixed hybrids. That would be insane."

Satia thought for a minute. "Sabursa?"

"Ubers?"

They both laughed, and Wolfe turned toward her. He smiled so wide it crinkled his eyes, and her ursa chuffed.

Satia was right.

But she had no idea if he felt the same about her.

After dinner and a movie, Satia, Stix, and Andre went upstairs, while her mom and dad left, saying they would be back in the morning to help with Andre, when Satia and Stix left for work.

"Do you work tomorrow?" asked her dad.

"No. Doc said to take the rest of the week off. I'll go back Monday."

"How is school coming?"

"Crap! I forgot my laptop. I'll have to get it."

Her dad gave her a knowing smile. "I think you'll probably be here at least through next week. So you might want to."

"Or maybe you'll finally move in with us," said her mom.

Opal rolled her eyes. Her parents were always trying to get her to move in with them.

"Your room is still waiting," offered her dad. "We decorated it especially for you."

Opal rolled her eyes. Oh, please don't let her dad have painted it pink with unicorns like he had to surprise her when she was ten. "We'll see."

Her dad hugged her, and her mom did, too. Her dad walked up to Wolfe, pulled him into one of his giant ursa hugs, and whispered something in Wolfe's ear. Wolfe smiled and nodded.

As her parents closed the front door, they sat on the couch, listening to Satia read a story to Andre up in his bedroom. Magnus curled near the fireplace, snoring loudly.

Wolfe tapped her arm. *"I love your family."*

She nodded. "They are pretty great."

"You are lucky to have them."

Thinking of all Wolfe had been through made her realize how right he was.

"I've put them through a lot. It hasn't been easy for them, but they have been there for me through everything. I am blessed."

Wolfe nodded and gazed at her. Opal's stomach flopped, and her ursa whined.

He lifted his hand and brushed her hair from her eyes. *"I love your eyes."*

Her body heated.

"I heard what you said."

"What... what do you mean?" she stammered.

"You think I'm hot. Totally hot, I think you said."

Opal swallowed hard. "Yes," she breathed.

He leaned in even closer. *"I think you are too."*

"You... you do?" She barely got the words out.

He moved until his body rubbed against hers. Slowly, he ran his fingers through her hair before stopping at the base of her neck and pulling her face to his. Tenderly, he touched his lips to hers. Her breath caught, and her ursa howled. Opal pressed her lips to his, suddenly. His arm slid around her waist, and he opened her mouth with his. Their tongues entwined, and she became lost. The scent of him. The feel. The taste. They all exploded, encompassing her and drowning out everything else in the world.

He pulled her to him, lifting her onto his lap. She laced her arms around his neck, their kisses heating.

He gripped her hips and dug his fingers into them, making her pant. He broke the kiss and ran his lips down her neck, licking and kissing her.

Opal's brain swirled as she took in every inch of contact his body made with hers. She ground her hips against his as heat flooded her core and her nipples grew sensitive, brushing against him. He pulled her face to his again, his teeth clashing against hers. His kiss forceful and needy, and she reciprocated.

He broke the kiss and threw his head back, eyes squeezed shut.

"Are you okay?"

He shook his head. Every muscle in his body tensed, and his grip on her hips grew tighter to the point of pain.

A ripple traversed his skin, and the hair lengthened on his arms. She understood.

"It's your wolf. He's trying to take over."

He nodded once and grunted.

She cupped his face. "Wolfe, open your eyes. Look at me."

He grimaced.

"Wolfe." She kissed his eyelids before rubbing her thumbs over his furrowed brow, forcing the muscles to relax. "Wolfe, open your eyes. It's ok."

His eyes flew open. Glowing in the dim light.

She smiled. "It's okay. Breathe with me, and tell him to back down."

His mouth opened, and he tried to say something, but she couldn't read his lips.

She slid her hands down his arms, feeling the velvety fur. "You're okay. This is natural. It happens. Probably never for you before because you've kept your wolf chained up. Now that he's had freedom, he's going to want more. Tell him to back down. Take control. Force him to calm down."

He stared at her intently. His eyes never moved from hers as she rubbed his arms, his cheek, his neck. Finally, his eyes returned to normal, and he pried his fingers from her hips.

He sighed. *"I don't know how you're able to help me so much."*

She smiled. "You're welcome."

He took another minute to breathe before signing, *"Will that happen every time I... get excited?"*

She chuckled. "Yes and no. From what I've been told, he will want out, but you'll be able to hold him back. You did awesome this time, and you've never even tried before."

His brows knit together. *"From what you've been told?"*

Heat flushed up her neck to her cheeks. "Uh... yeah. I mean, I wouldn't know because I've never... I mean, I'm..."

"A virgin?"

She nodded and dropped her gaze.

He lifted her chin. *"Are you ashamed?"*

"Well, not exactly. I mean, sort of, I guess. You've been with lots of women, and I've never-"

He shook his head and cupped her face with one hand. *"I'm glad you've never."*

"You are?"

"I wish I had never."

"Guys never say that."

He paused. *"I won my first match against a champion fighter at fifteen. He beat me so bad I thought I would die, but I won. And my uncle said I had proved myself to be a man in the ring, so I deserved to be rewarded like a man. He took me to the penthouse for the first time. He introduced me to alcohol and hired some girls to come up and reward me some more."*

Opal couldn't help her mouth falling open. "Wolfe... that's... that's awful."

"At the time, I didn't know better. I just knew I was finally not being treated like a pet anymore."

"But you were a child. That's not right. That's rape. Abuse. A million other things which aren't legal."

He snorted. *"Mo doesn't do legal."*

"But..." Tears sprang into her eyes as anger bubbled inside her so rapidly her ursa jumped to her feet and growled.

Wolfe wiped the tear from her cheek. *"I'm sorry. I shouldn't have said anything."*

"No," she said forcefully. "I want to know. I want to know you. The good parts and the bad parts, too." She shook her head. "I just don't understand. How have you been through so much and still remained so... kind? Sweet. Not hate the world."

He thought for a minute. *"Honestly, I just am who I am. But, after being here with your family, I will never go back. Can never go back. To go back would do those things to me. Make me hard. Make me hate. To have experienced peace and kindness from people who weren't paid to give them to me, I'm changed. You have changed me, Opal. I can never be what my uncle wants me to be again. Never."*

She wiped her nose on her sleeve. "If I ever meet your uncle, I can't promise I won't kill him."

Wolfe smiled and pulled her lips to his.

Opal meant it. The rage coursing through her at what he'd been through was nothing like anything she'd ever experienced. And she wasn't altogether sure she'd be able to hold her ursa back if she and Mo ever came face to face.

She wasn't sure she'd even try.

CHAPTER FIFTEEN

Wolfe woke to the scent of pancakes and bacon drifting through the unfamiliar room. Sunlight streamed through curtains he didn't recognize, casting warm patterns over a bed that wasn't his. Panic seized him- then memory rushed back. Stix's house. Deacon's bedroom. Safety.

He sat up, running a hand over his stubbled jaw as last night with Opal replayed in his mind. He'd told her so much- yet he'd still held back. The part about being "rewarded" to wealthy female patrons who'd paid premium prices to spend time with Mo's prized fighter... That, he couldn't bring himself to share. Not yet... maybe not ever. What would she think of him? His virginal Opal?

The memories alone made his skin crawl. Those nights in the penthouse suite, Mo's instructions ringing in his ears. *"Make her happy. Whatever she wants."* The women with their hungry eyes and grasping hands, treating him like an exotic pet, a novelty to be sampled and discarded. Their perfume choking him as they whispered demands, his body responding mechanically while his mind retreated to some distant place.

He couldn't tell Opal. The anger that had flashed in her gray eyes when he'd mentioned the "rewards" had been enough. To see her gentle face contorted with rage and pity- he couldn't bear it. Not when her opinion of him had somehow become the most important thing in his world.

Wolfe swung his legs over the bed, feet touching cool hardwood. His wolf stirred within him, content in a way it never had been. The run's freedom lingered in his muscles, a sweet ache reminding him what it felt like to be whole.

Not only had the shift changed him. It was Opal, as well. The way she'd gazed at him on the couch, her eyes filled with desire and something deeper. The way she'd tasted- honey and popcorn and something uniquely her. The way her body fit against his, curves pressing into his hardness as if they'd been designed as complementary pieces.

For the first time in his life, he'd wanted to kiss someone. Not because it was expected, not because it was a transaction or a duty, but because he craved the connection. The connection with her. He'd wanted to taste her, to feel her respond to him, to lose himself in the sensation of her lips against his. To give to her, but also selfishly to take for himself and his wolf as well.

In all his encounters with women, he'd never truly been present. He'd done what was necessary- touched where they wanted to be touched, moved how they wanted him to move- but he'd never allowed himself to feel. Half the time, he didn't finish, treating his own pleasure as irrelevant to the exchange. He'd been a tool, nothing more.

But with Opal, everything was different. Her touch set his skin on fire. Her smile made his chest ache with an unfamiliar fullness. When she'd sat in his lap, her weight against him had been like coming home to a place he'd never known existed.

A knock interrupted his thoughts. He grabbed the sweatpants Stix loaned him and pulled them on as the door cracked open.

"You awake?"

He nodded, self-conscious about his bare chest and the marks that mapped his torso; a testament to all he'd endured.

Opal slipped into the room, a tray balanced in her hands. She wore simple jeans and a faded T-shirt, her dark hair pulled back in a loose braid. Beautiful.

"Mom insisted on making you breakfast in bed."She laid the tray on the nightstand. "She thinks you're too thin."

The tray held a stack of at least a dozen pancakes

drizzled with maple syrup, crispy bacon, scrambled eggs, and a tall glass of orange juice. The sight of so much food prepared for him made something tighten in Wolfe's throat.

"Tell her thank you."

Opal sat on the bed, her thigh brushing against his. "Sleep okay?"

He nodded, though in truth, his dreams had been a tangled jumble of past and present. The cage. The hotel. Mo's icy smile. All surfaced, interspersed with flashes of Opal's face, her touch, her scent.

"I brought you something." She reached into her pocket. She pulled out a small black rectangle. "It's a phone. Stix activated it this morning. It's got my number and everyone else's programmed in. I figured... You might need a way to communicate when I'm not around to translate."

Wolfe took the phone, turning it over in his hands. The gesture so thoughtful, so practical, his throat clamped down again.

"Thank you." He opened the contacts, found her name, and typed out his first text message.

Thank you.

Opal's phone buzzed in her pocket. She pulled it out and smiled at the screen. "You're welcome," she said, then tapped out a reply.

Wolfe's new phone vibrated.

Good morning, handsome.

Heat flooded his face. No one had ever called him that before- at least not in a genuine way, rather than appraising. A blush stained Opal's cheeks.

"Sorry," she said. "Too much?"

He shook his head and typed.

No, Beautiful. I like it.

Her smile returned, brighter than before. "Good. Because I mean it." She gestured to the tray. "You should eat before it gets cold. Mom will be offended if you don't clean your plate."

Wolfe reached for her hand instead, pulling her in until their faces were inches apart. He wanted to kiss her again, hoping it would feel as right as it had last night, but uncertainty held him back. Were there rules? Was he allowed to touch her, to want her?

Opal closed the gap between them and pressed her lips to his.

"In case you were wondering," she whispered against his mouth, "that's definitely not against the rules."

Relief and desire coursed through him. He deepened the kiss, one hand cupping the back of her neck, fingers threading through her braid. She tasted of maple and toothpaste, and something beneath that was purely Opal- a flavor he was already addicted to.

When they finally broke apart, both breathing harder, Opal's eyes darkened with desire. "You should definitely eat," she said, her voice breathy. "Because

Caleb called. His father wants to meet you. But first, you need stuff of your own. So you don't have to keep borrowing from Stix."

Wolfe paused. *"I don't mind borrowing. It's fine."*

She studied him. "You don't need to worry about the money. I'll take care of it."

"No."

She cocked her head to the side. "Yes," she said slowly.

"I don't want you paying anymore for me. Food. Housing. Now a phone. It's wrong."

She sighed. "I understand how you feel. But take the help. This isn't charity, and it isn't pity. It's what we do. Shifters help each other and don't ask for anything in return."

He'd never had anything given to him without strings attached.

"Okay," he finally signed. "*But as soon as possible, I need a job so you don't have to keep paying for things. Problem is... I can't do anything but fight."*

"We'll figure it out. You can go to college. Or work in town. Don't stress now. Let's start simple and acclimate to not living in a hotel. You know, things like making your own bed and helping with the dishes. And occasionally cooking me another amazing meal. Then we can talk about next steps, alright?"

Wolfe nodded. The mention of the future and money and meeting the Alpha brought reality crashing back- Mo, the sheriff, the uncertainty that stretched before him. Yet even with those shadows looming, the light Opal brought couldn't be dimmed.

As he reached for the fork, his wolf rumbled within him. For the first time, both man and beast were in perfect agreement- whatever came next, they would face it together, with Opal by their side.

After breakfast, Wolfe showered and dressed. The jeans hung low and tight on his hips, and the shirt stretched tight across his torso. As he studied his reflection in the bathroom mirror, he couldn't help but think how different he looked from the fighter who had fled Seattle less than a week ago. His face had filled out slightly, the hollowness in his eyes replaced by something calmer, more settled.

Opal waited for him downstairs, car keys dangling from her fingers. "Ready for the grand tour?"

Wolfe nodded, following her out to her old blue Jeep parked in the driveway. The crisp, clean morning air carried the scent of pine trees and falling leaves. His wolf stirred, eager to explore the new territory that might become their home.

"Buckle up," Opal said as they settled into the Jeep. "Wolf River isn't huge, but there's more to it than meets the eye. And some of the roads can be a little bumpy."

As they drove from Stix's house, Wolfe soaked in the scenery. The town lay nestled in the valley like a secret, shielded by mountains on all sides. Unlike the concrete and glass of Seattle, Wolf River seemed carved from the earth, buildings of wood and stone which complemented rather than dominated the landscape.

She turned down a tree-lined street, slowing as they passed a modern yet vintage-looking building, mostly wood and glass. "That's the school," she said. "The Reeds built it about fifteen years ago. Before then, most pack kids were homeschooled or bused to the human school in the next county."

Wolfe studied the building with interest. Children played in a fenced yard, their laughter carried on the breeze. He tried to imagine growing up in a place like this, surrounded by others of your kind, free to learn and play without fear.

"It goes from kindergarten through high school. They teach all the regular subjects, plus shifter history and culture. There's a gym designed for young shifters to learn control."

She drove on, pointing out various landmarks- the community center, Doc's clinic, a small park with walking trails that disappeared into the surrounding forest. Each place she described sounded more incredible than the last, a haven designed specifically for beings like them.

"That's the main square." Opal pointed to a central plaza where several streets converged. In the center sat a grassy area with a huge firepit in the middle.

“Most of the businesses branch off from this street."

As they approached the town square, delicious aromas wafted through the open windows. Opal slowed in front of a charming storefront with "Wild Flour Bakery" painted in elegant script across the window.

"That's Caleb's wife's place. Makayla makes the best muffins ever. We'll have to stop in when we're not in a hurry."

Wolfe's stomach rumbled despite his recent breakfast, making Opal laugh. "We'll come back."

They circled the square, Opal pointing out each business- the grocery store with locally sourced produce, the hardware store which doubled as a hunting supply shop, the diner her parents owned.

"And this," she pulled up in front of a converted log cabin, "is us. The Exchange."

The building stood with a wooden porch wrapping around the front and sides. A simple wooden sign hung above the entrance, painted with the silhouettes of various animals- wolf, bear, cougar, falcon- arranged in a circle.

“This was the original home the Reeds built way back when they bought the land and settled here.”

As they got out of the car, Wolfe instinctively moved to Opal's side, opening the door for her. Just before stepping inside, the hairs on his arm stood up, and his wolf growled. Glancing across the street, a man watched them from the shadow of a storefront. He couldn't see the man clearly as he wore a baseball cap pulled down.

Without thinking, Wolfe raised his hand in greeting. The man started, scanned the street, nodded once, and hurried away.

"What is it?"

Wolfe shook his head. *"Nothing. Just someone watching us."*

Opal followed his gaze, and the man rounded the corner and disappeared.

"Probably curious," she said. "It's going to happen because of us."

"Us?"

"Yeah, you aren't the only curiosity in town," she chuckled. "Remember when I told you I never fit in because I'm an ursa? That only got worse after my suicide attempt. Seeing me is as much of a gossip starter as you moving in."

His gut twisted tight as a wet rope, thinking about Opal hurting herself. If she'd succeeded, he'd never have met her. The thought hurt him more than he could articulate.

Inside, the store appeared both quiet and spacious. The old house flowed together in an open floor plan. Racks of clothing, shelves of books, displays of household goods- all arranged with care but without the polished merchandising of commercial stores.

"Welcome to The Exchange." Opal gestured

around them. "It's kind of like a thrift store, but with a twist. People bring things they no longer need, and others take what they can use. When they're done with those items, they bring them back or contribute something else."

"No money?"

"No money," Opal confirmed. "It's a way for everyone to help each other out. Need a winter coat? Take one. Outgrown your shoes? Bring them in for someone else."

She led him toward the back of the store, where men's clothing hung on simple racks. "The one rule is to take only what you need, and give when you can."

Wolfe fingered the sleeve of a flannel shirt, the fabric soft from wear but still in excellent condition. The concept of helping and trading, foreign to him. Items freely given and received, no transaction required, no debt incurred.

"How does it stay stocked? What if people take but don't give back?"

Opal smiled, pulling a few shirts from the rack to hold up against him. "That's where the Reeds come in. Since they own the place, they often buy new items. They take the tags off and wash them a few times. Everyone knows they are brand new, but it's a way, no one feels like they're receiving charity, and there's always enough for people in need."

"I've never heard of anything like this." He selected a dark blue Henley.

"Jeremiah Reed has a lot of money." Opal moved to a shelf stacked with jeans. "Like... a lot. He made his fortune in software back in the early days of computers. But instead of hoarding it, they've dedicated those resources to building the pack and Wolf River, helping anyone who needs it."

She handed him several pairs of jeans. "Because of their investment, the town has grown. The bakery, the school, the grocery store, construction jobs, even the church, funded by the Reeds initially."

As they moved through the store, gathering socks, shoes, underwear, pajamas, and a sturdy coat, Opal elaborated. "But they don't simply hand out money. They help pack members start their own businesses. Doc's clinic, my parents' newest restaurant, a small flower shop, and a coffeehouse are owned by pack members, but the Reeds helped them."

Wolfe's arms loaded down with clothing. He searched for a checkout counter.

She took some of the items from his arms. "When you're settled and have something to contribute- whether it's items, time, or skills- you'll give back to the community in your own way. Maybe you'll make food for one of the widows when they aren't well. Or perhaps you'll donate some hours to help with the kids at school, or teach boxing, or go to Moscow to the mall and buy some stuff to replace what you took today."

"It sounds too good," he signed after setting his armload on a nearby table.

"By human standards." Opal folded the clothing. "But in pack life, everyone helps everyone. It's how we've survived."

A middle-aged woman emerged from a back room, smiling when she spotted Opal. "Opal Reed, it's been ages."

"Mrs. Dawson," Opal greeted her with a hug. "This is Wolfe. He's new here and needs some basics."

Mrs. Dawson's eyes flicked over Wolfe, taking in his size and the ill-fitting borrowed clothes. "Welcome, Wolfe. Do you need a bag?"

Wolfe nodded, offering a small smile.

As Mrs. Dawson bustled away to find bags, Wolfe turned to Opal. *"Everyone is so... accepting."*

"That's how packs are supposed to be."

They left The Exchange with three packed bags of clothing and essentials. As they loaded them into the Jeep, Wolfe touched Opal's hand, turning her to face him.

"Thank you. Not only for the clothes. For showing me a place like this can exist."

Opal's eyes softened. She reached up to touch his face, her fingers tracing the line of his jaw.

"You're part of it now. Don't thank me. Thank your friend Zaden when we find him. And the Reeds."

He nodded, his heart full of emotions he couldn't name. For the first time since he was a child, he might belong somewhere, with someone who saw him for who he truly was.

As they drove back toward Stix's house, Opal reached over and squeezed his hand, her touch grounding him in his new reality.

His wolf settled within him. Finally, a home. And if he had his way, with Opal.

CHAPTER SIXTEEN

Caleb returned to Stix's house after lunch, his expression serious as he greeted them. "My father would like to meet you, Wolfe. If you're up for it."

Wolfe glanced at Opal, who gave him an encouraging nod. "We'll go together."

The Reeds' house stood on a hillside overlooking Wolf River, its wide windows capturing sunlight and forest views. The house was formidable but not imposing- natural wood and stone made from the surrounding vegetation.

As they approached the front door, Wolfe's wolf stirred anxiously. If Caleb's presence had been intimidating, what would the Alpha be like?

The door swung open to reveal a woman with silver-streaked dark hair and kind eyes that reminded Wolfe of Caleb.

"You must be Wolfe," she said, her smile genuine. "I'm Mary Reed, Jeremiah's wife. Please, come in."

She embraced Opal with the familiarity of family before leading them through the house to a spacious living room where enormous windows framed the forest beyond. The furnishings comfortable rather than formal- well-worn leather couches, bookshelves lined with actual books rather than decorative objects, and a stone fireplace dominated one wall. Family photos sat on every surface available.

"Can I get you something to drink?" Mrs. Reed asked. "Water? Coffee? Tea?"

"I'm fine, thank you."

"*Water would be nice, please.*"

Mrs. Reed nodded and disappeared, returning moments later with a tall glass of water which she handed to Wolfe with a smile.

Footsteps approached from the hallway- heavy, measured footsteps vibrated through the floorboards. Wolfe's wolf immediately snapped to attention, hackles rising as a towering figure entered the room.

Jeremiah Reed carried himself with the quiet confidence of a man who had never needed to prove his strength to anyone. His presence filled the space completely, an invisible energy radiating from him made Wolfe's skin prickle. Unlike Caleb's power, which had felt like pressure, Jeremiah's was more like gravity- a natural force that simply existed.

"Wolfe," he said, his voice deep and resonant. "I'm glad you've come."

Wolfe rose, instinctively straightening his spine. Though uncomfortable under the weight of the Alpha's gaze, he didn't feel threatened- merely aware of the power the man possessed.

Jeremiah gestured for him to sit, taking a seat across from them. "Caleb told me about your situation. I'd like to learn more, if you don't mind."

For the next half hour, Wolfe answered Jeremiah's questions through Opal's translation, explaining what he remembered of his childhood, his years with Mo, and his escape. The Alpha listened without interruption, giving nothing away, beyond attentive concern.

"Where are you from originally?" Jeremiah asked. "Before Mo found you?"

"I don't know. Somewhere with mountains. I remember forests, lakes. My parents and I lived away from other people."

"And what do you plan to do now? What future do you see for yourself?"

The concept of planning a future had never existed in his world. Each day had been about survival, about making it to the next match. The idea that he might choose a path, build something for himself, was as foreign as seeing all the stars in the night sky.

"I..." His hands faltered. *"I've never thought about it."*

Jeremiah nodded. "That's understandable. You've

been focused on surviving, not living." He studied Wolfe. "You're strong, physically capable. We're always building- new homes, expanding businesses. Construction work might be a place to start. It would give you income, useful skills, and a way to contribute."

Wolfe considered this, the idea of building rather than destroying, appealing on a fundamental level. *"I'd do whatever is needed. I'm willing to learn anything."*

"Where will you be staying? Caleb mentioned you've been with Opal at their family cabin."

Opal and Wolfe exchanged a glance. "We'd like to stay up there, at least for now, but... Holden has been nosing around. I've been meaning to call and talk to Logan. I found him trying to break in two days ago."

Jeremiah's expression darkened. "It's best you stay in town for now. The cabin is too isolated if he tries to come back again."

"We'll stay with Stix and Satia for the time being," Opal said. "But I need to go back to get some of my things."

"I'll have Caleb go with you," Jeremiah offered.

Opal shook her head. "I'll be fine."

Jeremiah nodded. "Okay. But take precautions. Call if anything happens."

He turned his attention back to Wolfe. "You're a good man who has been through a lot. You are welcome to stay here as long as you want. Whatever is going on with the fake warrant and your uncle, I'll have Logan dig into it. If for some reason the sheriff shows up in town, I'll handle him, but just in case, Logan is Wolfe's lawyer now, so call immediately if there's trouble."

Gratitude washed over Wolfe, so strong his chest ached. He bowed his head, unable to find the right signs to express his feelings.

"You'll need to learn our ways. The laws of our pack, the boundaries of our territory, and how we live among humans while protecting our kind. I am assuming you won't have trouble with the last one."

Wolfe nodded, ready to learn anything necessary to be able to stay.

"I'd be happy to teach you myself," Jeremiah offered.

Wolfe's eyes widened in surprise. *"I don't want to impose."*

"It's no imposition," Jeremiah assured him with a smile. "And if I'm being honest, there's something familiar about you, but I can't quite place it."

The words sent a jolt through Wolfe. Could Jeremiah have known his parents? The possibility was tantalizing.

"Thank you," he signed simply, hoping the depth of his gratitude evident despite the limitations of his communication.

"Caleb will help you settle into a job. Sarah will make sure you have everything you need for your stay with Stix and Satia." He extended his hand to Wolfe. "Welcome, Wolfe. I hope you find the home you've been searching for."

As they shook hands, something shifted inside Wolfe- his wolf settling, as if finally recognizing where it belonged. He glanced at Opal. Her smile made his heart flip.

For the first time, the future didn't loom as a threat but as a promise.

"I'll walk you out," Mrs. Reed said. At the door, she pressed a small card into Wolfe's hand. "My number. Call anytime, for anything. We take care of our own here." She smiled at Opal. "Make sure he has Logan's number. We've already informed Logan to be on the lookout for a possible text."

"Thank you."

Mrs. Reed pulled Opal into a tight hug and breathed in deeply. "It is wonderful to have you back, Opal. We missed you so much."

Opal hugged Mrs. Reed, and Wolfe turned away from them to give them a moment of privacy.

"I look forward to seeing more of you both soon," said Mrs. Reed.

Wolfe turned back to her and waved. Opal took his hand, and together they walked toward her Jeep.

In the car, Opal turned to him. "So? What did you think?"

"I like them. Jeremiah is... intimidating."

"That's the Alpha for you. Everyone feels that way around him."

"You don't."

"Well... It's complicated. Technically, my dad is my Alpha because he is the head of our family. Ursas don’t have packs the way other species do. But we do have families. Our family is our pack. But Jeremiah is the Alpha of Wolf River, and my father defers to him. I guess it's that I've never had to deal with him as an Alpha before. Honestly, I don't know what would happen if he commanded me to do something. He's never had to."

As they drove back toward town, Wolfe couldn't shake Jeremiah's words from his mind. *There's something familiar about you.* The possibility of answers- that he might discover pieces of his past both thrilled and terrified him.

Opal smiled as she drove, her profile illuminated by the afternoon sun. Whatever came next- whatever truths might be revealed- he wouldn't have to face it alone. He had someone by his side. Someone who chose to stay despite what she knew about him. Someone of his own.

The road wound through the forest, the trees casting dappled shadows across the windshield.

"I need to stop by the cabin to grab some stuff and my laptop," Opal said, breaking the silence. "Do you want to come with me or should I drop you at Stix's?"

"I'll come," he signed. *"To be safe."*

"My hero," she teases, her eyes filled with genuine affection. "We'll take the back road to be safe."

CHAPTER SEVENTEEN

Opal pulled up to Stix's house, and Caleb's truck sat out front.

"Looks like Caleb is here to talk to you again. Maybe about a job."

Wolfe smiled at her.

Stix's house buzzed with tension as Opal and Wolfe opened the front door, but no one spoke.

"Something's wrong," said Opal as her ursa swayed foot to foot.

Caleb and Jeremiah sat in the front room exchanging tense glances.

"What's happened?"

"Logan has had news," said Jeremiah.

She grabbed Wolfe's hand, and he closed the front door behind them.

She and Wolfe walked in.

"Tell us." She barely got the words out.

Jeremiah motioned for them to sit. Opal pulled Wolfe to the couch, and they sat.

Jeremiah looked at Wolfe. "Apparently, your uncle has put out a bounty on you."

"Bounty?" Opal asked.

"How much?"

"Two million," said Caleb.

"Two million dollars?" Opal gasped.

"He put the word out all over in less than reputable circles."

Wolfe sat utterly still, his face a careful mask that betrayed nothing of his thoughts.

"Two million dollars is a lot of motivation," Caleb said.

"What exactly does Mo want with Wolfe?" Stix entered. "Beyond the obvious revenge for escaping."

Opal glanced at Wolfe. "Mo sees Wolfe as his property- the star who brings in big money."

"We've faced threats before," said Jeremiah. "We'll face this one together. We protect our own, and Wolfe is one of our own. We'll send out word. If anyone sees anything or anyone suspicious, they are to phone immediately."

"Did Logan say anything about the warrant?"

"It's real, apparently. Circumstantial, based on Mo's word of what he said happened. Mo knows which palms to place bribes in to make things go the way he wants."

"Will he come into town to look? Can he?"

"Only if he has probable cause. The laws are murky around Wolf River- though it's private land, it's still in the county. Let's wait and worry about that bridge when we reach it."

Jeremiah stood, so did Caleb.

"It's okay if they stay with you, Stix?" Jeremiah asked.

"Of course," said Satia. "We've already started preparing a space for them."

Opal and Wolfe glanced at each other.

"What does she mean?"

Opal shrugged.

"We'll check in tomorrow," said Caleb. "For now, try to relax and rest. I'll reach out and see if any other packs have heard anything."

Satia nodded. "I'll reach out to Affina."

"Thank you."

Caleb and Jeremiah left, and Opal's mom locked the door. She turned to the group. "How about I make some food?"

"Thanks," said Stix. "I need to head back to the restaurant."

"I'll show you what we worked on today," said Satia.

Opal took Wolfe's hand. Together, they followed Satia to the door leading down to the basement.

Satia flipped on the lights as they descended the wooden stairs. Magnus barreled past them down the stairs, almost knocking everyone over. He immediately sniffed everything.

The basement had been transformed from what Opal remembered as a cluttered storage space into something cozy. A queen-sized bed with a sturdy wooden frame occupied one corner, complete with fresh linens and a pile of throw pillows. A small sitting area with a loveseat and a coffee table filled one corner. And someone hung curtains over the small windows along the top of the walls.

"We've been converting this for a while." Satia gestured around the space. "It's not finished yet, but it's private and comfortable."

Opal took in the space, noticing the thoughtful touches- a small dresser, bedside lamps, even a vase of fresh wildflowers on a desk tucked against one wall.

"It's perfect. I had no idea you guys were doing all this."

Satia tucking a strand of hair behind her ear. "We thought it might be more comfortable to have a guest space that's more private than Deacon's room. Especially when Deacon eventually comes back."

"I thought you'd want to stay together," she said, "but Deacon's room is free for now if you want separate spaces."

Heat flushed Opal's cheeks as she realized what Satia implied. Her family expected her and Wolfe to be sleeping together. Wolfe's expression remained carefully neutral, though a faint blush colored his neck.

How was he an expert at that? Probably years of practice.

An awkward silence stretched between them as Opal struggled to find the right words. Were they together? They'd kissed, and there was undeniably something powerful between them, but they hadn't discussed what it meant.

"I'll let you get settled," Satia said. "Call if you need anything."

"Thank you," Opal managed, her voice sounding strangely high to her own ears.

As Satia's footsteps receded up the stairs, Opal turned to find Wolfe sitting, staring at the floor. His shoulders hunched, tension evident in every line of his body.

"Are you okay?" Opal sat beside him.

He didn't look up as his hands moved. *"I don't want to bring trouble to you or your family."*

Opal laughed, the sound escaping her before she stopped it. "Wolfe, we're shifters. There's always some kind of trouble."

His eyes finally met hers. *"This is different. Mo is dangerous. And now he's offering enough money to tempt anyone."*

"What do you want? Do you want to stay in town?"

He nodded without hesitation. *"Yes."*

"Is it too much, staying with my family? Would you rather have your own place?" The questions tumbled out as her own insecurities bubbled to the surface. "I'd understand if you need some space. Everything's happened so fast, and my family can be a lot, and-"

Her words cut off as Wolfe clamped his lips to hers. He cupped her cheek with surprising tenderness. When he pulled back, his eyes were bright with an emotion that made her breath catch.

"I want you," he signed. *"If that's okay. I think... I think I want you for the long term."*

Opal's heart hammered as she processed his words. A swirl of joy, fear, and disbelief tangled within her, making it hard to breathe.

"My wolf keeps telling me I need to be with you." His gaze never left hers. *"I know we've only known each other a few days, but I've never felt for anyone the way I feel for you."*

"Are you sure? You're not just grateful or-"

He shook his head firmly, cutting off her doubts. His hands moved again, the signs flowing more confidently. *"What I feel for you isn't gratitude. It's something else. Something... bigger."*

Opal reached for his hand, twining her fingers with his. "I feel it too," she admitted. "From the moment I found you in my yard, something inside me recognized you. My ursa knew you were important before I did."

Relief washed over his features, followed by a smile that transformed his face.

A hint of mischief crept into his eyes. *"Does this*

mean we're staying down here together? We don't have to do anything. I mean, you're a virgin. I don't want you to think I want you to stay here to sleep with me." He shook his head. *"Yes, sleep, not sex, sleep.*

Opal laughed, the tension breaking. "I understand."

His smile widened, and his lips found hers again. Opal melted into him, her arms winding around his neck as his hands settled on her waist.

When they finally broke apart, Opal rested her forehead against his. "We should probably go upstairs and get the rest of the stuff from the Jeep."

"Can it wait? I want to hold you, if that's okay."

Opal smiled. "I'd love that."

They settled onto the bed, Wolfe's strong arms encircling her as she rested her head against his chest. The steady rhythm of his heartbeat soothed Opal's frayed nerves. Despite the danger lurking beyond Wolf River's borders, in that moment, she felt safer and more at peace than she had been in her entire life.

"This is nice," she murmured, her fingers tracing idle patterns on his forearm.

Wolfe rumbled, and he kissed the top of her head. The warmth of his body and the rise and fall of his breathing lulled her into a state of peaceful drowsiness. Her eyelids grew heavy as the events of the day caught up with her.

"Five more minutes." She snuggled closer. "Then we'll go get our stuff..."

Wolfe's arms tightened in response.

"Opal? Wolfe? Dinner's ready."

Her mother's voice filtered down the stairs, pulling Opal from a dreamless sleep. She blinked groggily, disoriented by the unfamiliar surroundings. Wolfe stirred beside her, his eyes opening as he came awake.

"Mom's calling us for dinner," she said, reluctantly extracting herself from his embrace. "We must have been more tired than we thought."

Wolfe sat up, running a hand over his stubbled jaw.

"Coming, Mom," Opal called back, her voice still thick with exhaustion.

They made their way upstairs, Opal's stomach rumbling as the aroma of her mother's cooking grew stronger. The aroma of roasted chicken and herbs filled the warm, bright kitchen.

"There you are," her mom said. "I thought you might skip dinner entirely."

"Sorry," Opal said, stifling a yawn. "I guess we needed the rest."

Wolfe moved past her to the cabinet, gathering a stack of plates, and began setting the table without being asked. He worked with quiet efficiency, arranging silverware and napkins with careful precision.

Her mom smiled with approval. "Thank you, Wolfe."

He nodded, offering her a small smile before continuing.

He gave her a wink. She smiled, and her ursa bounced in a circle.

"Mom, Wolfe's an amazing cook," Opal said. "You should've seen what he made with almost nothing."

Her mom's eyebrows rose with interest. "Well, perhaps you'd like to cook for us sometime, Wolfe. I'm always happy to have another chef in the family."

Wolfe paused. *"I would be honored. Though I'm not sure my cooking will be as good as yours."*

Her mom snorted. "False modesty won't get you out of it now that you've offered. How about tomorrow night? I'll buy the ingredients for whatever you'd like to make."

Before Wolfe responded, the patter of small feet announced Andre's arrival. The little boy burst into the kitchen, his face lighting up when he spotted Wolfe.

"Wolfe!" he signed, racing across the room and launching himself into the air.

Wolfe caught him effortlessly, lifting the child to eye level and pretending to growl at him.

Andre bared his teeth back at Wolfe.

Wolfe set the boy down and crouched to his level. His hands moved again, and Andre watched with rapt attention.

"What's he saying?" Her mom came to stand beside Opal.

"He's asking Andre about his day." Opal's chest warmed at the sight of them together.

Andre nodded, his small hands moving in what appeared to be his own invented signs mixed with a few proper ones. Remarkably, Wolfe seemed to understand, nodding and signing in a way the toddler could follow.

"Wolfe's so natural with him." Her mom watched the exchange. "It's like they've been friends forever instead of a day."

"He's pretty amazing."

Her mom glanced at her, a smile playing at her lips. " Have you possibly given any thought to settling down? Starting a family of your own?"

"Mom," Opal hissed. "We only met a few days ago."

Her mom laughed, the sound warm and full of maternal mischief. "I'm saying, a man who cooks, is good with children, and looks at you the way he does comes along only to the fortunate few. Like with your dad and me. And Stix and Satia. And-"

"Mind your beeswax," Opal muttered, though she couldn't help the smile tugging at her lips as Wolfe and Andre continued their conversation.

"Fine, fine," her mom conceded, laughing again. "But don't wait too long. Your father and I aren't getting any younger, and we'd like more grandchildren while we can still chase them around."

“Well, Satia and Stix have that covered already.”

Her mom patted her cheek. “Yes, but I’m sure they don’t want to have to take on the role of increasing our family all on their own. Besides, having wolf pups in the family would be so cute. Imagine our family with ursa, sabers, and wolves. Talk about a blended family. It would be so much fun.”

Opal rolled her eyes. As much as her mother's teasing embarrassed her, she couldn't deny the image of Wolfe with children- their children- had already crossed her mind more than once.

"Dinner's ready," her mom called, breaking into Opal's thoughts.

As they gathered around the table, Wolfe took the seat beside Opal, his thigh pressing warmly against hers under the table. She glanced up to find him watching her, his eyes full of an emotion that made her heart skip.

Her ursa rumbled, settling contentedly within her as Stix began passing dishes around the table.

They were safe. They were together. And that was enough.

CHAPTER EIGHTEEN

The following days settled into a rhythm both new and strangely right. Each morning, Wolfe woke beside Opal, her warmth and scent the first things he registered before opening his eyes. They would dress and head upstairs for breakfast with the family- Andre's excited signing, Stix's humor, Satia's soothing presence, and occasionally Joyce and Robert stopping by with fresh pastries or fruit from their garden.

After breakfast, Wolfe accompanied Caleb to various construction sites around town. Jeremiah had arranged for him to apprentice with Caleb, learning carpentry and building skills. Being able to use his hands to build and create, rather than to break and harm, brought him a sense of peace and fulfillment. His strength and quick learning earned respect from the other workers, who treated him as one of their own despite his inability to speak.

In the evenings, he would return to Stix's house, shower away the sawdust and sweat, then help prepare dinner. Sometimes he cooked, teaching Opal and Satia recipes he'd learned from the hotel chefs. Other nights, they all pitched in, the kitchen filled with laughter and warmth as Andre "helped" by stirring bowls and taste-testing everything within reach.

After dinner came his favorite part of the day-shifting with Opal and running through the forest. In wolf form, they communicated freely, his thoughts flowing into her mind without the barrier of his damaged throat. They wandered through the trees, exploring farther each night, learning the territory that quickly became home.

Tonight, they'd ventured to a small lake nestled in the mountains, its surface reflecting the full moon overhead. Wolfe stood at the water's edge, taking in the breathtaking view. Beside him, Opal's massive ursa form gleamed in the moonlight.

"It's beautiful," he said through their mental connection.

Opal's bear snuffed. *"We used to come here as cubs. My father would bring us on full moon nights to swim and fish."*

Wolfe's paws sank into the cool mud at the lake's edge. *"Can we swim?"*

Her laugh rippled through his mind. *"Of course. The water's freezing, though."*

"I don't mind." He waded deeper until the water lapped at his torso. The bracing cold invigorated him, his thick fur keeping the worst of the chill at bay.

Opal's ursa followed with more hesitation, a grumble of complaint escaping her as the water reached her belly. *"Cold, cold, cold,"* she chanted, making Wolfe's wolf chuff with amusement.

"Bears don't like cold water?" he teased.

"This bear doesn't," she retorted, plodding forward until she swam beside him, her precise strokes carrying her through the dark water.

They swam for a while, circling in the small lake under the watchful eye of the moon. Wolfe reveled in the movement, the weightlessness of his wolf body in the water.

"I have to start work again next week," Opal said, as they paddled toward shore. *"I've already missed too many days."*

Wolfe's gut twisted at the thought. *"Will you be gone all day?"* He liked coming to the house and having lunch with her.

"Just mornings."

They reached the shore and shook the water from their fur, droplets flying in all directions. The night air chilled his wet coat, but he didn't mind as he settled on the grass.

The sounds of the forest surrounded them- owls

calling, small creatures rustling in the underbrush, the gentle lapping of water against the shore. Wolfe's wolf stretched out beside Opal's ursa, their fur touching.

"Wolfe?" Opal's voice in his mind was soft, almost tentative. *"Can I ask you something personal?"*

He turned to her. *"Of course."*

"Do you ever think about finding a mate? Having a family someday?"

His wolf perked up. *"I never thought it was possible,"* he admitted. *"In Mo's world, I was a commodity, not a person. The idea of having someone who chose me, who wanted to build a life with me... someone I chose as well... wasn't even a dream I allowed myself to have."*

Opal's ursa moved closer, her warm body pressing against his side. *"And now?"*

Wolfe's heart thundered as he considered her question. Since coming to Wolf River- since meeting Opal- everything had changed. He'd begun to imagine a future where he belonged somewhere, with someone.

"Now," he said. *"I want that. A mate. Cubs, eventually."* He paused, gathering his courage. *"I think I might have already found her."*

Opal's breath caught, the sound carrying through their mental connection. *"Wolfe..."*

A howl pierced the night- urgent, commanding. Caleb. They both jumped up, ears pricked toward the sound.

"That's a call to gather."

Wolfe fell into step beside her ursa as they ran through the trees toward town. The peace of their evening shattered, giving way to a growing sense of foreboding.

The forest blurred around them as they ran, moonlight dappling the ground between the trees. Despite the urgency of Caleb's call, Wolfe couldn't help but reflect on their interrupted moment. He had been on the verge of telling Opal what had been growing increasingly clear to him. That his wolf recognized her as his mate, that the connection between them was more than attraction or gratitude. It went deeper, longer.

Now, racing through the night with danger potentially waiting ahead, he wished he had spoken sooner. Some truths shouldn't wait for perfect moments.

They approached the area where they'd entered the woods, and slowed. Lights glowed in the distance, but there were too many cars, too much movement.

"We should shift back," Opal said. *"I don't like this."*

They retreated into the cover of trees where they shifted in privacy. The transformation was smoother now for Wolfe, his body accepting the change with only minor discomfort. As he emerged, he found Opal already dressed in the clothes they'd stashed in a hollow tree before their run.

"Here." She handed him his jeans and T-shirt.

When he finished dressing, Opal texted rapidly on her phone.

"It's Stix," she said, her face illuminated by the screen's blue glow. "The sheriff is in town with a warrant. They're searching now."

Wolfe froze. Mo had found him, and the fragile peace he'd discovered would be shattered.

"Jeremiah's gathered everyone at the community center."

She dialed a number and put it on speakerphone. It rang once.

"There you are," Stix said. "We were worried."

"We were on a run and heard Caleb's call. What's happening?"

"The sheriff showed up at the Reed house with the warrant."

Wolfe's hand tightened around hers.

"You two need to go. You need to hide."

Wolfe shook his head. *"I should go back. Face the charges."*

"That's exactly what Mo wants," Opal countered.

"Logan will be here by morning. Hide until then."

"I don't want to run anymore. I don't want to bring more trouble to your family, to this town."

"This isn't about running. It's about buying time until we can prove the charges are false. Either way, we're going to sort this out. No one here is going to let you go back."

“She's right,” said Stix. “The whole pack is in agreement. No matter what it takes.”

Wolfe stared at her for a long moment, conflicted,

but if the members of the pack were willing to go to such lengths to protect him, then he wouldn't give up either.

"Where should we go?"

"Back to the cabin," Stix replied. "The sheriff already searched it top to bottom. Didn't find anything, so to go in again, he'd need another warrant."

"But the Jeep-"

"No car," Stix cut her off. "Too visible. You'll have to go on foot. And no Magnus either- he'll draw attention."

Jeremiah's voice rose in the background. "I've asked the sheriff to allow us time to consult our legal counsel. He's stationed deputies at the town limits. No one is to leave town tonight."

"Go," said Stix. "Stay off the roads. Keep the lights off, in case the sheriff decides to make another visit."

"Be careful, baby," her mom whispered into the phone.

"We will." Opal ended the call.

"We should shift," Opal said. "We'll move faster."

Wolfe nodded, already pulling his shirt off. They undressed, stashing their clothes back in the hollow tree. Opal held her phone, staring at it as if contemplating what to do with it. She undressed and shifted, then picked up her phone with her teeth.

As they tore through the forest, Opal's ursa took the lead with Wolfe's close behind.

Minutes ago, they had been swimming in the moonlight, contemplating a future together. Now they were fugitives, running from a law that had been twisted to serve a monster's purposes.

"We'll be okay," she told Wolfe through their mental connection. *"Logan will sort this out."*

THEY REACHED THE CABIN THIRTY MINUTES LATER, approaching cautiously from the rear. The building stood dark and silent, with no signs of anyone. Still, they circled it twice before shifting back.

"Stay low."

They slipped inside and locked the door behind them.

Her ursa growled. Even in the darkness, she sensed the disruption. They found some clothes in the dryer and walked through the laundry room into the hallway. The scents of half a dozen humans had her ursa huffing and snorting in distaste. She continued further in. Furniture had been moved, drawers left open, the lingering scent of strangers permeating her private space.

"Assholes," she growled, running her hand along the wall until she found a small flashlight she kept for emergencies. She flicked it on, keeping the beam pointed downward to minimize the chance of being seen from outside.

The cabin was a disaster. Cushions overturned, drawers emptied onto the floor, the refrigerator had been searched, its contents scattered across the kitchen. Her books had been pulled from shelves, photographs removed from frames, rugs upturned.

“What the hell did they think I was hiding you in the cabinets or behind my books? He did this out of spite. He’s such a prick.”

Opal laid the flashlight on the floor, and they attempted to restore some order to the chaos. Opal righted furniture while Wolfe gathered scattered belongings, both of them moving by the narrow beam of the flashlight. When they’d done as much as they were able in the dark, Opal yawned.

"We should sleep. We can finish in the morning when it’s light."

Wolfe nodded. They made their way to her bedroom, which had suffered the same thorough ransacking. The mattress had been flipped, the bedding strewn across the floor. She shook her head, and they went to the guest room, finding it in the same state. Together, they righted it, smoothing the sheets and comforter.

As they lay down, Wolfe pulled Opal against him, his arms encircling her. His heart beat against her back, steady and comforting with everything they'd been through.

Wolfe pressed a kiss to the top of her head, his body relaxing against hers.

"I won't let them take you," she vowed.

Wolfe tipped up her chin, and his brow furrowed.

"What's wrong?"

He got up and walked to the curtain, opening it enough to let the moonlight shine across the bed before he sat back down.

"It's me who won't let anything happen to you. Now that I've found you, my wolf has found you..."

She waited for him to finish instead he kissed her. Really kissed her. Not soft. Not tentative. A real kiss. One that told her what he and his wolf wanted from her.

He pulled away from her enough for him to sign. *"I don't know how to do this. I don't know anything about mating or bonding. All I know is I want to be with you, and my wolf wants to be with you forever."*

Her ursa chuffed in happiness. What they had between them was the real thing. Wolfe was meant to be her mate.

Opal nodded. "My ursa and I feel the same."

"I'm never letting you go."

She locked her fingers with his. "I'm going to hold you to it."

His mouth found hers again, the gentle press of his lips growing more insistent as his hands slid under her shirt, warm against her skin. Opal's breath hitched as his fingers traced her spine, leaving trails of goose-bumps in their wake. She tugged at his shirt, desperate for his skin against hers.

They undressed each other, each new expanse of skin revealed becoming a canvas for exploration. Wolfe's mouth moved down her body. Licking and kissing her neck, over her breasts, down her belly to her hip. His hands moved with reverence over every curve, every sensitive spot, making her gasp and want more.

Opal's fingers traced the scars etched into his skin, silently acknowledging each scar as part of the man she'd come to love. She ran her fingers down his waist to his rear and squeezed as he groaned and nipped at her neck. His fingers traced over her nipple and sent a pulse of desire through her that she'd never experienced.

"Wolfe." Her voice trembled. "I want you to make love to me."

His hands stilled, eyes searching hers in the dim light. *"Are you sure?"*

"Yes," she breathed.

He swooped in and claimed her mouth with his. His hips settled on hers, his length warm on her belly. Nervousness wound inside her, but her ursa lay ready and willing.

Wolfe broke the kiss and made eye contact with her. His hand slid down her hip and between her legs. He brushed over her sensitive skin once, softly as if waiting for permission. Opal bucked toward his hand, her own nails digging into his back. Anticipation swirled in her belly, and warmth settled between her thighs. Her skin grew sensitive with every swish of his fingers, making her gasp.

She shut her eyes, but he nipped her lip, and she opened her eyes again.

He nodded.

Okay, he wanted full eye contact.

He swished his fingers up and down her folds, making her moan. When her eyes started closing again, he nipped her lip, and she chuckled.

"Sorry."

Gently, he dipped his finger inside her, and she moaned. He waited until she nodded.

Gently, he worked his finger inside her, and when she gripped him harder and moved against his hand, he pushed two fingers inside her, making her pant. She reached between them and stroked him. His eyes shut momentarily as he blew out a harsh breath. When he opened his eyes again, he bent in and kissed her. She stroked him again, and he growled. He removed his fingers and positioned himself at her entrance. Before he entered her, he kissed her again, long and slowly. Then, he rocked his hips into hers. When he entered her, there was a brief flare of pain that made her catch her breath, but it dissolved into something far more electric. Her ursa rose within her, not to take over but to share in the joining, purring as their bodies intertwined.

Wolfe moved with careful restraint at first, his eyes never leaving hers, watching for signs of discomfort. But as pleasure built between them, his movements became more urgent. Opal welcomed the change, her body arching to meet his, urging him deeper. Pleasure wound inside her, making her reach for a release of some sort, though she didn't know what.

Wolfe kissed her again and set his forehead on hers as he groaned and his body tensed. He rocked into her hard, his hips rolling down hers, and her body exploded.

She whispered his name, and he lifted his head, staring at her, his face a mix of strain and pleasure. When she thought the sensations couldn't get more intense, it washed over them both in a wave of pleasure so all-consuming that Opal cried out, her fingers digging into Wolfe as he shuddered above her and mouthed her name. Her body tensed and relaxed all at once in a cacophony of pleasure.

As the waves crested and waned, his body dropped onto hers, and he rolled on his side, pulling her to him and kissing her as if trying to convey all his thoughts and feelings.

In the stillness that followed, their breathing slowed, bodies still joined. Wolfe's hands framed her face, his eyes bright with emotion.

"For as long as I live," he signed. *"I will never make love to another woman. Only you. Always you."*

Tears pricked at the corners of Opal's eyes. "Wolfe..."

"I love you. My wolf loves your ursa. We are yours, if you'll have us."

"I love you too," she whispered, her voice thick. "Both of you. The moon goddess brought us together. No one will ever be able to come between our bond."

He gathered her in his arms, pulling her against him. For the first time, the broken pieces of Opal started to knit back together.

As sleep claimed them, their bodies stayed intertwined.

CHAPTER NINETEEN

Wolfe jolted awake, heart pounding. Beside him, Opal slept undisturbed, her dark hair spilling across the pillow. The digital clock read 3:17 AM.

He slid from the bed, careful not to disturb her, tucked the quilt around her, and tiptoed to the door. The floorboards whispered beneath his bare feet as he crept toward the kitchen. Moonlight poured through the windows, casting shadows across the rooms.

He grabbed a glass and filled it with cold water. The drink chilled him as he peered out the front window at the driveway and the forest beyond. The trees stood as sentinels in the golden moonlight, undisturbed by chaos.

His thoughts drifted to Opal, to the warmth of her body against his. The taste of her skin. The sound of her whispering his name in the dark. Making love to her had been unlike anything he'd ever experienced. The genuine connection made him whole for the first time in his life. He finally understood the difference between sex and making love, between physical release and connection.

With Opal, every touch mattered. Every kiss promised more. Each breath bound them tighter together. He ached to return to bed, to hold her forever, sheltered from the world.

Wolfe placed the empty glass in the sink with a clink. A floorboard creaked behind him.

He whirled toward the hallway.

Mo stood in a tailored suit, his cold eyes gleaming in the moonlight. He blocked the path to the bedroom where Opal slept, unaware of the danger.

"Hello, Wolfe," Mo said, his voice carrying the same cultured tone that had ordered countless beatings. "You've led me on quite the chase."

Wolfe's wolf exploded with a roar of protective fury that drowned out all rational thought. He lunged forward, hands outstretched, intent on ending the threat to his mate.

Mo didn't flinch. "I wouldn't." He produced a gun from his jacket. "Not if you want your little girlfriend to live through the night."

Wolfe froze, his wolf held in check by the threat to Opal.

"That's better. You were always trainable. Now, here's what's going to happen. You're going to come without a fuss. In return, I'll leave your friend and her family alone. Refuse, and my men will ensure she never wakes up. Then I'll let the sheriff end the rest of her family."

Wolfe's mind swam. How had Mo found them? How many men had he brought?

"Time's running out." Mo's voice hardened.

Wolfe's wolf snarled and snapped as a shift ripple trapesed over his skin. Could he reach Mo and rip his throat out before Mo reached Opal? He wasn't willing to risk Opal, her family.

Inside his wolf raged against its confines, demanding blood, demanding vengeance. The rational part of him said to comply. To go with Mo to keep Opal safe. But his wolf, freed after years of suppression, would not be denied again.

With a snarl, Wolfe's control slipped. His wolf surged forward, seizing their body. He launched at Mo, hands morphing to claws, teeth lengthening into fangs.

Mo's expression didn't change as he raised the weapon and fired. Instead of a bullet, a dart embedded itself in Wolfe's arm. Almost instantly, his limbs grew heavy, his vision blurring as the tranquilizer flooded his system.

He crashed to his knees, the room spinning. Through cloudy vision, he spotted two men behind Mo; hulking figures with faces blank as they eyed him.

"Pick him up," Mo ordered. "Get him in the car."

"Wolfe?" Opal called groggily from the other room.

Wolfe fought to get to his feet, his wolf raging inside him, wanting to protect her.

The men moved toward him, and Wolfe resisted the darkness encroaching on his consciousness. He needed to warn Opal, needed to fight, needed to protect. But the drug was too potent.

Before unconsciousness claimed him, Wolfe witnessed Mo turn toward the bedroom and fire a dart at Opal.

Wolfe's mouth opened as his wolf roared in his head. With his last ounce of strength, Wolfe struggled to his feet and dove at Mo, knocking him into the wall. Mo brought his elbow down on the back of Wolfe's neck, and darkness dragged Wolfe under. His final thought was a desperate prayer that Opal wouldn't be harmed.

CONSCIOUSNESS ROUSED HIM IN PAINFUL FRAGMENTS- THE vibration of an engine, the bite of metal against his wrists, voices murmuring nearby. Wolfe kept his eyes closed, assessing his situation.

He lay on his side, his hands cuffed behind his back. His ankles similarly bound, and a collar encircled his neck, the pressure against his scar a cruel reminder of his captivity.

"...should have killed her," said one of Mo's men. "She'll alert others."

"No. By the time she wakes and raises the alarm, we'll be well beyond their territory. Besides, dead shifters attract more attention than live ones. Killing her would have brought Jeremiah Reed to our door. This way, it's more likely no one will care."

"What about the sheriff?" the other man asked.

"He served his purpose. He'll find his payment wired to his account, as agreed. Whether the pack discovers his corruption is not our concern."

Wolfe's heart thumped as he processed their words. Opal was alive. She would wake to find him gone, would alert the pack. There was still hope.

He cracked his eyelids. Through his lashes, he made out the interior of a luxury SUV. Mo sat in the front passenger seat. Two men occupied the middle row seats.

Outside, trees flashed by in the darkness. With each mile, the distance between him and Opal grew, and the bond between them stretched thinner almost painfully. His wolf stirred and growled, groggy. He tried to rise but couldn't.

"He's awake," one of the men announced, his eyes meeting Wolfe's from over the middle row of seats.

"Welcome back, nephew. I'd apologize for the rough handling, but you brought this on yourself."

Wolfe glared at him, though Mo couldn't see it.

"Don't worry," Mo continued. "Once we're back in Seattle, you can return to your comfortable quarters. The penthouse has been waiting for you. Your match is already scheduled- a special event to celebrate your return. The fans are frantic."

Rage boiled within Wolfe, his wolf straining against the effects of the tranquilizer still lingering in his system.

Wolfe grunted in response.

"I had hoped your little adventure might have gotten this rebelliousness out of your system. But you still need to be reminded of your place, apparently."

The collar around Wolfe's neck burst with a jolt like lightning shooting through his head and shoulders. His body jerked and spasmed, and he involuntarily kicked the seats and the window. Finally, the lightning stopped, and he panted for breath as every muscle in his body ached with fire. His nose began to run, and his eyes watered as he coughed.

"You want to act like a dog, I'll treat you like one. Since nothing else seemed to work, we are back to a shock collar. You haven't had to wear one of those for more than a decade?"

A man in the middle seat produced a syringe.

Wolfe thrashed against his restraints as the needle pierced his neck. His wolf floated away, locked behind a chemical barrier that had imprisoned him for most of his life.

No. No!

Wolfe's body relaxed from the chemicals, but still twitched from the shocks.

The separation from his wolf tore at him, like

having a limb severed. After freedom and connection with his wolf, the forced division was worse than any physical pain Mo inflicted.

I'll get you back. I'll get us free.

Wolfe sagged against the seat, his body heavy. Without his wolf's strength, escape seemed impossible. The cuffs, the collar, the drugs- Mo had prepared for every contingency.

As the SUV sped through the night, carrying him back to a life of captivity and violence, Wolfe squeezed his eyes shut and focused on the one thing Mo couldn't take from him- the memory of Opal's touch, her scent, the way she looked at him in the moonlight as they'd made love. Her promise to be his forever.

She would come for him. As much as he didn't want her to, he didn't want her to put herself in harm's way... Hope lingered inside him. For the first time in his life, he had people who would fight for him, who would not rest until he was free. Family.

The knowledge fortified him as the miles unspooled between him and Wolf River, between him and the woman who'd shown him what it meant to be truly alive. She would come. She had to. He belonged to her.

CHAPTER TWENTY

Opal woke to emptiness. The bed beside her cold, the sheets abandoned. A chill that had nothing to do with the morning air settled in her skin as she sat up.

"Wolfe?"

Silence answered her.

She tried to stand up, but her vision blurred, and her limbs grew heavy and sluggish. She pushed to her feet, only to immediately fall.

What the hell?

Her ursa snuffed and tried to lift her head, but wasn't able.

What was going on?

"Wolfe!" she called again, and again got no answer.

Her heart galloped as she tried to get up again. Finally, she managed to sit against the wall. She breathed deeply, trying to calm herself and focus. Sunlight streamed through the window, but it was all wrong. She tried to spot the clock on the other side of the bed, but couldn't from where she sat. Finally, her eyes lit on her cellphone. She reached for the cord and yanked on it. Her phone clattered to the floor, and she pulled it toward her with the cord.

She picked it up and turned it on. The phone beeped with messages from Stix and her mom asking if they were okay and telling her Logan had arrived. Then, more texts told her the sheriff had left. Finally, a text saying it was safe for them to come back. She looked at the time on her phone. Noon? What the hell?

"Wolfe!" she screamed, panic lacing her voice.

She dialed her brother.

The phone rang once.

"Hey. You guys okay?"

"Stix," she slurred.

"What's wrong?"

"Wolfe is gone, and I feel weird. Drugged."

"I'm on my way."

Opal's ursa forced her to her feet. Leaning on the walls for support, she scanned the room, forcing herself to focus. On the bed lay a small silver dart with a yellow tail.

"Son of a bitch."

She pulled the sheet off the bed and flung it around herself.

She hobbled to the living area, but no Wolfe.

Opal's heart thundered, and she fought to stay calm. Tears flooded her eyes, and rage bubbled to the surface. They'd taken him. Her Wolfe. Her mate. Her ursa roared to life, raging against the lingering effects of the tranquilizer. She had to get herself together. She needed to go to Seattle and rescue her mate.

Stix's car came screaming up the road. She stumbled to the door and crumpled as she reached the front porch.

Stix's car spit gravel in all directions as he tore up the drive and stopped next to her Jeep.

He jumped out along with her mom, dad, and Magnus.

Magnus barked and ran to her, licking her face before charging inside and sniffing every surface.

"Opal!" Her mom gathered her in her arms.

Stix and her dad stormed inside, looking around.

"They took him," she sobbed. "Mo took Wolfe while I slept."

"Are you hurt?" Her mom looked her over.

She shook her head. "They tranquilized me. I'm fuzzy, but I'm fine. But Wolfe- " Her voice broke, unable to form the words.

"I called Jeremiah," her dad said. "He should be here soon." Her dad reached down, picked Opal up, and carried her to the couch.

Stix rushed back in with Magnus in tow. "They're all gone. Scents are at least six hours old."

Opal hugged herself as sobs wracked her body.

Wolfe's scent still clung to her skin from their love-making, a cruel reminder of what she'd lost.

The sounds of a convoy of trucks and SUVs racing up the gravel drive came to an abrupt halt.

Jeremiah was first through the door, his alpha presence filling the room as he surveyed the scene. Behind him came Caleb, Griffin, and another man she didn't recognize.

"Tell me what happened." Jeremiah's voice remained gentle despite the authority behind it.

Opal wiped tears from her cheeks. "I woke up, and he was gone. I found a tranquilizer dart in my bed. Someone took him while we slept."

Caleb examined the door frame, running his fingers along the wood. "No signs of forced entry. They must have come in the back."

"I don't remember locking the doors before bed. I should have made sure, but usually Magnus is here, so I don't need to."

Caleb paused, his eyes darkening. "He might have gone willingly."

"He wouldn't. He's my mate," Opal said fiercely. "Wolfe would never leave me. Someone took him."

"Easy." Jeremiah placed a calming hand on her shoulder and crouched in front of her. "We're not accusing him of anything. But we need to understand how they got to him."

Stix emerged from the kitchen holding a second dart. "Another tranquilizer."

"We need to go," she said. "We need to find him."

"No," Jeremiah cut her off. "Mo planned this carefully. He'll be expecting pursuit."

"I don't care," Opal snapped, her ursa's protective instincts overriding her respect for the alpha. "They have Wolfe. They're probably torturing him right now."

Jeremiah's eyes flashed. "I understand what he means to you. But rushing in blind will only get you both killed. We do this smart. I've reached out to our allied packs along the route to Seattle. They are going to search the highway all the way up to Seattle."

"I have several friends searching for Mo, and which hotel is his. They are trying to get more information on his operation," said the man she didn't recognize.

Opal nodded, while her mind raced, desperate for a plan. The pack's methodical approach made sense, but every minute they spent planning was another minute Wolfe spent in Mo's hands. The memory of his scars, the stories he'd told her about his captivity, made her stomach churn with fear for what he might be enduring.

She sniffed the air. The man she didn't know was a feline shifter. His scent similar to Satia's. A saber... Razor's Edge. Her mind plucked the name from conversations overheard between Satia and Stix.

Opal retreated to the bedroom under the pretense of packing. In reality, she needed space to think, to plan. She remembered Wolfe's words from the night before. The fierce determination in his eyes as he'd signed, he would never let anything happen to her. He had protected her at the cost of his own freedom, had gone with Mo to keep her safe.

Now it was her turn to protect him.

She found a backpack and stuffed it with essentials- clothes, cash she kept hidden in her dresser, and energy bars. If she went after Wolfe alone, she'd need to travel light and fast.

She slipped the bag under the bed. When the others went back to Wolf River, and she was alone, she would begin her own hunt. Mo thought he could threaten them and use their love as a weapon.

He was about to learn how dangerous a bear could be when protecting her mate.

The plan dissolved as quickly as it had formed when Jeremiah appeared in the doorway.

"You need to dress. We're heading to my house." His tone left no room for argument. "Logan's found something."

Opal sat in Jeremiah's spacious living room, surrounded by her family. Her mother's eyes red-rimmed from crying, her father's jaw set in a hard line. Stix paced near the window while Caleb stood beside his father, both men radiating a controlled fury which charged the air.

When Logan strode in, his usual easygoing

demeanor was nowhere to be seen. He carried a laptop under one arm and a thick folder in the opposite hand, his face grim as he nodded to Jeremiah.

"What did you find?" Opal asked, unable to wait for pleasantries.

Logan placed his laptop on the coffee table, opening it to reveal a series of documents and photos. "I know who Mo is. His name is Maurice Black." Logan tapped a key, bringing up an old photograph. "Years ago, he came to town."

Jeremiah's eyes widened. "The fighter. I remember him."

"You know him?" Opal leaned forward, her heart racing.

"He was a human MMA fighter who'd heard rumors about werewolves. Came here demanding to be turned, said he wanted the advantage in the ring. Offered money, threatened exposure when I refused. We escorted him out of town."

Logan nodded. "After, he went to Seattle and started building his own operation. An underground club. Started by fighting himself, then recruited others. Eventually bought the hotel and established the club in the basement- exclusive, and high-end."

He scrolled through several photos of a modern hotel in downtown Seattle, stopping on an image of an opulent underground room with a cage at its center, surrounded by luxury seating.

"He recruits anyone to fight for him- willing

participants are paid well. But he's always looking for shifters. Using them, he rigs fights to ensure his guys win against human opponents."

"And Wolfe?" Opal's voice trembled.

Logan's expression tightened. "That's where it gets strange. I couldn't find anything about Wolfe. No records, no history. It's like he doesn't exist. I dug as deep as I could, but there's nothing- no birth certificate, no school records, nothing to tell us who he is."

"That's impossible," Opal insisted. "Everyone leaves some kind of trail."

"Not if someone deliberately erased it," Caleb suggested.

"Where are they keeping him?" Stix finally stopped pacing.

Logan nodded, pulling up another image- a detailed floor plan of the hotel. "The Obsidian Hotel in downtown Seattle. The club is in the basement, but there's a private suite on the top floor where I believe they're holding Wolfe."

"I'm going." Opal stood.

"You can't go alone," her mother protested, reaching for her hand.

Her father stood, his massive frame casting a shadow across the room. "She won't be alone. Wolfe is family."

"Damn right," Stix agreed, moving to stand beside their father.

Caleb exchanged a glance with Jeremiah, who nodded once.

"We're going too," Caleb announced. "Mo has operated in the shadows for too long. And I want to find out what happened to Zaden."

"This won't be easy," Logan warned, scrolling through more images. "The hotel has security, and the club itself is even more protected. We'll need a plan."

"We'll make one on the way," Jeremiah said. "Everyone, gather what you need. We leave in an hour."

“Wait,” said Razor. “I have an idea.”

CHAPTER TWENTY-ONE

Consciousness rolled in slowly, like swimming through tar. Wolfe's eyelids felt impossibly heavy. He forced them open, blinking against the harsh light from familiar floor-to-ceiling windows. The fine cotton sheets beneath him confirmed what his heart already knew. He was back in the penthouse of the Obsidian.

His prison.

He tried to sit up, but his limbs refused to cooperate, weighed down by whatever cocktail of drugs Mo had pumped into his system. His wolf lay distant and muffled, as if blanketed in layers of cotton. He reached for the connection, the wild strength that had sustained him through his escape and the weeks of freedom, but found only a hollow echo where his wolf should be.

The realization struck him with brutal force-a

punch that left him gasping. Mo had locked his wolf away again, severing the bond he'd fought so savagely to claim. Grief crashed into him, raw and fierce, followed by a rush of rage so scorching it burnt away the drug-induced haze, leaving every nerve alive with anguish and fury.

With trembling arms, he forced himself upright and swung his legs off the massive bed. The room spun violently. He gripped the mattress until the vertigo passed. When he could focus, he took in his surroundings. Sleek modern furniture, abstract art on the walls, and plush carpet. Everything as he'd left it, as if the past weeks had been nothing but a dream.

But it hadn't been a dream. Opal was real. The life he'd glimpsed in Wolf River was real. The love he'd found, the family who had accepted him, the freedom he'd tasted- all of it had been real.

He would give anything to save it. The memory of Mo leveling the dart gun at Opal nearly shattered him. Terror, sharp and absolute, pierced his heart. He prayed she was still safe.

Wolfe forced himself upright, every muscle stiff, and his legs shaking under his weight. The drugs coursed through his blood, making his movements clumsy, his arms heavy, and his fingers slow to respond. He staggered toward the front room of the suite, supporting himself with one shaky hand on the wall to steady his off-balance, stumbling steps.

Mo had spared no expense in creating his gilded

cage. The kitchen boasted top-of-the-line appliances, though Wolfe never used any besides the fridge. Leather furniture crowded the living area, a massive television dominated one wall, and floor-to-ceiling windows offered a panoramic view of Seattle's skyline. It was a beautiful prison, but a prison nonetheless.

He reached the kitchen and pulled open the refrigerator door, the blast of cool air prickling against his overheated skin and throbbing face. Grabbing a bottle of water, he twisted it open with trembling fingers. His parched throat burned and scraped as he gulped the whole bottle in greedy, shuddering swallows. The water sent a brief chill through his aching belly, helping clear the edge from his fogged mind, although his arms and legs remained frustratingly heavy and stiff.

The sound of a key card in the door made him tense. The door swung open, revealing Mo in a tailored charcoal suit, a guard behind him pushing a food cart laden with covered dishes.

"Ah, you're up!" Mo's cheerful voice rang out more as a greeting to a friend after a brief absence rather than that of a captor who had drugged and kidnapped someone. "How are you? Rested, I hope?"

Though hatred burned within him, he maintained a calm demeanor. Mo either didn’t notice or chose to ignore the hostility radiating from him. Silence stretched between them.

"I've brought your favorites." Mo gestured to the

cart as the guard positioned it near the dining table. "Steak, perfectly rare. Those little roasted potatoes you like. Even the chocolate cake from the bakery downtown."

He moved around the suite with ease, straightening a pillow here, adjusting a curtain there. "We've got a spectacular night ahead of us. Your homecoming, as it were. I was going to wait to save you for a fight on Friday, but I got an idea, and as soon as it was announced, the tickets sold out within hours. People are so excited to have you back in the ring after your... vacation."

Mo's pause before the word "vacation" carried an unspoken threat. Wolfe watched him.

Mo removed the covers from the dishes. "Special occasion. The buyers have paid a premium for this event."

Wolfe's jaw clenched. His body was in no condition to withstand even one match. But arguing would be pointless; Mo had him where he wanted him. And he was going to make sure Wolfe was punished for his escape.

Wolfe moved to the counter where a notepad and pen lay, part of the suite's standard amenities.

Who am I fighting?

Mo smiled, the expression never reaching his cold eyes. "That's a surprise. Don't want to ruin the anticipation, do we? But he's a worthy opponent. You'll need to be at your best."

Wolfe's wolf stirred weakly and grumbled. He couldn't break through the chemical barriers Mo had erected. He wanted to refuse, to tell Mo he would never fight for him again, but the threat to Opal and her family hung unspoken between them.

As if reading his thoughts, Mo's smile hardened. "I should mention I've taken precautions to ensure your cooperation. Some of my men are near Wolf River. One word from me, and your friend and her family will suffer most... unpleasant consequences. Which would be a shame. She's cute. Not beautiful like the women you usually get, but cute in a natural way, I suppose."

The casual way he delivered the threat made it all the more chilling. A cold surge of fear shot through Wolfe. His hand tightened around the pen until his knuckles turned white, and it snapped in half.

"So," Mo continued, "it's quite simple. You fight, they live. You refuse, they die. I should thank you for running, actually. Before I knew, there was always a chance you might try to leave. But now... now that I finally found something you care about, now I am certain you never will again."

Mo waited for confirmation.

Rage burned inside him so in that moment, he was capable of killing someone. Wolfe gave a single, terse nod, fury and despair warring within him. He would fight. He would do whatever it took to keep Opal safe and to stay alive until he got back to her.

Mo clapped his hands. "Excellent! Now, eat. Build up your strength. You'll need it for the fight."

Wolfe turned back to the notepad, a question burning in his mind since he'd learned of Mo's deception.

What is my real name?

Mo's smile faltered. "Your name is Wolfe. That's who you are."

Wolfe wrote again.

What did my parents call me?

A strange expression crossed Mo's face- something between annoyance and discomfort. "It doesn't matter."

Wolfe's pen moved across the paper with renewed urgency.

You're my uncle, you know my real name.

The façade of friendly concern dropped from Mo's face, replaced by cold anger. "Listen carefully. Whatever name you had before, whatever life you think you remember- none of it matters. That boy is gone. You are Wolfe. My fighter. My property. Nothing more, nothing less."

Mo straightened his jacket, composure returning as fast as it had slipped. "You fight at eight. Be ready."

With that, Mo turned and left, but the guards remaining stationed at the door. The electronic lock engaged, a final reminder of his captivity.

He stood motionless for a long moment, staring at the door. Then, with deliberate steps, he returned to the bedroom, closing and locking the door behind him. The act was meaningless in practical terms- Mo had keys to every lock- but it gave him the illusion of privacy, of control.

He scanned the room, searching for anything which might help him contact the outside world. The phone had disappeared, as had the tablet he'd played games on. Mo had learned from his escape and removed anything that might aid another attempt.

Wolfe sank onto the bed, the weight of his situation crashing down upon him. After tasting freedom, after finding love and family with Opal, the return to captivity was almost unbearable. A sob crept up his throat, breaking free despite his efforts to contain it. Tears spilled down his cheeks as he buried his face in his hands.

He allowed himself a moment of weakness, a brief surrender to despair. But even as he wept, a resolve hardened within him. He would fight, would give Mo the show he wanted. But this was not the end. Somehow, he would find a way back to her.

And when he did, Mo would pay for every moment of suffering he had caused.

Wolfe wiped the tears from his face, drawing a deep breath to steady himself. He needed to conserve his strength, to prepare for the fights ahead.

Whatever opponent Mo had chosen, Wolfe would face them. He would win. He would survive. For Opal.

For the life they might still have together, if he made his way back to her.

With renewed determination, he moved to the bathroom to splash cold water on his face and made a vow to himself. Mo's victory would be temporary. He would not be broken.

Because now, he had something worth fighting for. And whether she came for him, or he made his way back to her, they would be together again.

CHAPTER TWENTY-TWO

"We're in," said Logan. "It wasn't easy, but I got seats."

"What do you mean?" Opal asked over Stix's car's speakerphone. "How?"

"Razor has a lot of connections in Seattle."

"So he got tickets for all of us?"

"No," Logan replied. "For you, Razor, his mate Affina, and Stix."

"What about you and Caleb and our dads?" Stix asked.

"My dad and your dad will get in through the kitchen and come in from the fighters' entrance. Mo will most likely recognize Dad, so he will stay out of the way with your dad unless needed. I will be going in a different way. Caleb will wait at the entrance."

"Okay," said Opal. "That's great for us to get in, but how do we get Wolfe out?"

"I'm still working on it, but probably a lot like last time. Wait for him to go to the locker room, and grab him."

"That won't stop Mo from coming for him again. And again and again and-"

"Then we make sure he can't," said Stix. "End of story. Whatever it takes."

Stix looked at Opal with the seriousness her older brother used to give her when they were in high school, and he promised he wouldn't let someone bother her.

"Let's keep that as a last resort," said Jeremiah. "If needs be, I'll step in, and Logan can negotiate."

"There's nothing to negotiate," said Opal. "He's not property, he's a person."

"True," said Logan. "But sometimes money can make people see things the way you do."

Opal's ursa didn't like it, and neither did she. They shouldn't have to pay for Wolfe to be free of slavery. If it were up to her, Mo would be lucky to leave with his life.

"When we reach Seattle, we need to go shopping," said Logan. "We all have to look the part, but time will be tight. We'll only have about an hour. Affina will meet us at a clothing store she frequents, and we will go from there."

It was after one thirty p.m. They had four hours left in their drive and then shopping. Her ursa growled. Opal hoped she'd be able to keep her ursa under control until they were able to save Wolfe.

Affina studied Opal in the boutique mirror with a critical eye, directing the makeup artist to add another layer of highlighter to Opal's cheekbones.

"More contour," she instructed, gesturing to Opal's jawline. "We need to change the shape of her face as much as possible."

Opal sat rigid in the plush velvet chair, trying not to flinch as the makeup artist applied yet another product to her skin. She barely recognized herself beneath the foundation, eyeshadow, and false lashes. Her hair had been styled into an elegant up-do that pulled her features taut, making her appear older and more sophisticated.

Her nails had been shaped and polished to match her dress. The waxing had been painful but mercifully quick, leaving her skin smooth and sensitive.

"Are you sure this is all necessary?" she asked. "I feel like I'm wearing a mask."

Affina nodded. "These events are as much about appearance as they are about the matches. The women who attend dress to impress- designer clothes, professional makeup, perfect hair. If we want to blend in without drawing attention, we need to look the part."

The makeup artist admired her work. "You're stunning."

Opal stared at her reflection, unable to reconcile the glamorous stranger in the mirror with the woman who spent her days in nursing scrubs or running through forests in ursa form. The gold dress Affina had selected clung to every curve, the fabric catching the light with each breath she took. It felt foreign against her skin, like wearing someone else's life. As silly as it sounded, the high-heeled boots she wore made her tower a foot taller than usual. At least they were tight enough that she wasn’t afraid she’d fall out of them or break an ankle walking in them.

"Besides," Affina added. "In case Mo saw you, we need to make sure he doesn't recognize you. This transformation should be enough."

Opal nodded, understanding the necessity even as she chafed against it. For Wolfe, she would endure far worse than mile-high boots and cakey makeup. Even if Opal felt like she'd been remade from the outside in.

"I can't imagine what all this cost," she murmured as they prepared to leave, eyeing the small army of stylists who had worked on her transformation.

Affina waved a dismissive hand. "Don't worry about it. Razor and I would pay a million dollars for your outfit, and it still wouldn't be enough to cover the debt we owe to the Reeds."

"What debt?"

Affina's expression softened. "When my father died, and our clan was in chaos, Jeremiah helped us. Without him, we might have lost everything. And

Satia..." She paused, emotion coloring her voice. "Satia is family, which makes you family."

The simple declaration warmed Opal's heart. Family. The word carried so much weight, so much meaning- especially when they were all risking their lives to save Wolfe.

"You're beautiful, not that you weren't before," Affina said, surveying the final result. "Though I understand not liking all this. Believe it or not, I still prefer to walk around in my pjs than to get all this done."

Opal chuckled. She couldn't imagine the towering beauty in anything less than designer everything.

"Let's go show the others."

They exited the boutique into the cool evening air, where a sleek limousine sat at the curb. The driver opened the door, revealing Razor, Caleb, and Stix inside. Both Caleb and Stix dressed in expensive suits that transformed them as completely as Opal's makeover had changed her. She'd never seen either of them out of flannels and jeans before.

As she scooted into the vehicle, Stix's eyebrows rose.

"Damn, who are you, and where is my little sister?"

Opal smiled despite her nervousness.

Caleb swallowed hard. "You look..."

"Beautiful," Razor finished. "You're both beautiful." He reached for Affina and kissed her knuckles. She smiled at him and kissed his hand in return.

Stix tugged at his collar.

"I've never seen you in a suit before," Opal remarked.

"That's because I've never worn one before." He grimaced. "I feel like I'm being strangled."

Opal snorted despite the tension coiling in her belly. "It looks good on you. You should save it to show Satia."

Stix snorted, a hint of his usual humor breaking through. "What about you? Going to wear that gold dress for Wolfe back home?"

Heat flushed to Opal's cheeks, and she shrugged, trying to appear nonchalant. "I will if he asks me to."

"If we're all finished discussing fashion," Razor interrupted, his tone light. "We should review the plan one more time."

The mood in the limousine shifted, playfulness giving way to focused determination. Razor pulled out his phone and displayed a detailed floor plan of the Obsidian Hotel.

"The fights are held in the basement level, accessible through private elevators requiring key cards. As VIP guests, we'll receive cards. Once inside, we locate Wolfe and assess the situation."

"What if he's not in the arena?" Opal asked. "What if they're keeping him somewhere else?"

"Our intel suggests Mo keeps his fighters close

before matches," Caleb replied. "There are locker rooms adjacent to the main arena. That's likely where we'll find him. But after what he tried last time, there will definitely be beefed-up security."

"And if we don't find him?" Stix pressed.

"Then we move to plan B," Razor said. "I create a distraction while you and Opal search the hotel with your fathers. Logan will disable the security systems temporarily, giving you access to the upper floors."

"What kind of distraction?"

Razor threw her a calculating smile. "The kind that involves an extremely wealthy, extremely drunk client making outrageous demands. Trust me, I can keep Mo occupied for as long as necessary."

Opal nodded, trying to quell the anxiety churning inside her. So much might go wrong. So many variables they couldn't control.

"Remember," Caleb said, his voice steady and reassuring, "you're simply four rich people going in. Jeremiah and Robert are already in position near the service entrance. Logan has eyes on the security feeds. We're coordinated, we're prepared, and we're here for one of our own."

The limousine slowed at the Obsidian Hotel, its glass-and-steel facade gleaming against the night sky. A red carpet stretched from the entrance to the street, where valets in crimson uniforms assisted arriving guests.

Opal centered herself as her ursa stirred restlessly

within her. The gold dress felt like armor, her makeup a war paint applied for battle rather than beauty.

Affina gripped Opal's hand. "Ready?"

Opal nodded.

As the limousine stopped and the driver opened the door, Opal stepped out, her head held high, despite her wobble in the unfamiliar, tall footwear. Stix took her elbow, steadying her.

“It’s weird seeing you like this,” he said.

“It feels weirder than it looks.”

Stix ushered her up onto the curb. Somewhere in the enormous, flashy building, the man who kidnapped him prepared for a night of entertainment at Wolfe's expense. Somewhere inside, people paid to watch her mate in pain. Somewhere inside, her mate waited for her, and she wouldn’t let him down.

Wolfe’s trafficking would end. One way or another, they were bringing him home.

The lobby of the Obsidian Hotel epitomized luxury-marble floors, crystal chandeliers, staff in immaculate uniforms moving with practiced efficiency. Razor led their group toward a discreet elevator bank at the far end, separate from those used by regular hotel guests.

A suited attendant stepped forward, his face blank. "Evening. Invitations, please?"

Razor produced black cards embossed with gold lettering, handing them to the attendant with the casual confidence of someone accustomed to exclusive access. The man examined them before nodding and gesturing toward the elevators.

"Enjoy your evening, Mr. Edge. The event begins in fifteen minutes."

As they entered the elevator, a chill ran down Opal's spine. The doors slid shut, and they began their descent into the hotel's hidden underworld.

"Remember," Razor whispered. "Stay calm, stay focused. We're here to observe first, act second."

Opal nodded, though every instinct screamed at her to tear through walls and doors until she reached Wolfe. Her ursa prowled in a circle, ready to emerge at the first sign of danger.

The elevator opened to reveal another attendant waiting to escort them into what appeared to be an exclusive lounge. The dimly lit space sported plush seating and a well-stocked bar where richly dressed patrons sipped champagne and whispered among themselves.

"This way, please." Their guide led them to a reserved section with an excellent view of what lay beyond- a circular arena with a cage at its center, surrounded by tiered seating for spectators.

Opal's heart hammered as she took in the scene. This was where Wolfe had been forced to fight for years, where he had suffered for the entertainment of the wealthy and cruel. Her fingers curled into fists, nails digging into her palms as she struggled to maintain her composure and keep her ursa reined in.

"Easy." Stix placed a steadying hand on her arm. "We can't help him if we're thrown out."

She nodded, forcing her muscles to relax as they were shown to their seats. The area around them filled with other patrons- men smoking cigars and holding glasses of expensive liquor, women dripping with jewelry, all of them exuding an air of entitlement and anticipation.

Anticipation for the blood of her mate.

CHAPTER TWENTY-THREE

Wolfe sat in the penthouse, watching the sun's slow descent behind Seattle's skyline. As afternoon faded into evening, the room darkened, and shadows lengthened across the plush carpet. He hadn't touched the food Mo had brought. With his soul so hollow, the thought of eating sickened him. His mind whirled with desperate thoughts of escape.

The clock showed 7:30 PM. Thirty minutes until the fights began. Thirty minutes until he would be forced back into the cage. Usually, he would have already been down in the locker room, shown off to Mo's best clients. But with all that had happened, he supposed Mo wasn't taking chances anymore.

He paced the bedroom. Muscles knotted and battling the drug's lingering pull. His wolf stayed maddeningly remote, muffled. Without the bond, he was incomplete, vulnerable in ways that cut deeper than simple frailty.

As the minutes ticked by, he found himself drawn to the window. He laid his palm against the cool glass, staring at the city sprawled below, anxiety twisting in his gut. He clung desperately to the hope that Opal and Stix and Jeremiah and Caleb would come for him. They would get him out and back to freedom. Each moment, the uncertainty gnawed at him, but he forced himself to believe she would find a way to reach him. He had to believe. If he didn't believe, he would succumb to the darkness shadowing him.

The clock hit 7:45 PM with quiet precision. Seconds later, a sharp knock sounded on the bedroom door.

"It's time," barked a gruff voice. "Boss wants you downstairs."

Wolfe stayed motionless, staring out at the darkening sky. For a heartbeat, resistance flashed inside him-he wouldn't make this easy for them. Still, a wave of resignation dulled the edge of his defiance. Whatever punishment came, he would endure it. He'd endured worse. But afterward, he would do whatever he had to do to be free once and for all. Even if it meant he had to die to get it.

Another knock, more insistent this time. "Don't make this difficult, Wolfe. Open the door."

He still didn't respond. A muttered curse followed, then the metallic click of a gun being cocked. A deafening bang echoed through the room as the lock shattered. The door blew violently inward.

A burly man in a black suit filled the doorway, pistol still raised. His face twisted in annoyance and resignation as he scanned the room and found Wolfe by the window.

He lowered the gun. "I've been instructed to take you downstairs by any means necessary, short of killing you. I'd rather not hurt you, so can we just do this?"

Wolfe crossed his arms and planted his feet on the carpet. His defiance silent but unmistakable.

The guard holstered his weapon. "I figured you'd be difficult." He reached into his jacket pocket and pulled out a smartphone, tapping the screen a few times before turning it toward Wolfe.

The image froze the blood in Wolfe's veins. Opal. Asleep, her dark hair spread across a pillow, peaceful and unaware. The timestamp in the corner showed the photo had been taken mere hours ago.

"Mo has men watching her," the guard explained, his voice almost apologetic. "Says if you don't cooperate, they have orders to bring her in."

A growl rumbled in Wolfe, primal and protective. His wolf strained against its chemical restraints, desperate to break free.

"So what's it going to be? You coming downstairs, or do I make the call?"

He couldn't risk Opal's safety, couldn't bear the

thought of her being dragged into this nightmare. A pang of defeat twisted inside him; Wolfe slumped as determination drained away. The hope that she was looking for him flickered and died. He was on his own.

With a curt nod, he moved toward the door. Resigned.

"Smart choice." The guard let him pass.

In the hallway, four more guards waited, all armed and watching him. They moved in a tight formation around him as they walked toward the elevator-one in front, one behind, two flanking. The message clear-there would be no escape.

The elevator doors slid open, and they entered it. One of the guards inserted a key into a slot on the control panel and depressed the button marked "B3."

As the elevator descended, Wolfe's heart pounded and memories bombarded him.The roar of the crowd, the taste of blood, the bone-aching exhaustion after a match. His palms grew slick. He wiped them against his pants, trying to control the trembling in his fingers.

The doors opened onto a corridor with concrete floors and black walls. The distant sound of music and voices drifted through the air, growing louder as they moved toward the arena. Wolfe slowed instinctively, his body resisting even as his mind knew resistance was pointless.

A guard shoved him forward, not roughly but with enough force to keep him moving. "Don't drag this out," the man muttered. "Sooner you do this, sooner it's over."

They reached the locker room, where two more guards stood at attention. They nodded to Wolfe's escort and pulled open the heavy door, revealing a space that had once been as familiar to him as his own reflection.

The room hushed as he entered, a dozen pairs of eyes turning. Some faces he recognized, others were new, young men hungry and desperate. Those who had made Faustian bargains for a chance at money and fame. They gaped at him with a mixture of awe, fear, and curiosity. The legendary Wolfe back from the dead.

Wolfe scanned their faces, searching for the one person who had shown him kindness in this hell. Zaden. But his friend was nowhere to be seen, his absence a painful confirmation of Wolfe's worst fears. Had Mo killed him for his role in Wolfe's escape? Was he being held somewhere, suffering for his betrayal?

Moving with deliberate calm, Wolfe crossed to his old locker. The combination came back to him automatically. Muscle memory guided his fingers as he turned the dial. Inside, everything was as it had been-his shorts, hand wraps, and the small towel he used.

He stripped, ignoring the stares of the other fighters. The routine natural shoes off, shirt over head, pants folded on the bench. He tied his shorts at the waist.

When he finished, he sat on the bench, staring at the floor- the oppressive hush in the room broken only by the occasional shuffle of feet or clearing of a throat. No one spoke to him. No one dared.

Minutes dragged before the door swung open again. Mo strode forward in a suit that likely cost more than most made in a month. His slick-backed hair glinted in the fluorescent lights, his smile radiant yet utterly cold.

"Gentlemen!" he announced, clapping his hands together. "It's going to be a big night. Are we ready?"

No one answered. The fighters inspected their hands. Some fixed their eyes on the floor. Others studied the walls- anywhere but at the man who controlled their fates.

Mo remained unbothered by the lack of response, his attention already fixed on Wolfe. He crossed the room, stopping in front of him.

"I can't tell you how pleased I am to have you back, Wolfe," he said. "The crowd has missed you. I've missed you." His smile widened, showing too many teeth. "Win, and I'll consider your vacation paid for in full. Bygones and all that. I'll even leave your friend alone. You have my word."

Wolfe's eyes narrowed.

Mo bent close, his breath hot against Wolfe's ear. "Sadly, I don't think you'll manage it. Not tonight. Not in your condition."

Before Wolfe reacted, Mo drove a syringe into the

side of his neck. Wolfe's hand shot up and yanked it free.

Rage exploded through him. He lunged at Mo, hands reaching for his throat, intent on ending the nightmare once and for all. But the guards tackled his arms, hauling him backward before his fingers closed around Mo's neck.

Mo chuckled, straightening his tie as Wolfe struggled against the guards' hold. "Always so predictable, nephew. So easy to manipulate."

Wolfe continued to struggle, even as the new drug crept through his system. His vision blurred at the edges, and his limbs grew heavier. The guards' grips became iron bands, impossible to break.

"Sit him down before he hurts himself." Mo laughed.

The guards forced Wolfe back onto the bench, where he slumped against the lockers. His body no longer responded to his commands. The room tilted and swayed around him. Faces blurred into indistinct shapes.

"Good luck, Wolfe." Mo patted his cheek. "You're going to need it."

With that, he turned and swept from the room. Wolfe slumped on the bench, battling the encroaching blurriness.

Panic clawed at his insides. His reflexes dulled, his reaction time lagged, though he stayed fully conscious. The perfect drug for a fighter who might otherwise refuse to enter the cage. The perfect insurance for whichever opponents Mo had lined up.

This wasn't a match- it was an execution. Fear morphed to despair. The truth settled in- Mo didn't want him to win; he wanted him broken, humiliated, possibly dead. In his current state, Wolfe stood little chance, even against a mediocre opponent, let alone Mo's champions.

He tried to stand, to prove to himself he could still fight, but his legs barely supported his weight. The room spun, faces and lockers blurring together in a nauseating kaleidoscope. The other fighters watched with pity and relief- glad it was him and not them.

Through the haze of drugs, a single thought crystallized in Wolfe's mind. Opal. He had to stay alive for her. Had to endure whatever came next. Had to believe that somehow, she would find him, save him from this nightmare.

The thought anchored him. He might not be able to win tonight's fights, but he'd survive. Had to survive. For Opal and for himself.

The door opened again, and two guards entered.

"Sanchez, Jones, you're first. Five minutes."

Two men stood and moved toward the exit, stretching and shaking out their limbs.

CHAPTER TWENTY-FOUR

The lights dimmed, and a hush fell over the crowd. A spotlight illuminated the center of the cage as a man stepped up to a microphone. Opal's ursa paced and snuffed, sniffing the air, trying to catch a whiff of Wolfe. Wanting to know he was unharmed.

"Ladies and gentlemen." The man's voice was smooth and practiced. "Welcome to tonight's special event. We have an exceptional program for you this evening, featuring the return of our champion after a brief vacation."

A murmur of excitement rippled through the audience. Opal's grip tightened on her champagne flute until Affina gently removed it from her hand before it shattered.

"But first, please welcome your host for the

evening, the man who makes these extraordinary encounters possible- Mr. Mo Black!"

The crowd cheered as a spotlight swung to illuminate a figure emerging from a private entrance. Mo was exactly as Wolfe had described him- tall, silver-haired, impeccably dressed in a tailored suit screaming of wealth and power. His cold smile made her squirm.

"Evening, friends," Mo said, taking the microphone. "Tonight is indeed special. Not only do we have several exceptional matches for your entertainment, but we also celebrate the return of our undefeated champion, the Killer Wolfe!"

More applause, louder this time. Mo raised a hand for silence.

"For those who have placed wagers, the odds have been updated. So if you wish to change your bet, now is the time. But before our prime event, we have two other matches."

There was a groan from the crowd and several boos.

Mo chuckled. “I know, I know. Waiting is painful. But anticipation can be true pleasure. So drink up. Get your wagers in, and be ready for some action-packed fights.”

He strode out, and Opal’s grip on her chair arm made the metal groan. She and her ursa wanted to jump over the railing and shred him, but Stix’s hand clamped down on her arm.

“Hold it together, sis.”

"Where are Dad and Jeremiah? Why haven't they and Logan checked in?"

Stix checked his phone.

"Be patient." Razor motioned the waiter over. "Order some food. The Reeds have this under control."

The waiter approached, and Razor ordered another round of drinks for them as well as some food, not that Opal would eat any of it. She doubted she would ever eat again unless Wolfe was safe with her.

THE FIRST TWO FIGHTS LASTED SO LONG OPAL HAD TO excuse herself. The tense air had her at the end of her tether. Between the waiting, her ursa, the makeup, and the clothes, she couldn't take any more.

Affina walked with her. "Laugh," Affina said lowly. "Smile. Laugh. Look like you are enjoying yourself, or you'll draw attention."

Affina promptly giggled as they passed the guards. "Seriously? I knew Sanchez would win. He was so hot."

The guards eyed them as they walked to a small hallway and into the first door for the ladies' room.

Opal rushed to the granite countertop and slammed her fists onto it, making it shake.

Affina came up behind her and rubbed her back. "Breathe. I know this is hard, but we have to keep it together. That's our job. Your job. Probably the hardest job of any of us. If Raze was in there… I can't imagine what I would do."

Opal took a shuddering breath, meeting Affina's eyes in the mirror.

"I feel like I'm going to explode," she whispered. "My ursa is clawing to be unleashed. I don't know how much longer I can keep her caged."

"I know," Affina said. "But you can't let her out. Not yet."

"Have you heard anything from Logan? From Jeremiah?"

Affina shook her head. "No updates. But that's not necessarily bad. They're being careful."

The bathroom door swung open, and two women entered, their laughter cutting off abruptly when they spotted Opal and Affina. They were dressed similarly-expensive gowns, perfect makeup, jewelry that probably cost more than Opal's cabin.

"First time?" one of them asked, her smile sharp as she assessed Opal. "You look a little green."

Affina snickered, the sound so natural it surprised Opal. "Her first time seeing this level of violence. I told her it would be intense."

The woman nodded knowingly as she moved to the mirror. "Wait for the Wolfe. He's something else entirely."

Opal's heart stuttered at the mention of Wolfe. "The Wolfe?" She tried to keep her voice casual.

"Mo's champion." The second woman applied fresh lipstick.

"He's been gone for weeks. Everyone thought he was dead or something, but Mo brought him back." She capped her lipstick and turned to face them. "Word is he's not in the best shape, though. The odds have shifted dramatically."

Opal's blood chilled. "What do you mean?"

The first woman shrugged, checking her reflection one final time. "My husband heard from Mo's people that the Wolfe might not be... himself. Something about needing to be reminded of his place."

“Are you going to bid on him tonight?” the first woman asked.

The second woman primped her hair and applied more lipstick. “I don’t know. I mean, he is definitely worth the money, but... if he’s not in shape to perform...”

The first woman snorted. “Trust me, that man can perform with all different parts of his body besides his dick.”

Both women chuckled, waved to Opal, and left, their heels clicking against the marble floor. Opal gripped the counter so hard her knuckles cracked. Her ursa roared inside her, and her mind swirled.

Bid on him? Women bid on him?

Her stomach roiled, and Opal hurried into the first stall. She fell to her knees and heaved into the toilet.

He’d been prostituted. Her Wolfe. Her sweet and

gentle Wolfe. Tears flowed from her eyes, hitting the toilet bowl, creating tiny ripples.

The stall door clicked behind her, and Affina knelt and hugged her.

Affina spoke soothingly to Opal in a language she didn't understand. She hugged Opal as tears fell and sobs wracked her.

"They drugged him," she cried. "They drugged him so he can't win. And worse... he was sold. Sold to women..."

Affina kissed Opal's hair. "It won't happen again. We won't let it happen to him ever again. No matter what we have to do. We are getting him out. We need to stay strong. He needs you now more than ever. You have to hold it together a little while longer. You can do this. He needs you. Needs you to be out there. Needs to know you are fighting for him no matter what."

Opal's heart shattered for Wolfe. For the little boy, he never got to be. For the teen forced to fight in a ring. And for the man who had been sold body and soul to the highest bidder.

She gulped down a huge breath. She had to keep it together. If he could endure what he'd been through, she could endure hearing about it.

"For as long as I live, I will never make love to another woman. Only you. Always you." His words echoed in her head.

She swiped at her eyes and got clumsily to her feet before turning to Affina. “How bad is my makeup?”

Affina gave her a smile. “Don’t worry. We can fix it.”

THEY REACHED THEIR SEATS AS THE ANNOUNCER'S VOICE boomed through the arena again.

“Are you okay?” Stix asked.

Opal shook her head but couldn’t speak.

Affina sat next to Opal and watched Razor. He leaned in, a concerned expression on his face. Affina spoke to him in a different language.

“What’s going on?”

But Opal couldn’t tell him. It wasn’t her trauma to discuss. “We need to get him out.”

“We will. I promise.”

Opal leveled her gaze on her brother. “I don’t care what happens to me. You promise me you will take him home with you.”

“Opal-”

She gripped his arm, her claws lengthening. “Promise.”

Stix searched her face and swallowed hard. “I’m not going to let anything happen to either of you. But I promise. We aren't leaving here without him tonight.”

She nodded.

"Ladies and gentlemen, the moment you've all been waiting for,” the announcer called. “Please welcome back, the one, the only, winner of over two thousand fights... Killer Wolfe!"

The crowd erupted. The sounds of the screams, clapping, and whistling pierced her ears, making her flinch.

A gate at the far end of the arena opened, and Wolfe staggered in. His usual fluid grace gone, replaced by an unsteady gait that spoke of drugs. His shoulders hunched, his head hanging as guards flanked him on either side.

She sniffed the air, trying to catch his scent, but she was too far away. A sob clenched Opal's throat. Her ursa roared, and Opal jumped from her seat to grasp the balcony railing. Stix called her name, but she couldn't answer. She couldn't move. She couldn't take her eyes off Wolfe. She clocked his every movement. His breath. The way he couldn't control his own limbs. His gait appeared heavy and off. His eyes unfocused. Then Affina was next to her. Cheering and yelling Wolfe's name. She wrapped an arm around Opal and held her tight.

"Breathe. You need to breathe, or you'll pass out."

Opal blinked rapidly, trying to keep tears from rolling down her face again.

A phone rang behind her. Razor looked at it and moved it to his ear. He talked so low Opal couldn't hear him over the roar of the crowd. He glanced at her, stood, and walked out of their box toward the bathrooms.

Wolfe swayed back and forth. The announcer grabbed Wolfe's arm and lifted it high.

"We need to move," Opal hissed as they forced Wolfe into the center of the mats. "He can barely stand."

"And his opponent tonight, undefeated in over one hundred and fifty-two matches, the Southern Slayer, Zaden Redpaw!"

The opposite gate opened, and a man entered. Easily six feet tall, his muscled body covered in tattoos, and his eyes flashed an unnatural blue.

"Oh no." Horror washed through her. "Is that?"

"Yes," said Raze, returning. "Zaden. The one who helped him escape."

"We have to do something," said Opal

"We can't," Raze replied. "Security is beefed up. Double what's normally here. If we try anything now, it will be a mess. Jeremiah doesn't want to risk it with so many humans around."

Opal stared at Wolfe, willing him to see her, but if by some miracle he did look, she doubted he'd recognize her with how glazed his eyes appeared.

"Sit," said Stix. "We wait for the Reeds."

Opal turned to her brother. "The Reeds aren't my alphas."

"No," said Stix. "But they are Wolfe's. And they have helped us every step of the way. We wouldn't be here if it weren't for them. We do as we're told."

“What if it was Satia? Or Andre? Would you sit and wait?”

Stix swallowed hard. “I promise you, if it comes down to it, I’ll go myself and carry him out. And I’ll kill every one of those assholes if I have to. Okay?”

Her breathing burst out of her in a harsh exhale. She swallowed and nodded.

Affina and Stix led her back to her seat as the announcer called for everyone to quiet down. Then Mo stepped up.

“These two are not only friends; they are best friends. Zaden is the one who helped Wolfe plan his whole vacation. I’ve never met two fighters closer than these two. Like brothers.” Mo clapped both men on the back in turn. “So sit back, and watch these two titans as they battle for the new top spot on my roster.”

The referee stepped between the fighters, explaining the rules merely for show. There were no rules here, no protections. This wasn't a sport. They were gladiators in the coliseum. Blood sacrifices for the entertainment of the wealthy.

Zaden leaned close to Wolfe, his voice barely audible over the crowd's roar. "I'm sorry." His eyes flashed with anguish. "They have my sister. They'll kill her if I don't-"

Wolfe lifted his head, and clarity pierced through

the fog. Anguish laced his friend's eyes, and Wolfe understood the impossible position Mo had engineered.

With tremendous effort, he raised his hands, signing deliberately. *"Do what you have to do."*

Zaden's face crumpled before he steeled himself and backed up as the referee finished his meaningless speech. The bell rang, and the crowd erupted in cheers.

Zaden circled Wolfe, neither of them eager to begin.

“Do something,” Zaden mouthed. “Hit me.”

Wolfe blinked several times, trying to keep on his feet. He tracked Zaden’s movements, glad he hadn’t eaten anything, or he would throw up from the dizziness rolling through him.

The audience grew restless, shouting for action, but both fighters hesitated.

"Come on, you bastards!" someone yelled from the crowd. "Fight!"

Mo's voice cut through the noise, speaking into a small microphone. "Gentlemen, I'd hate to have to remind you both of what's at stake."

The threat was clear. Wolfe looked up toward where Mo sat, and his wolf growled, trying to stand. As Wolfe glared at Mo, his vision cleared a fraction more.

It had been what? An hour? An hour and a half since Mo had shot him up with who knew what. But little by little, his vision cleared, and his limbs lightened. But that didn't do much for him at the moment. Zaden sagged, and he threw the first punch- a half-hearted jab Wolfe dodged. Even in his drugged state, Wolfe's instincts remained sharp. He swung at Zaden, catching him in the shoulder. Zaden spun half away but recovered. Wolfe couldn't be sure if Zaden had let him land the blow or if he'd done it himself, but it didn't matter because Zaden's eyes flashed and he came at Wolfe with force.

Zaden's fist connected with Wolfe's ribs, the impact driving the air from his lungs in a painful whoosh. Wolfe staggered backward; his weakness made it impossible to maintain his balance. The crowd roared its approval, bloodlust evident in every cheer.

Wolfe tried to counter, his movements sluggish but impactful. Zaden tried dodge the swing, but took the jab to his chin, his face a mask of professional detachment that couldn't quite hide the anguish in his eyes. This was theater, nothing more.

"I'm sorry," Zaden whispered again as he landed a blow to Wolfe's midsection. "I'm so sorry."

The words were lost in the crowd's roar, but Wolfe read them on his friend's lips. He managed to grab Zaden's arm and pull him into a bear hug.

Zaden's jaw clenched as he broke free from Wolfe's grip. "What did he take from you? What's he got over you?" He threw another punch to Wolfe's shoulder, rather than anywhere that might cause serious damage.

Wolfe deflected the punch and landed an unsteady kick to Zaden's ribs, making him stumble.

Wolfe leveled his gaze on Zaden and signed two words. *"My mate."*

Zaden's eyes widened. It didn't matter what Mo wanted. Didn't matter that they were friends. And it didn't matter what Zaden had thought Wolfe would do to help him rescue his sister. Wolfe was not going to lose. Not with the safety of his mate on the line.

Zaden rushed in, but Wolfe grabbed him around the waist and tossed him away. Zaden rolled across the mat and slammed into the chain link. Wolfe glared at the box where Mo sat. His vision still swam in the corners, but not as much as before. He stared Mo in the eye. He would win. Whatever it took. Whatever he had to do, he would do it because he refused to live one more day without Opal. One more day in captivity. One more day as a slave. He would win, and he would tear apart anyone who stopped him from getting back to Opal. Mo had said Wolfe was a murderer. Had gotten even the police and a judge to believe it. So be it. If it got him back to Opal, that's what he'd be.

He scanned the crowd of cheering faces. He breathed in the odor of sweat, pheromones, perfume and-

He sucked in breath again. He'd recognize that scent a mile away. His wolf lifted his head and howled.

Wildflowers and sunshine. His head whipped to the side, and his eyes stopped on a box to the far right. There, sitting, watching, sat Stix, and next to him, a beautiful, posh woman he would know even if she wore a blowup chicken suit.

But… it couldn't be. The guard had shown him a photo of her asleep in bed… And yet, she was there. She'd come for him. Opal. His Opal. His mate.

It had been fake. The photo had been a lie. His wolf howled again, and Wolfe couldn't help the smile that planted on his face a second before Zaden's fist slammed into the side of his temple.

CHAPTER TWENTY-FIVE

Opal sprang to her feet as Wolfe collapsed on the mat, his body motionless. Her ursa surged within, claws bursting through her skin before she restrained them. Stix seized her wrist, his grip iron-strong.

"No." Stix pulled her back into her seat.

Zaden stood over Wolfe's prone form, his expression both anguished and relieved. The referee began counting, each number echoing through the hushed arena. The crowd leaned forward, hungry for more.

"Six... seven..."

Wolfe's fingers twitched.

"Eight..."

His eyes fluttered open, unfocused but determined.

"Nine..."

With a surge of will, Wolfe rolled to his side and

scrambled to his knees. The crowd erupted into some cheers and some disappointed groans as bets were won and lost on his resilience.

Zaden's shoulders drooped.

"He saw you," Affina said over the crowd. "Before he went down, he looked right at you and smiled."

Opal nodded, unable to speak. She had seen it too-a spark of recognition in his eyes, a fleeting lift in his face before Zaden's fist landed.

The knowledge both strengthened and devastated her. Wolfe staggered to his feet and faced Zaden again. His movements still uncoordinated, but with a new determination in his stance.

Zaden hesitated, clearly reluctant to continue the assault. This hesitation earned him a sharp rebuke from Mo, whose voice cut through the arena like a whip.

"Finish it!"

Zaden advanced on Wolfe, throwing a combination of punches Wolfe barely managed to block. One caught him in the ribs, driving him back against the chain link barrier. The crowd roared its approval as Zaden brought up a knee to Wolfe's midsection.

Opal's hands gripped the railing. Beside her, Stix's phone buzzed. He glanced at it, then bent close.

"It's happening. Five minutes."

She nodded, not daring to take her eyes off where Wolfe rallied, pushing back against Zaden's assault with a series of surprisingly effective counterpunches.

One caught Zaden square in the jaw, sending him stumbling backward. Zaden's eyes widened with surprise.

Opal's ursa surged with fierce pride as Wolfe pressed his advantage, landing two more solid blows to Zaden. His chest heaved as he drew in breaths. He ran on pure adrenaline and willpower.

"Beautiful, isn't he?" Mo's voice drifted from behind her, and Opal forced herself not to stiffen. "My nephew's a natural fighter."

The casual possessiveness in his tone made her skin crawl. She kept her face neutral, playing the part of an interested spectator as Mo moved to the railing.

“He is.” Razor stood and approached Mo. “When I learned about him, I had to witness for myself. And of course, bring my wife. She adores these kinds of things.” He extended his hand to Affina. Affina stepped forward, and placed herself between Mo and Opal, deliberately blocking Opal from view.

Mo chuckled. “I wondered who these new patrons were who wanted late entrance to this evening's fights. I searched you out, and it became clear. You own property near Wolf River, Idaho, and do business with Logan Reed.” Mo looked over Affina’s shoulder to Opal. “And you’re the girl from the cabin. Opal isn’t?”

Opal’s ursa roared, and she clenched her jaw before standing and staring straight at Mo. Finally, the charade ended.

“Yes.”

Razor pulled Affina into his side and out of Mo's path.

Mo nodded and walked toward Opal. Stix stood and growled, and Mo appraised him. "Do you fight? You'd make a ton of money in the ring."

Stix clenched his fists.

Mo chuckled. "Pity." Then he turned his attention back to Opal. "It's nice to meet you, while you're awake."

Opal's longer, sharper nails dug into her skin. "I can't say the same."

"It's interesting. You're not his usual type."

Opal's ursa roared. "I think you mean, I'm not your type. Clearly, you don't know your nephew as well as you believe. If you did, you'd know I'm exactly his type- his only type." Opal met Mo's eye, her words challenging.

Mo assessed her for a moment.

Zaden recovered and circled Wolfe. Both men breathed hard, sweat and blood mixing on their faces. Zaden feinted left, then dug his shoulder into Wolfe's midsection, driving him backward. The metal rattled with the impact.

Wolfe's knees buckled for a moment, and Opal's heart stopped. But then he straightened, his gaze finding hers.

Mo bent toward Opal's ear and ran a finger down her arm. "You're welcome to stay here if it will make him happy. But I'll kill him before I let you take him."

Opal snarled and shoved Mo away. She didn't use her full strength, but it was enough to send Mo stumbling toward the railing. Shock registered on his features.

Stix jumped next to her. "Touch my sister again, and I'll rip your arm off."

Razor and Affina both bared their teeth at Mo.

Suddenly, Wolfe launched himself across the mats and up the cage wall. People gaped as he clambered up the chain-link fence to the opening at the top. Wolfe launched himself across the divide and slammed straight into Mo, tackling him into the seats.

The arena erupted into chaos as Wolfe slammed his fist into Mo's face once, twice, three times. Screams pierced the air as patrons scrambled away from the violence. Security guards rushed forward, but Stix and Razor intercepted them, their shifter strength making quick work of them.

Blood poured from Mo's nose, and his left eye already started to bruise. Wolfe's hands closed around Mo's throat. Mo clawed at Wolfe's wrists, his face rapidly turning purple as he clambered for air.

Mo's eyes bulged.

"Wolfe!" Opal fought her way toward them, pushing against the panicking crowd as Affina forced a clear path ahead of her.

Wolfe's head whipped up, and he spotted her, his eyes wild and unfocused.

"Wolfe," she called again.

His grip on Mo loosened enough for the older man to gasp in a desperate breath.

"Kill me," Mo wheezed, his cold black eyes meeting Wolfe's, "and you'll never find out who you are. Your real name. Your family."

OPAL REACHED HIS SIDE AND TOUCHED HIS SHOULDER. HIS wolf howled, regaining his strength. Her touch invigorated him. She was there. Really there. Under the makeup and hairspray that masked her real face, she was there. Her gray eyes full of tears, but her lips smiling.

"Don't let him manipulate you anymore, baby. Forget him. I'm here. Right here." She kissed him, and his entire body ignited. She'd come for him. They all had.

Mo's lips curved into a bloody smile. "Do you remember anything before the age of seven? Anything at all?"

The question hit Wolfe like a physical blow. He remembered fragments, glimpses of a life before the ring. *A woman's laugh. The smell of pine trees. A voice calling a name that wasn't Wolfe.*

"That's right." Mo's voice grew stronger as Wolfe's grip weakened. "I found you broken, dying. Your family left you to rot after the hunters finished with you. I saved you. I gave you purpose."

"You're nothing more than lying human scum," Opal snarled. "You aren't related to Wolfe. You smell nothing like him."

Around them, more chaos ensued. More armed security guards poured into the arena. Below, Zaden stood frozen, torn between escaping and helping.

Stix appeared at Opal's side and sniffed. "She's right," he said. "He's not related to you, Wolfe. You are a Blood Born wolf. He's a human. It's not possible."

Mo's eyes flared, and Wolfe's grip tightened again. Not related? Not his uncle? How had he not noticed? Never questioned? If Mo wasn't his uncle... who the hell was he?

A brawl broke out below, and a gun went off. Jeremiah, Logan, and Opal's father, Robert, fought their way into the room. The guards tried to keep them out, to no avail. They were no match for Alphas. Zaden helped take down a guard.

"You don't have to kill him." Opal wrapped her warm arms around him. "He's not worth it."

For a moment, Wolfe's wolf fought to be released, but he wasn't strong enough yet. His claws lengthened and dug into Mo's flesh. It would be so easy. So easy to rip out his throat. Break his neck. End him.

"Don't be what he accused you of, what he wants you to be. Be you. The you I know you are."

Opal's words burst through the fog of rage, and his wolf backed down.

He peeled his hands from Mo's skin, finger by finger.

Mo collapsed against the seats, gasping and coughing as air entered his lungs.

"You're right," Wolfe signed. *"He's not worth it."*

Mo's cough turned to a cackle. "Cute trick. You teach him that? He's always been a teachable little doggie."

Wolfe lunged for Mo again, but Opal grabbed his face. "He's not worth it, my love. He's not worth you."

Wolfe searched her face, and she brushed a curl from his forehead. He wrapped his arms around her and inhaled her neck. Opal, his Opal.

Opal kissed his neck. He clung to her. She was there. She was safe. He let out a shuddered breath. Opal stiffened in his arms, and she screamed.

"Gun!" She shoved Wolfe sideways as a shot rang out.

Wolfe toppled onto his side as Opal flattened her body on his.

THE SHOT SLAMMED INTO OPAL'S BACK, MAKING HER CRY out. Stix's roar, followed by her father's, rang in her ears. Her ribs crushed inward as if a cinderblock had dropped on her. She struggled to suck in air, trying to breathe. Her torso burned like wildfire.

Wolfe's mouth opened and closed as he pulled her

to him and tried to talk. She wanted to tell him it was ok. She would be okay. Not to worry. But her voice wouldn't work, and trying to lift her arms felt like trying to lift her Jeep.

There was a thunderous crash as her father's massive ursa landed on the balcony. Stix raked his claws across Mo's body. Mo reached for the gun, but Stix swatted it away.

Shouts and gunshots rang out below them. Opal clawed at Wolfe, fighting to catch her breath.

Zaden appeared beside them. Blood streaked his face, but his eyes were clear and determined. "She needs a doctor. A shifter doctor. I know one, but he's twenty minutes away."

Wolfe's face swam in and out of focus, his lips forming words she couldn't read. Pain blossomed outward from her back, hot and sharp, consuming everything. More shouting and chaos erupted around them. She coughed, and something sticky leaked out of her mouth and down her chin. She swallowed several times and tried to breathe in slowly, even as her brain told her she needed more air.

Zaden grabbed Mo by the shirt. "Where's my sister?"

Opal's father's massive ursa loomed protectively over them, his roars vibrating through the floor. Stix pinned Mo to the floor, his partially shifted form terrifying in its controlled rage.

"Opal," Wolfe mouthed, his hands framing her

face. Tears streaked through the blood on his cheeks. His hands moved frantically, signing words she couldn't focus enough to understand.

Her ursa stirred, wanting desperately to heal the damage. Her strength ebbed with each labored breath. Her vision blurred as wildfire coursed through her.

"Move!" Jeremiah's Alpha command. He appeared beside them, his face grim as he assessed her wound. "We need to get her out of here. Now."

Jeremiah ripped off his shirt and tied it around Opal's torso, pulling it tight. She tried to scream, but had no air.

Wolfe nodded, gathering her up, ignoring his own injuries. She wanted to protest- he was hurt, drugged, in no condition to carry her- but her body refused to respond.

"The service entrance," Logan directed, clearing a path through the panicking crowd. "Caleb's got a vehicle waiting."

Opal's vision tunneled, the edges darkening as Wolfe carried her through the chaos. She focused on the steady beat of his heart against her ear, the warmth of his arms around her.

Behind them, her father roared in fury, followed by Mo's scream.

“Wait!” Jeremiah commanded.

Her father’s roar cut off.

“My sister,” Zaden begged. “Tell me where she is!”

"Bring him. We'll find your sister. He doesn't get out of this that easily."

Zaden's sister? Mo kidnapped Zaden's sister to make him fight? Her ursa roared in protest. Opal wanted nothing more than to go back and rip Mo apart with her teeth, but she doubted she'd live through the experience.

Didn't matter. The Reeds didn't show mercy. Whatever Jeremiah had in store for Mo would be much worse than the simple swipe of her father's massive paw or the snap of her jaws.

The scene around her changed as Wolfe cradled her and kissed her head repeatedly. Bright lights, then darker, sounds of feet slapping against a hard surface, before a metal door slammed against the wall, the scents of food, and finally, cool air whooshed over her skin.

Spots clouded her vision as the sensation of drowning gripped her.

"Lay her down in the back," Caleb said.

"Stay with me." Wolfe set her down, his face coming into focus above her. *"Please, Opal. Stay with me."*

She managed to lift her hand to his face, her fingers leaving a smear of blood on his cheek.

"Always."

Darkness pulled her under. The last thing she heard was Wolfe's anguished whine.

CHAPTER TWENTY-SIX

Consciousness floated back in fragments-beeping machines, hushed voices, the odor of antiseptic. Opal's eyelids felt impossibly heavy as she struggled to open them.

"She's waking up."

Opal forced her eyes open, blinking against the sunlight. She lay on a large bed, surrounded by medical machines of all kinds, but it wasn't a hospital room.

“She’s waking,” her mother said louder.

Opal continued to blink, trying to clear her vision and focus.

Footsteps hurried into the room, and the mattress shifted as a heavy body sat next to her. She breathed in.

Wolfe.

He let out a huff and rubbed his cheek on hers as he gripped her hand.

“Wolfe.” Her voice came out hoarse, and her chest burned, but no longer felt like live coals had been shoved inside her.

He pushed at her hair, sniffed her neck, and kissed her. He wore a simple green T-shirt and sweats. His bruises and cuts had begun to heal.

On the other side, a familiar soft hand took hers.

“Baby girl,” said her mom.

Opal tried to speak but ended up coughing.

“Easy,” said her mom. “You’ve been through a lot the last twenty-four hours.”

Wolfe ran from the room and returned with a bottle of water. He opened the bottle and tipped it to her lips. She swallowed slowly, thinking how interesting it was that their roles were now reversed. She nodded, and he removed the bottle. She took in a breath, realizing she breathed easier. Her ribcage ached and her side burned, but she was alive. Wolfe was alive. And they were together.

“What happened?” she finally managed.

“You were shot. You had a collapsed lung. Several broken ribs. They had to do surgery.”

A tube stuck out of Opal's skin, taped to her ribs.

“You’re going to be fine,” her mom said. “Jeremiah and Razor took care of everything.”

“Where am I?”

“We’re in Razor and Affina’s place. Still in Seattle.”

She nodded.

"I'm sorry," Wolfe signed. *"This is my fault."*

"Stop. This is not your fault."

"You could have died."

"Yeah, but I've been there before. And like that time, I made it through. I promised I wouldn't leave you, didn't I?"

"I don't know what I would do if I lost you."

She smiled. "Well, let's not find out."

He laid his forehead on hers, and a tear dripped onto her nose.

Zaden's words floated back to her. "Zaden. Your friend. Did he find his sister?"

Wolfe nodded. *"She was in the hotel."*

Opal sighed in relief. "Where are Dad and Stix? Are they okay?"

"They're fine," said her mom. "Murderous, but fine."

She looked at Wolfe. "Mo?"

His eyes flashed and hardened. *"Not dead."*

"Jeremiah has him with your dad and Stix. They were waiting for you to wake up before deciding what to do with him."

She nodded. "Well, before he gets his final punishment, I have a few questions."

Wolfe shook his head.

"Yes," Opal said. "There are things only he has the answers to."

"I don't want you near him," Wolfe signed.

"Neither do I," said her mother.

"That may be true, but it doesn't change the fact that I want answers. Not for me, for Wolfe."

She and Wolfe stared at each other for a moment before he nodded once.

She gave her mom a tight smile. "Will you arrange it, please?"

Her mom chewed her lip for a moment before standing. "Five minutes. That's all."

"That's all I need."

Her mom walked to the door and out into the hallway before pulling out her phone.

Wolfe's face held a cacophony of emotions.

"I can't live without you. That sounds dumb, but I can't. I've never known love before you. If I lost you, I think my heart would literally stop beating."

She pulled him in and kissed him. "Then I'm glad you don't have to."

Wolfe lay down next to her and slid his arms around her, running his fingers up and down her arm.

Being in his arms was the most peaceful thing ever- but it also hurt like hell. She decided to wait a minute before telling him, though.

CHAPTER TWENTY-SEVEN

Wolfe tightened his grip, forming a protective barrier around her. She was okay. She was alive and okay.

His wolf sniffed her, searching for any further injuries or possible signs of infection, but there weren't any.

Wolfe's heart boomed. They would be together, and no one would ever tear them apart again.

He kissed her head and rubbed his cheek on her hair.

"Wolfe, my love? You're hurting me."

Oh my gosh, he was such an asshole. Horrified, he started to pull away.

"No," she caught his hand. "Don't go. Just... gentle. I'm not healed yet."

He stared at her, questioning, making sure she meant it.

She smiled and tugged him back to her.

He settled beside her, his touch light as he stroked her hair.

She looked up with soft gray eyes, so different from before-no heavy makeup, no false lashes like the women Mo made him entertain. Simple natural beauty- the curve of her cheek, the small freckles on her nose, her pillowy peach lips. All natural. All real. No garish lipstick or glitter, only her beautiful face.

"What are you thinking?"

"You are so beautiful."

She snorted. "I'm sure."

He drew his eyebrows together. *"You are. You are the most beautiful woman I've ever seen, and you are all mine."*

"Does this mean you don't want me to keep wearing the makeup?"

He scrunched up his face and shook his head.

She laughed. "Thank heavens, because that was hella uncomfortable."

He remembered her gold dress and matching boots and smiled.

"What?"

"I wouldn't mind the boots every once in a while."

She laughed again, coughed, then groaned and gripped her side.

"Sorry. Sorry. Sorry." He covered her face with kisses.

"As long as I can pick a different dress, I think I can manage the boots," she croaked.

"Do you need more water?"

She nodded.

"I'll get it," her mother said. Wolfe smiled at Joyce as she reached for the bottle and gave it to Opal. She'd been an anchor in the past twenty-four hours. Tending his wounds, making sure he was okay, holding his hand through Opal's surgery, whispering words of encouragement, assuring him their girl was too strong to die.

"They have Mo down two floors in Razor's office."

Wolfe tensed.

"I'm up to it," Opal said. "I want to talk to him."

Her mother frowned and walked out the door.

She turned to Wolfe. "Will you help me?"

A snarl rumbled in his body, and he tensed. Wolfe's wolf bristled; he did not want Opal anywhere near Mo.

She touched his cheek. "The sooner we do this, the sooner we can go home. You shouldn't have to live the rest of your life wondering."

He nodded. She was right. He needed answers so he could put the past behind him and move on.

Affina entered holding two hangers. "I have some clothing for both of you."

GETTING DRESSED TOOK PATIENCE AND PAIN. EACH movement sent twinges through her chest; the drainage tube complicated even simple tasks. She asked her mom to call the doctor to see if they could remove it. She couldn't help the groan of agony that escaped her as her mother slowly removed the tube and covered the small wound with gauze. She never wanted to do anything like that again. Tube removal from the body ranked right above cake makeup and tight gold dresses on the list of things she vowed never to do again.

Wolfe helped her with care, guiding her into a loose sweater to avoid her wounds and IV.

When dressed, Wolfe lifted her into his arms despite her protests. His expression brooked no argument, and she relented, resting her head on his shoulder as he carried her from the room, rolling the IV beside them.

The hallway led to a lavish, spacious living area where the others had gathered. The odor of iron and salt mingled with the faint scent of urine and sweat. Stix loomed by the windows, knuckles raw and bloodied. Her father sat in an armchair, massive frame tense with fury. Jeremiah and Caleb stood by the bar, speaking with Logan and Razor.

All conversation ceased when Wolfe carried her in.

"You should be resting," her father said immediately, rising from his chair.

"I'll rest after." Opal's voice came out stronger than she felt. "Where is he?"

"Downstairs," Logan answered. "We've... prepped him for you."

The clinical way he said it chilled Opal. She wasn't naive- it was more than apparent what had happened to Mo while she was unconscious. The blood on Stix's knuckles and cold satisfaction in Jeremiah's eyes told a story of retribution already underway.

"Take me to him," she said.

Wolfe carried her to the elevator, the other men joining them. Her mother looked as if she might say something, but Affina led her to the couch as the group exited the apartment.

They descended to the lower level with Wolfe's heart hammering against her. His body taut, his arms secure yet light around her.

The elevator opened on a sleek corridor of glass-walled offices. Razor led them to frosted glass at the end. Logan knocked. Footsteps sounded inside, and Griffin, Jeremiah's youngest son, opened the door.

Wow. All of the Reed boys had come.

Wolfe hesitated, his muscles bunching around her as if preparing to turn and carry her back upstairs. Opal touched his face.

"I need to do this. We need answers."

After a moment's resistance, he nodded, carrying her through the doorway.

The sight that greeted them made even Opal's ursa

recoil. The entire office had been covered in clear plastic sheeting, the kind used by serial killers in movies. In the center sat a shirtless Mo, bound to a metal chair with zip ties. Blood pooled on the plastic under him and splashed the room. Blood, piss, and sweat hung thick in the air.

His once-immaculate appearance was gone- his hair matted with blood, his expensive suit torn and discarded on the floor. One eye had swollen shut, and his split lip oozed fresh blood when he smiled at their entrance.

"The happy couple," Mo rasped, his voice rough. "How touching."

A growl rumbled through Wolfe, the vibration traveling into Opal's side. His eyes blazed with palpable hatred.

Logan brought another chair forward, positioning it a safe distance from Mo.

"For Opal," he explained.

Wolfe ignored the offered chair, instead taking the seat himself with Opal cradled in his lap. She tried shifting to sit separately, but his arms tightened, refusing to let her go.

"Wolfe, I can sit-"

His head shook once, definitively. His facial bones shifted, and his canines lengthened before returning to human. She understood. Separating from her would push him over an edge he already teetered on.

Instead of arguing, she settled against him,

focusing on Mo. Behind the prisoner stood Jeremiah, her father, and Stix.

Mo's eyes flicked between her and Wolfe, calculating. "To what do I owe this pleasure? Come to gloat before they finish me off?"

Opal studied him, taking in the man who had caused so much suffering. Wolfe's rage trembled with the effort of restraint. The depth of his anger shocked her- not its existence, but its intensity. This wasn't about what Mo had done to him over the years. This was personal, immediate. It was about the bullet that had torn through her body.

"Who are you?" she finally asked.

Mo's eyebrow cocked up. "Mo Black. I believe we've been introduced."

"No," she said evenly. "Who are you to Wolfe? He's a Blood Born. You are human."

The question hung between them. Mo's functioning eye narrowed slightly as he considered his answer. A muscle in his jaw twitched.

"His father used to work for me," he finally said. "As a fighter. Left before his debt was paid. When I found him, I decided to take the boy as payment instead."

"Did you kill his parents?"

Mo shrugged, wincing as the movement pulled at unseen injuries. "Not personally."

Stix's fist connected with Mo's jaw before anyone

could react. The older man groaned and gasped for breath.

"Answer the question," Stix growled.

When Mo straightened, blood leaked through his teeth. "As I said, not personally. But I saved him. The boy was bleeding to death when I found him. Throat slashed open. Would have died within minutes if I hadn't arrived."

"So there is no blood relation between you and Wolfe?" she pressed.

"No." Mo's lips twisted into something meant to be a smile. "But I think of him as my son. I raised him, after all."

Bile rose at the words. "You imprisoned him. Drugged him. Forced him to fight for your entertainment and profit. You're not a father, you're a trafficker."

Mo's expression hardened. "I gave him purpose. Direction. Without me, he'd have died in those woods, another victim of the ones who killed his parents."

“The ones who killed his parents because you told them to?”

He didn’t deny it.

A brutal cough wracked Opal, agony slicing through her and robbing her breath. Pain burned her torn lung, every gasp scraping her raw and helpless.

Wolfe's wolf couldn't take it. He couldn't handle Opal's pain. Couldn't handle the smug expression on Mo's face. Couldn't handle being so near to the man who had almost killed his mate without ripping his throat out.

Wolfe's hands moved frantically. She needed to go. She needed rest.

Plus, he didn't want her to see what he planned for Mo.

"Not... yet," she gasped between coughs, her eyes strong and determined.

Wolfe's wolf snarled and snapped his jaws, wanting to be released. *Just a couple more minutes.* A couple more, and he would give his wolf what he wanted.

"Where... did it happen? Where... did you find him?"

Mo watched her detached. "Montana. Outside a small town called Black Wolf Rock. Ironic, isn't it?"

Black Wolf Rock. The name hit Wolfe like a physical blow. *A wooden sign flashed into view through the front windshield of an old van. A small general store where his mom bought groceries. A long winding road to a group of cabins in the woods. A stone fireplace with a single photo of them sitting on the mantle.*

"What was his name?" Opal managed. "His real name?"

Mo's lips curved into a cruel smile. "Why don't you ask him? He remembers. Don't you, boy?"

Wolfe's breathing became erratic, as memories crashed through him.

"I think we've learned enough for today." Jeremiah stepped forward. "Robert, Stix- take our guest back to his accommodations. We'll continue this later."

“No,” said Opal. She moved to stand, but he held on to her. She looked at him, her gaze stern. “Let go, babe. I’m fine.”

He searched her pale face.

“Let go,” she said again.

He loosened his grip on her, and she stood shakily and took a step forward, using her IV stand for support. Wolfe’s wolf growled at the distance forming between them, so he stood behind her, needing the connection with her as much as he wanted to lend her strength.

She shuffled slowly toward Mo until she stood inches from him.

"What is Wolfe's real name?"

Mo's lips curled into a smirk. "His name is Wolfe. That's the name I gave him. That's his name."

"What was his name before?"

Mo remained silent.

Opal moved closer, ignoring Wolfe's protective growl.

"Fine. Have it your way."

Her hand shot out. Her nails lengthened into bear claws, the sharp tips pressing into Mo's skin enough to draw tiny beads of blood.

"You tried to kill my mate," she said, her voice dropping to a dangerous purr. "You may have dealt with my father and brother, but there's a reason people call for mama bear when there's a problem, not papa bear."

Mo's pulse fluttered beneath her claws, his breathing shallow as she applied the slightest increase in pressure.

"And even more dangerous than a mama bear," she leaned in until her lips grazed his ear, "is a bear whose mate was almost killed by an asshole like you."

Wolfe stepped forward and placed his hand on her back. Part of him wanted to pull her away to safety, another part urged her to finish what she'd started. His wolf reveled in the power she wielded.

"If you want any chance of me not eviscerating you excruciatingly slowly, you'll tell me his real name."

Mo's eyes darted to Wolfe, then back to Opal. For the first time, real fear flickered across his face.

"I see now why he likes you. You may not have the looks of some of the women I know, but you sure do have more balls than most of the men," he rasped against the pressure of her claws. "Reuger McConnell."

The name hung in the air, and Wolfe gasped.

"Reuger. Where are you?" his mother's voice echoed through his head. "I'm coming to find you, my little pup."

Reuger covered his mouth as he giggled, waiting for her inside the closet.

Her shadow passed in front of the crack between the doors.

"Are you under the bed?"

He giggled again.

"Nope. Not under the bed. Are you in the sock drawer?"

The drawer scraped open and closed.

"Not in the drawer. Where can you be? Maybe you're in... the closet!"

The door swung open, and Reuger leapt on his mom, tackling her to the ground and laughing.

"I caught you," she laughed.

"No," he said. "I caught you!"

She pulled him close and nuzzled his face.

The memory made Wolfe gasp. Reuger. He was Reuger McConnell.

Opal released Mo and turned to Wolfe's. She leaned into him, and he pulled her close.

His eyes stayed on Mo as he signed the word. "*Reuger.*"

"That's how I know you," said Jeremiah. "The McConnells were a well-known pack in Montana. A solid Blood Born family. Strong and kind. Years back, one of the sons returned with his wife and pup after getting himself in some trouble. We talked about them coming and joining us. But before we settled anything, they were massacred. Everyone. Twelve wolves. We thought the entire family had been killed."

"Not everyone," Mo said.

Wolfe stared at Mo. More images flashed through

his mind. *The cabins in the woods. Warm laughter around a packed dinner table. A plump, older woman with red hair and kind eyes singing lullabies to him. An older man with a weathered face teaching him to track deer through fresh snow. The mixture of apple pie and cedar wood. Home.*

"Your father was the best fighter I had before you," said Mo. "Like you, he was a complete natural. And because he was a werewolf, like you, he beat everyone. Until one day, he decided he was done. And he ran. Just. Like. You."

Wolfe's hands clenched into fists.

Mo smiled, cold and satisfied. "Your father owed me a lot of money. When he refused to honor his debt, I had to collect it another way. I gave him options-return to the ring, or I'd take his family."

"But he refused," Opal said.

"I found you. Half-dead, flayed open, your parents' bodies already starting to rot. You should have thanked me."

Wolfe's wolf exploded to the surface, no longer suppressed by drugs or shock. His eyes flashed as his canines lengthened. A sound part growl, part roar tore from his damaged throat- raw and primal and filled with years of buried rage.

He shifted in an instant, not registering the pain. Leaping through the air, he knocked Mo's chair backward and pinned him to the floor.

Terror and satisfaction shown in Mo's eyes.

Wolfe raked his claws down Mo's chest, flaying open the skin.

Mo cried out, and the sound rang through Wolfe's ears like a sweet lullaby. Faces flashed through his mind.

His mother. His father. Grandfather. Grandmother. Uncles. Aunts. Cousins.

Everyone Mo had taken from him.

Wolfe lifted his claws and slashed again. Over and over and over. One slash for each family member. Mo screeched and squealed like a pig. Blood sprayed Wolfe's muzzle. He wanted to yell at Mo. To curse him for what he had done. To crush his windpipe and watch him suffocate slowly. Every ounce of his wolf roared at him to do it. To kill Mo.

He sucked in a ragged breath, and Opal's words floated back to him. *"He's not worth it, my love. He's not worth you."*

Wolfe bared his teeth and forced his wolf back. He shifted to human, still poised over Mo. He sat on Mo's torso.

"I am not Wolfe. I am Reuger. I am not a murderer. I am not your nephew. I am a McConnell, like my father, my mother, and all the others you murdered. And after tonight, I will move on and forget you ever existed."

Mo stared at Wolfe. "What did you say?"

Wolfe spat in his face and stood.

Opal's small hand slipped into his.

He turned. *"Let's go."*

"What did he say?" Mo croaked.

Opal spat on Mo as well before Wolfe lifted her into his arms, grabbed the IV rolling cart, and headed for the exit.

"What did he say?" Mo croaked.

Wolfe didn't turn. Didn't stop. Didn't slow.

"What did he say?" Mo yelled.

Wolfe walked out the door to the elevator.

To him, Mo Black was already dead.

Razor opened the door to the apartment for Wolfe as he carried Opal inside. Joyce and Affina stood from the couch when they entered, but said nothing as Wolfe walked down the hall.

Not a sound permeated the apartment except for his and Opal's breathing as he moved to the large bed and lay her down on it. He stood for a moment with Opal, searching his face.

"I need to shower."

Opal sat up. "Let me help you."

He shook his head. *"Stay in bed. I'll be back."*

She looked like she might argue.

"Please," he signed.

Opal nodded and lay back on the pillows. He padded to the bathroom and locked the door. The lights came on automatically, and he stared at himself in the full-length mirror. Blood caked his naked form. He took in his features, his build, his hair.

He was Reuger McConnell. Reuger McConnell. Not Wolfe. Not Killer Wolfe. But Reuger McConnell.

He stared at himself until the chill of the air forced him into the shower. He didn't bother to let it warm before he got inside and crumbled to the travertine floor. He shook with silent sobs as years of suppressed grief finally broke free.

CHAPTER TWENTY-EIGHT

Opal's heart squeezed so hard she thought it might stop. The broken look in Reuger's eyes as he'd picked her up and carried her back upstairs shot right through her. His naked, bloodied body rippled with tension and pain as he lay her on the bed and then went to shower. She'd wanted to protest. Wanted to go with him. Wanted to hold and console him, but she hadn't. She'd been where he was. Knew the pain and confusion. And in that moment, he needed to be alone to process. When he was ready, he would come to her, and she would be there in every way.

A knock sounded on the door, and Affina and her mom entered. They glanced toward the bathroom door and went to Opal's bed.

"Is he okay?" her mom asked.

Opal shook his head. "He will be."

Affina took her armful of clothing and laid it on the bed. "I got you both some clean things."

Opal smiled. "Thank you. I think I'm gonna owe you a lot of new clothes at this point."

Affina waved her off and walked back toward the door, but stopped and turned. "When you come face to face with the person who murdered your family... You go through a lot of emotions. Especially if you chose not to, or don't get the chance to avenge what has been done to you. It's going to be rough for the next little while. Be patient with him, he'll work it all out. And until he does, if either of you needs anything at all, Razor and I would be happy to help, or listen."

"Thank you, again," said Opal. "I appreciate your kindness more than you possibly know."

Affina nodded. "Call me any time."

Opal's mom took her hand. "Are you okay?"

"I'm grateful he's out and alive, but I'm worried for him."

"As any mate would be."

Hearing her mom acknowledge Wolfe as her mate warmed Opal's heart. "His name is Reuger McConnell."

"Reuger. I like it. It fits him."

The water turned off, and Opal's ursa whined.

Her mom patted her hand. "I'll let you two rest. I need to check on your father and brother anyway."

Opal wanted to roll over on her side, but the IV restrained her. She looked at the drip to find it empty.

She lifted a tissue and removed the needle from her arm. She held the tissue to the puncture for a few seconds and bent her elbow.

The door opened, and Reuger stood wet with a towel loosely around his hips. The bruises he'd sustained from Zaden still marred his sides.

"Do you want me to sleep in another room?" he signed.

"Why?"

"Because of what I did. What you saw."

His words made Opal's ribs crush inward so hard she could hardly breathe. She got out of bed and walked to him. When she reached him, she touched his face.

"Reuger, you are my mate, and I love you. Nothing you do will change that or make me feel anything less for you than I do."

His eyes swam. *"But... there are things I've done. Things I was made to do..."*

She stepped into him and wrapped her arms around him. "I already know everything. You don't need to tell me, and you don't need to talk about it unless you want to. I love you," she said. "I love you. You are my mate."

A moment passed, and then Reuger grabbed onto her and held her against him. *"I don't deserve you."*

He rested his cheek on her head, breathing in deeply. Her ursa whined, wanting to comfort him.

"You are an honorable person who was used for

other people's greed and satisfaction. You deserve every beautiful thing in this world for the rest of your life, and if I can help, I will. You deserve much more than I can give you, and I will spend the rest of my life showing you that."

He kissed her head again. She led him to the bed and sat on it. He walked around to the other side. She stripped off her bloodied sweater and leggings and tossed them to the floor. Reuger dropped his towel and slid between the sheets. She scooted toward him, and he gathered her into his arms.

Reuger stroked her hair with infinite tenderness. His touch different. Not desperate protectiveness, but something deeper. Reuger's love, reclaimed along with his name and his past.

"Reuger," she whispered, the name natural on her lips. "I love your real name."

His breath hitched, and he kissed her temple. Tears streamed down his face again- but not tears of grief. Tears of gratitude, of wonder, of a man who had been given back his identity.

"I love you, Opal," he signed, his movements slow and reverent. *"My mate. My everything."*

Her ursa chuffed happily before lying down satisfied.

She smiled, her eyes drifting closed. "I love you, too, Reuger McConnell. All of you."

His arms settle around her with careful precision,

mindful of her injuries but unwilling to be separated from her. His warmth surrounded her like a cocoon.

Reuger watched Opal sleep, his mind reeling from the revelations of the past few hours. Memories continued to surface- his mother's laugh, his grandfather's patient teachings, the scents of his childhood home. But underneath the grief for what he'd lost, there was something else- hope.

He had a name. A history. And most importantly, he had Opal- and a future worth fighting for.

Outside, Seattle's lights twinkled in the darkness, but Reuger's attention focused entirely on the woman sleeping in his arms. Tomorrow would bring the long journey of healing from years of trauma.

But tonight, he was simply Reuger McConnell, holding the woman he loved, and finally free.

CHAPTER TWENTY-NINE

Opal awoke to Reuger kissing her face. She slid her hand over his skin, and he rolled to her, his hard body aligning with hers. Her ursa mewled, and Opal's skin heated as he ran his hand down her back and rested on her rear.

Sleepiness vanished in an instant, and she moaned. He kissed her, his mouth hot and needy.

She broke the kiss. "Are you okay?"

He shook his head. *"I need you. I need to be inside you. But I don't want to hurt you."*

"I'm fine," she said, though her side twinged. "I want you too."

Reuger rolled onto her, and Opal's body heated further. Ropes of muscle flexed as he lowered himself between her legs, his erection pressing against her. She arched. He cupped her face and his lips slammed into hers, his tongue probing and claiming her mouth.

Without waiting, he thrust inside her in long, slow strokes which stretched and filled her in the most delicious way. She moaned into his mouth. He withdrew from her and thrust inside her again. Her ursa whined, wanting more of him.

They found their rhythm, their bodies moving in sync. Reuger groaned, biting down on her bottom lip, making her open her eyes as he picked up the pace. Opal's nails dug into his rear in response, urging him onward. The bodies joined sensually in a frenzy of need and desire. Reuger's scent filled her, making it almost too thick to breathe.

"Bite me," Opal panted. "I need you to bite me."

Reuger's canines dropped into his mouth, and he bent in and pierced her neck with his fangs. Her fangs lengthened, and in an instant, she bit into his neck. Her ursa howled, and Reuger let out a primal growl as he emptied himself inside her, causing waves of ecstasy to ripple through Opal's body. Her fangs disengaged as she threw her head back and rode the waves of pleasure that crashed over her. Reuger thrust into her until he locked eyes with her. They both held their breath, and for a split heartbeat, she swore their animal spirits touched.

Opal had no words. The connection between them grew in a way she couldn't understand. From that moment forward, everything in her life would revolve around Reuger. Every moment, she would want him.

Every hour, she would need to see his face. And every night she would need him inside her.

He kissed her like she was the most delicate thing in the world. Then he lowered himself beside her and pulled her flush against him. She clung to him, afraid if she moved away, the feeling would fade.

"I can't explain in words how I feel."

"Me too."

"This is it, right? The mating bond?"

She kissed his chest. "Yes."

They lay for several minutes.

"I never thought I would feel this way about someone. I didn't know it was possible to be so connected."

She nodded. "Me neither."

"How am I going to work a job or do anything but want to be in bed making love to you?"

She laughed. "I don't know. Shifters do it all the time, though, so I guess we learn to live with it?"

"I'm not sure that will help. I am so sorry, Opal."

"Why?"

"Because you are going to be sick of me fast. I'm gonna be following you around like a lost pup forever."

"Not if I follow you first."

Opal crawled up Reuger's body. She fisted her hand in the hair at the base of his neck and claimed his mouth.

She reached between his legs and stroked him. He groaned as Opal straddled him and stroked him again.

She sat up, and he ran his hands down her body, pinching her nipples and making her gasp.

"I think we're both gonna have trouble holding down a job."

Reuger's chest rumbled, and she poised above him, looking into his eyes. She'd never seen a hotter male in her entire life. And he was all hers.

CHAPTER THIRTY

Three weeks later, the convoy of vehicles wound its way through Montana's mountain roads. Reuger sat in the back seat of Jeremiah's SUV, his hand clasped tightly in Opal's. Behind them, her parents drove in their truck, while Mary Reed sat in the front seat helping Jeremiah navigate.

The landscape shifted from highway to back roads, from civilization to wilderness. With each mile, Reuger's memories sharpened; the curve of a particular hillside, the way sunlight filtered through specific trees, a creek which ran alongside the road for a quarter mile before disappearing into the forest.

"We're close," he signed.

Opal squeezed his hand.

His wolf inhaled the scents of the familiar woods. He wanted out. He wanted to explore. In the previous three weeks, Reuger and Opal had run almost nightly around their cabin. They'd spent hours running, exploring, talking. Some nights, they talked about the future. Some nights, they talked about the past. But most nights, they talked about things they liked. Favorite movies, music, books, and the eternal debate about pineapple on pizza. It didn't matter to him what they talked about, as long as they were together.

They'd spend several nights swimming and splashing in the cold lake. And then many more warming each other by making love in the grass, in their bed, or his favorite, by the fire.

The turnoff appeared suddenly, a narrow dirt road barely visible through overgrown brush. Jeremiah slowed, navigating carefully around potholes and fallen branches. After ten minutes of careful driving, the trees opened onto a clearing.

Reuger's breath caught.

There, weathered but still standing, were the cabins. His family's compound. Five structures in various states of decay, their logs silvered with age and weather. Windows gaped dark and empty. Porches sagged. Nature had begun reclaiming what had been abandoned.

The vehicles came to a stop in front of his grand-parents' cabin. Silence settled over the clearing, broken only by wind rustling through pine branches and the distant call of an owl.

Reuger froze, unable to move. Fifteen years had

passed, but the memories crashed over him with such force he couldn't breathe.

"Reuger." Opal's voice anchored him. "Look at me."

He turned to her, his eyes swimming.

"You can do this," she said. "And you don't have to do it alone."

Jeremiah cleared his throat from the driver's seat. "We'll wait as long as you need. Or we can come back another day."

Reuger shook his head. He'd come this far. He needed to see it. Needed to face the nightmares haunting him for so long.

Reuger opened the door, his legs unsteady. Opal stood beside him, her hand finding his. Behind them, the others emerged from the vehicles but hung back, giving him space.

"Do you want us to wait while you go in?"

"No. Come with me."

Hand in hand, they walked toward the cabin. Each step surreal, like walking through a dream. The porch creaked under their weight, the wood pliable from rot in places. The door hung slightly ajar, its hinges rusted.

Reuger paused with his hand on the door handle, his heart hammering. This was it. The last place he'd seen his parents alive. The last place he'd been as a child.

His wolf whined and pawed at the ground.

Reuger pulled the door open. The hinges squealed, and he stopped inside the threshold. The furniture sat where he remembered it, arranged exactly as it had been. A couch faced a stone fireplace. A wooden table with four chairs sat in the kitchen area. Curtains, faded but intact, hung at the windows. Someone had cleaned. There was no dust, no debris, no signs of decay.

And the scent. Faint but unmistakable. His mother's perfume still lingered, as if she'd recently walked through the room.

His knees buckled.

Opal caught him, her arms encircled him as he shook with sobs. She held him, saying nothing, just being there as years of suppressed grief poured out of him. He'd thought he'd gotten over the trauma. Moved beyond the worst of the nightmare. But being back where his parents had taken their last breaths... everything crashed down around him.

His wolf yowled in anguish and whined. For the first time, he didn't beg to be let out. Instead, he sat alone, sadness and pain draping over him.

Minutes passed as he crouched on the floor trying to gather himself, and through it, Opal held him and pressed kisses to his head and said nothing. Didn't question. Didn't pull away. Didn't fidget. Simply stayed with him.

He didn't deserve her.

When he finally breathed again, he lifted his head. "*I'm sorry.*"

"Don't be." She kissed tears from his cheeks. "Take all the time you need."

He nodded, sucking in a shuddering breath. Then, with Opal's hand still in his, he moved deeper into the cabin.

He pointed to the couch. "*That's where my father sat in the evenings, playing his guitar. He'd play until I fell asleep.*"

He almost saw his father's broad shoulders, his scarred hands moving over the strings, humming melodies Reuger had long forgotten but somehow still remembered.

They stood and moved through the small space. Reuger paused at the kitchen table, his fingers trailing over the wood.

"*My mother would make breakfast here every morning. Pancakes shaped like animals.*" He smiled through his tears. "*I always wanted bears.*"

Opal laughed, and the sound eased something tight inside him.

He showed her the fireplace, where his grandfather had taught him to whittle. The window where his grandmother had taught him to grow herbs in small pots. The corner where he'd played with toys his uncles had carved from wood.

Each memory both a gift and a wound, precious and painful in equal measure.

He walked to the back of the cabin and turned left. His hand hovered over the knob before he twisted it, and it swung inward. A faded yellow patchwork quilt spread across the brass bed. Under the bed, a rag rug his grandmother and mother had made from strips of old clothing. A solid wooden dresser sat across from the bed, with a wooden carving of three wolves sitting on it.

He waited for his wolf to do something, make a noise, anything. But he didn't. He sat immovable, taking it all in.

Finally, Reuger turned toward a doorway opposite his parents' room. His old room.

His steps slowed as he approached, dread pooling inside. This was where it had happened. Where his mother died protecting him. Where he'd nearly died himself.

Opal's grip tightened, lending him strength.

He stepped through the doorway.

The small room fit a bunkbed, a small dresser, and a wooden chest. Like the rest of the cabin, it had been cleaned. No bloodstains marred the floor. No signs of violence remained.

He pointed to a spot near the dresser. *"That's where my mother... that's where she died. And I almost died right beside her."*

Opal pulled him close, her cheek resting against his shoulder. "I'm so sorry, Reuger."

He stood, staring at the floor that showed no

evidence of what had happened. Nothing to indicate the horror that had unfolded.

"It's so clean."

"Jeremiah had a service clean before we arrived. He thought it might be easier to remember them as they lived, not how they died."

Gratitude swelled in Reuger. Jeremiah had known what he needed before he did.

His gaze drifted across the room, taking in the small details. The bed with its faded quilt. The dresser with its crooked drawers. And there, sitting propped against the pillow-

His breath caught.

A stuffed animal. Small and brown, with button eyes and a stitched smile.

He crossed to the bed in three strides, reaching out with trembling hands. When his fingers closed around the faded fabric, another memory surfaced-his mother's smile as she'd given it to him on his fifth birthday.

"For my little wolf pup," she'd said. "To keep you safe when I'm not here."

He picked up the bear, holding it carefully. Despite the years, it was remarkably well preserved.

He turned to Opal, a genuine smile breaking through his tears. *"It's a bear."*

She moved to his side, looking at the stuffed animal. "It is."

"It looks like you. My mother gave me this bear, and years later, I found you. My bear."

Opal smiled, bright and warm. "We were always meant to be together."

He nodded, pulling her into his arms, the stuffed bear pressed between them. *"Always."*

They stood in the small bedroom, holding each other, surrounded by memories of the past and the promise of their future. Outside, through the window, Reuger spotted the others waiting. Opal's parents and the Reeds, the people who had become his new pack. His new family.

He had lost everything in the cabin. But he also found himself again. Found his name, his history, his identity.

And most importantly, Opal.

"Thank you," he signed when they finally pulled apart. *"For being here. For coming with me."*

"Where you go, I go."

He kissed her forehead and tucked the stuffed bear under his arm.

They walked back through the cabin, and Reuger looked at each room. When they stepped out onto the porch, the others looked over.

"You okay?" Jeremiah asked.

Reuger nodded. *"Thank you. For cleaning it. For bringing me here."*

Opal interpreted.

"You're pack," Jeremiah said. "This is what pack does. What family does."

Jeremiah pulled out a piece of paper and handed it to Reuger. Reuger scanned it, confused.

"Logan found the deed to the land. As the last surviving member of your family, this is all yours. The land, the cabins, all of it."

Reuger read the paper again. His land. Something of his own. Of his family's.

"Which cabin would you like us to use?" Mary asked.

Reuger pointed. *"That was my grandparents' home. You should stay there."*

Mary nodded and carried several bags of groceries and supplies inside.

"What about us?" Robert asked.

Reuger pointed to one of his uncles' cabins, and they carried their things that direction.

"And us?" Opal asked. "Where do you want to stay?"

Reuger pointed to his cabin.

"Are you sure?"

"Like you said. I want to remember happiness and the love, not the bad."

She smiled. "Okay."

He walked to the car, pulled out his duffel bag and Opal's, and headed back to his house.

Dawn came slowly, pale light spilling over the treetops. They'd spent the last few days hunting for breakfast, walking through the woods, making love, talking about the future while in their animal forms, sitting in the big cabin with the others, eating, and sharing stories. Some nights, they watched the stars and moon travel across the sky.

On the fifth day, after the fire had long burned down to a crimson glow, the last embers crackled softly. Opal curled against Reuger, her fingers tracing the scar at his throat in absent strokes. Outside, the forest was still except for the whistle of the wind through the trees.

Reuger's arm flexed around her, pulling her closer beneath the stack of quilts, staving off the coolness of the chilled air. His breath warmed her neck. The steady rhythm of his heartbeat lulled her into that safe place between sleep and waking. She smiled, thinking of how strange it was to finally be home in a world that had once terrified both of them.

"Do we leave today?"

"Only if you are ready."

He breathed in deep and kissed the top of her head. *"I think I am. For now."*

"I'll tell everyone as soon as the sun finishes coming up."

He nodded. *"Guess that means we have more time then."*

She smiled and rolled on top of his hard, naked body. "I guess it does."

OPAL STOOD ON THE PORCH, HUGGING HERSELF AGAINST THE chill. The cabins looked almost golden in the morning sun, smoke trailing gently from the last of the dying fire from the chimney in the main cabin. Reuger shut the front door behind her and slid his arms around her waist.

"Ready?"

He nodded into her shoulder, his hand brushing hers. Together they looked out over Reuger's land.

"We can come back whenever you want."

He nodded again.

They walked down the steps, the wood creaking. At the corner of the cabin, Reuger stopped.

Opal slid her hand into his. "This isn't goodbye," she promised. "Next time, we should bring Zaden and his sister Ophelia. I think they'd like it here, too. Especially Ophelia after what she's been through."

He smiled enough to crinkle the corners of his eyes. *"I'd like that."*

Zaden and Ophelia had arrived in Wolf River a few days after Reuger and Opal had returned. They were renting a house from Jeremiah, while Ophelia got therapy to overcome the persistent fear and nightmares left by Mo.

Opal and Satia both spent time taking turns with Ophelia, helping her through her trauma. She'd begun to show signs of improvement, but true healing was still a long way off.

Opal never asked her father or Stix what they ended up doing with Mo, but she hadn't needed to. Jeremiah never left liabilities alive. And as for the sheriff, the fact that he hadn't shown his face near Wolf River or her cabin said everything. Either he'd stopped looking, or Jeremiah had made him stop.

Opal and Reuger joined the others in the vehicles, and Jeremiah drove down the dirt road. Opal lay her head on Reuger's shoulder and slid her arms around his waist.

With the cabins behind them and Wolf River waiting, they rolled toward the future no longer running from their pasts.

Two survivors made whole by their fated mate.

ALPHA MARKED

LYCAN KING WARS

Rebekah R. Ganiere

CHAPTER ONE

RIVER

"Did you take your medicine?"

River rolled her eyes. Every month, Cherry asked the same question, and every month since she'd been twelve, the answer had been the same.

"River?" Cherry wouldn't be ignored.

River looked up from her bowl of cereal and stared at her mom. "You know, I'm twenty-one now. Do you need to keep making me feel like I'm five?"

Cherry set down her cup of coffee and leveled her gaze on River.

That gaze had stopped working on River long ago, but with everything they had going on, River didn't want to give her mom any more reason to freak out.

"Yes, Mom, I took it. You know I took it. I saw you

go through my trash, looking for the empty bottle. So you know I took one every day this month."

Like clockwork, Cherry emptied River's trash at the end of the first day of the month. And Cherry didn't take the bag to the pack burn pile. Cherry put that trash with the glass bottle in the back of the old Corolla and drove it into town to dispose of, away from the pack.

River wondered for the millionth time why the hell her medicine made Cherry such a freak. But ever since the first time at age twelve when River had thought she would die, River never again refused to take the medicine. She figured Cherry didn't want anyone to know about it because something was wrong with River. River didn't know what, but it made Cherry both fearful and ashamed.

Cherry had never once let River run with the pack at the full moon. She'd never even let River shift in front of anyone except for her and Bianca and Strider on a few occasions. Those times had been on Bianca's first few shifts. Cherry and Strider had packed the girls into the Corolla and driven them back to where Cherry and River had lived with River's dad before he'd died. The four ran together in the abandoned pack grounds, teaching River and Bianca everything they needed to know to survive as wolves.

River always knew something was different about her and her wolf. Pack members talk about their bonds with their wolves. They made them seem like an extension of themselves, whereas River only ever connected with her wolf when she'd run with Cherry and Strider. There'd never been fights for control. No wolf emerging at the height of strong emotions. No cravings. No needing. And most of all, no heats. As far as River could tell, she was damaged, and everyone knew it. It was the only explanation for why her mom never let her shift or run with anyone outside her family.

"Have you showered?" Cherry asked.

River shook her head.

"Do it. This is the annual meeting. Not only our pack will be there-"

"All the packs across the state will be there. Yes, Mom. I am aware. Bianca won't stop talking about it."

Mating runs happened every full moon. But once a year, all the packs in the state got together for a run. Hundreds of unmated shifters showed up. To River, it was the most depressing of all runs. Seeing so many shifters with looks ranging from hope to complete desperation put River on edge.

At age twenty-five, if a shifter hadn't found their mate, they were ejected from their packs to find their mate elsewhere. They were only allowed to return if they found a mate. Most never returned, however. Seriously, who would want to go back to live with people who had tossed you out in your most significant time of need? Packs were more than neighbors; they were supposed to be family. Losing the connection with their packs sent most unmated shifters into a complete tailspin. The loss of family, connection, support, and, most of all, comfort. She'd heard of more than one shifter taking their own life to end the pain. Worse yet were the ones who fell into drugs to dull the pain. Would that be her fate?

"We need to be at the mating run in two hours. Hurry and shower and change into something nice."

Nice. Not comfortable. Not easy to shift in. Nice. For five years, River had gone to the mating runs wearing something nice. Other females wore soft, easy-to-remove clothes meant for shifting out of. But not River. Never River. Why? Because River never found a mate. Hell, the males barely noticed her, not that she cared. There wasn't one of them who had ever caught her eye. Even the Alpha's son Zade. Every other female in the pack had vied for his attention, primping and preening whenever he came within eyesight, but not River. River couldn't care less about the cocky jock.

In high school, he'd been the all-American favorite. But to River, he'd been like everyone else. Sometimes, River pondered if she was asexual. But in the end, she didn't care. All she wanted was to work on her art and keep to herself.

"River, did you hear me?"

River slammed her spoon into her bowl. "Yes, Cherry. I heard you."

Cherry growled. She opened her mouth, closed it again, and slammed her coffee mug into the sink.

Maybe River cared more about finding a mate than she realized.

"Problem?" Strider entered the kitchen, his eyes darting between them.

Cherry snatched her leather coat and slung it over her shoulders. Strider kissed her head, but Cherry's gaze remained locked on River.

"Spray yourself before you come," she said. "Extra spray since there are other packs."

River fought the urge to roll her eyes and simply nodded.

Cherry kissed Strider and walked toward the door. "I gotta meet with the Alpha."

Strider nodded. "We'll see you there."

Cherry exited the house without another word, and Strider looked at River.

"She doesn't mean to be like that. You know how she gets at the mating runs. She has a lot of responsibility."

River poked her bowl of mushy cereal. "Why do I have to go? It's not like anyone is going to want me. No one new has moved into the pack since us. And I am sure there won't be anyone new, either. And if there are, they will either be way younger than me or a rogue."

Strider walked to her and hugged her shoulder. "It's tradition, sweetheart. As long as you are in the pack, it's required."

"Yeah, well, maybe I should move away."

Strider stiffened. "Don't say that."

River shrugged. "I found a school in New York City. An art school. They have an amazing program."

Strider stared at her for a long moment. "You've already made up your mind, haven't you?"

River looked into her stepfather's soft brown eyes and nodded. He was so like her father, but not at the same time. They were both kind and diplomatic, but where her dad had been loud and fun, Strider was quiet and content to let her mom lead in every way.

Strider blew out a breath. "Does your mother know?"

River snorted.

He touched her shoulder. "Let's talk about it tomorrow. For today, let's get through this."

"Okay."

A squeal sounded behind her, and River's younger stepsister, Bianca, jogged into the room.

"What do you think?" she asked River, twisting from side to side and showing off her new jogging suit. "Dad got it for me. Cute, right?"

Strider smiled affectionately, making her heart squeeze. Her dad used to look at her like that.

"Super cute." River hopped off her barstool, dumped out her cereal, and put the bowl in the dishwasher.

"Are you gonna get ready?" Bianca bounced with energy.

"Yup. Doing it now."

Bianca bounced from foot to foot. "Well, hurry up. I want to be early and check out the males."

River couldn't help but smile. "It's the same guys we've seen for the last million years."

Bianca gripped River's hands. "Maybe this will be my year. I'll see one of them, and it will be like seeing them for the first time, and our wolves will connect."

River hoped it happened for Bianca. The girl had been dreaming about her mate for as long as she could talk.

River put on a smile. "I hope this is your year, sis."

Bianca hugged River. "I'll wait for you."

River walked through the narrow hall to her room and opened the door. She scanned the room with walls plastered in various art pieces she'd cut from magazines, printed from the internet, and taken photos of on trips into New York City with her mom.

She would miss her little room when she moved away for school, but she couldn't hang around the pack and continue to let Strider and Cherry pay her way for the rest of their lives. Her dad may have been an Alpha, but that legacy and respect only went so far for a female wolf with no mate or purpose in the pack.

She stripped off her pajamas and tossed them to the floor before wrapping in a towel and heading for the shower. She wanted to get the day over with and tell her mom she was leaving to focus on her future.

River walked to the camp center with Strider and Bianca. Bianca chattered and bounced around more than usual with frenzied excitement. River bore it patiently, smiling and nodding but not listening. Nervousness about talking to her mom about art school tied her in knots.

All around, scents of all the newcomers permeated the air. Unmated males and females of age milled about, chatting and laughing nervously. Their pack wasn't the biggest in the northeast, not by a long shot, but there were still close to fifty pack members, and with all the others who had shown up, there had to be two hundred unmated shifters out there.

A handful of males and females prowled the edges of the meeting spot with wild eyes. The sight made River's heart squeeze. The rogues. Some looked desperate, while others appeared like they might snap and claim anyone without permission. Those were the ones River worried about most. Not for herself; she was her mother's daughter and handled herself with no problem. But for Bianca. As much as River loved her, Bianca could be an airhead, and if one of those rogues cornered her, there was no telling what would happen. Of course, one of those rogues would have to be insane to try and do something to Cherry's stepdaughter. Her mom would rip out their heart with her bare hands and eat it while it still beat.

A bark resounded through the air, and the group

quieted. Bianca kissed Strider and ran over to join the group of unmated.

Their Alpha jumped on one of the picnic benches, and everyone in attendance bowed. He reached down, took his mate's hand, and gently pulled her beside him. Their pack Luna, Kawli, was one of the gentlest women River had met. Never once had River seen her angry or raise her voice. She was the calm to their Alpha's storm.

"Welcome," he said. "Tonight is our annual mating gathering, and I welcome everyone who has traveled to be here. We will begin with the run, followed by a meal, and finally, the sealing of all new matings."

The shifters howled, and the air electrified it with anticipation. She knew from experience the scents of every unmated shifter would rise with each minute. Her mother and Strider had taught her and Bianca how to control their senses so as not to become overwhelmed by them. Their sense of smell, hearing, sight, and more. River knew when to block them out and when to use them. River perked up her hearing and eyesight but clamped down her sense of smell to keep her brain from fogging over with all the pheromones flying around.

River gazed into the sky. The sun would set in the next hour, and the matings would begin as soon as it did. No one knew precisely why the moon held so much sway over their wolves, but the lunar cycles had been tied to shifters for as long as there had been shifters. They purposely picked a non-full moon night to hold runs for that reason. Currently, the moon was in its waning gibbous phase. The full moon had passed a week ago, and while in the waning gibbous phase, shifters were as docile and reasonable as they would ever be.

"It's starting," Strider whispered.

River tore her eyes back to the group as they began shifting, and part of her hoped something would happen with her wolf. As much as she hated that part of herself, she couldn't help it. Every time, the same thing happened. She wished and hoped for something to happen with her wolf. For her to wake up. Howl. Demand to be let free. Something, anything. But nothing ever happened. Nothing. Not a shot. Not a tingle. Not a twinge. She peered at the moon again. Was she even an actual shifter? She would seriously question her biology if she didn't have her enhanced senses and hadn't run with her mom and Strider before.

"I'm gonna go help prep the food."

Strider caught her hand.

She stopped, knowing what would come next. It had been like this every time. The sadness in his eyes at the fact that she hadn't found a mate. That she hadn't felt a twitch or twinge of desire for anyone. Ever. That she would remain alone until the pack kicked her out.

"I'll pay for art school," Strider blurted.

River stared at him. Had she heard him right? "What?"

"I'll pay for it. Whatever it costs. You figure out a plan and give it to me, and I'll talk to your mom."

River's mouth fell open. She liked Strider, even loved him, but she'd always kept him at arm's length because letting him in would somehow be disloyal to her father. Though for the last decade, Strider had been there for every moment of her life.

"I... Strider-"

He pulled her in and hugged her. "There's more to life than a fated mate, River. And I want you to find what you want for yourself."

She didn't know what to say.

An Alpha howl shook the trees, and Strider let go of her. "I have to chaperone."

River nodded, unable to form words. As Strider shifted and jogged down to the group, River smiled and turned toward the food kitchen.

It was going to happen. She would go to art school. A warmth of joy spread through her body, and as much as she didn't want to get excited, she couldn't help the skip that made its way into her step as she went off to peel potatoes. And Strider was right. There was more to life than a fated mate. Her mom and dad had been fated mates, and it hadn't gone well.

River peeled fifty pounds of potatoes with an ancient metal peeler that made her grip ache. Mates of other pack members helped prep food for when everyone returned. They would stroll back, starving, sweating, and stinking of sex. And it would be her cue to duck out and head back to her house. She breathed the fresh air, knowing it would be one of the last she would get for days. The afterscents of mating runs clung to every leaf in the woods.

She briefly shut her eyes and envisioned herself running with the pack like a wolf. Her eyes locking with some handsome timber wolf and then the heart-bursting unity which came from finding her mate. They would move toward each other, unable to resist the pull. Their wolves would demand to be unleashed together before the unbridled sex started. What would that be like?

She opened her eyes and peered into the darkness beyond. A light breeze blew in through the window, and a fragrance slammed into her. River stopped peeling and stiffened. The scent of honey and amber surrounded her, and for the first time, her wolf lifted her head and whined.

River's potato plopped into the sink, and she backed away so quick she slipped and landed on the floor with a thud.

"River, are you okay?" asked her Luna.

"What is it?" asked another mate she didn't recognize.

The women stopped talking, and one of them shut

off the radio, making the kitchen eerily quiet except for the sounds of food cooking.

"Do you smell it?" one of the women asked.

"What are they doing here?" said another mate shakily.

"They weren't invited," another whispered.

"Screw invited," said a fourth woman. "They make the rules. They can go where they want."

"We need to get the Alpha," said the first.

River's heart beat louder, and her wolf stood. What the hell? The scent grew more potent, and one of the women yanked River away from the back door.

When had she walked to the back door?

River's wolf lurched forward, and River doubled over, pain ripping through her. She screamed and gripped the potato peeler so hard she thought it might jam through her hand.

"River? River, what's wrong?" asked someone in a faraway voice.

River panted, and pain ripped through her again.

"I... I think River is shifting," someone called.

A woman knelt next to River, and through bleary eyes, River barely made out her Luna, Kawli.

No. No. No. Her mom would kill her. She needed to get out of there. Needed to get away. They couldn't see her. Cherry would kill her if they saw her shift.

"Everyone in the pantry," Kawli yelled.

"River, come on." Kawli dragged her backward.

The ripple stopped, and River took a breath. "I need to go home."

"No time," said Kawli. "They are coming. You need to hide. You are unmated, River."

Who? Who's coming?

The fragrance grew more potent, and River's wolf shook her head. River experienced her wolf's confusion. A mix of recognition swirled with fear.

Fear? Great. Her wolf decided to wake up just to be afraid. *Lovely.*

The women hurried into the pantry, dragging River with them. As they began closing the door, the back door's handle turned, and the wood swung inward.

The women huddled in the corner behind heavy metal shelves, but River couldn't bring herself to. She looked from them to the door and back again. Why were they so scared? She practically saw their heads hung and tails secured between their legs. Even Kawli moved to join the other women.

Her gaze swung back to the door, and her wolf growled. A ripple tugged at her gut again, but River quashed it. There was something else, though... something her wolf couldn't quite place. That scent... honey and amber... so invading, so masculine, so...

Heavy footsteps prowled to the pantry door.

"Ron," one of the women whispered into her phone. The woman whined. "Ronny."

A growl sounded through the phone, followed by

yelling from the other end. Ron, one of the pack's Betas, let out an emergency danger howl that cut through the night outside.

What the hell was going on?

River's wolf scratched to be loose, but River refused to let the bitch take over. No way her wolf was emerging because of some male.

Something sharp dragged across the pantry door, and the handle turned. The door creaked open.

River's wolf paced back and forth, becoming more and more agitated. A second later, the door opened fully, flooding the dark room with light and silhouetting the largest male River had seen. In wolf form, he stood almost five feet tall. His dark fur held patches of red, and his yellow eyes remained alert and terrifying.

A rogue. It had to be a rogue. But she'd never seen one so enormous before. He sniffed before growling.

River's wolf snarled and paced.

Something wasn't right with him. He seemed... feral.

The wolf stepped forward, and River brandished the potato peeler she still gripped.

Awesome, what was she going to do? Peel him to death?

Haha. Maybe it'll make him more appealing. She fought a snicker. Why did she always laugh at the worst times?

She should have been scared of the newcomer but remained eerily calm for some reason. Her wolf, however, started going haywire, and for the first time, River needed to protect not only herself but also her wolf.

"Stay back," River ordered. "There are no unmated females in here." It was a lie, but hell, it was worth a try.

The wolf sniffed again and took a step forward. River slashed at him with the peeler.

"I said, stay away. Trust me, dude; you don't want to mess with any of us. My mom is the pack enforcer, and these women are all mates of the Alpha and Betas."

The air shimmered, and the man shifted to human form. He remained crouched on the floor for a moment and then lifted his head.

He was handsome. Damn handsome. Blond hair with dark eyes. Tanned skin from being outside. Heavy chiseled jaw and cheekbones. Dirt smeared his naked body. Even so, she made out clearly ripped muscles and a dozen or so scars.

"You aren't mated." He stepped forward and sniffed again.

"Doesn't mean I want you."

His odor surrounded her, mixing her wolf up even more.

The man smiled, revealing bright white teeth. "Doesn't matter. I want you, and you cannot refuse me."

Of course, she could refuse him. It was the law. He

may be the best-looking guy she'd seen since the Australian Firefighters calendar on her bedroom wall, but that did not mean she would fall at his feet.

"An escape mental patient? I mean, only an insane man would say I can't refuse you. I can refuse anyone the hell I want," she answered. "Also, you'd have to be insane to come here and corner a group of mated females. If you leave now, you'll make it to the borders of our lands before the rest of our pack chases you down."

He took another step forward. "I smell you, wolf. You can hide all you want behind desensitizers with shifters, but not with me. I'm Lycan and an Alpha's son. Lycans take what they want. And I want you."

The man covered the distance between them in one long stride.

She backed up as he pounced and wrapped his arms around her. The women behind her screamed as River fell to the floor, the man crouched over her. He pinned her to the ground with his tremendous weight.

His eyes flashed blue, then yellow, and finally black. "Mine. Omega."

For a split second, everything slowed as he took her in. Her wolf quieted, and they both watched emotions play all over his face. His eyes morphed back and forth between colors as if he couldn't decide what he wanted to be.

Omega? What did he mean Omega? She wasn't an Omega. She wasn't anything.

River opened her mouth to say something, but a sharp pain pierced her throat.

River blinked, frozen in place as her wolf roared to life.

Bitten. He'd bitten her. He'd marked her. The icy chill of violation rained down on her.

No. No. No. Her wolf howled and snarled and fought against the restraint that appeared like a long red rope and snagged one of her legs.

Bonding. He was trying to bond with her.

A commotion sounded behind them, and Cherry roared. River's wolf whimpered as the red rope snaked up her leg.

River. Help.

The sound of her wolf's voice made River jerk to life. Rage burst through River like an explosion, and she roared and unpinned her right hand. She jammed the peeler downward into the male's back. His teeth disengaged from her throat, and he howled in pain. Again, River stabbed him. And a third time, reaching for his neck. Blood spurted from the wounds and splashed her face and arms.

Angry hands yanked the male off her.

"You son of a bitch! I'm going to rip your teeth out!" Cherry screamed.

River lay dazed for a minute before Strider rushed in. "River. Sweetheart. Are you okay?"

She fought to speak as her wolf squirmed in the red rope, howling and crying.

Strider inspected her. "Are you hurt? Is the blood his or yours?"

She fought to make coherent sentences, unable to process as the screams of her wolf echoed in her head.

Strider shook her gently. "River! Did he bite you?"

His voice pierced her brain fog, and she lifted her hand to her throat. A gash tore through her throat, spurting blood as skin dangled to the side.

"Shit." He picked her up and carried her out of the pantry, laying her on the counter. The other pack leaders rushed in and yelled for their mates. The noise and commotion overwhelmed her as dozens of people entered the kitchen.

Cherry appeared at her side. "What happened?"

River tried to use the edge of her sundress to staunch the bleeding in her neck. She healed as quickly as the next wolf, but she'd need stitches anyway.

Strider looked at Cherry and then River. "He bit her."

Terror flashed across Cherry's face, and she focused on River. "Do you see her?" she demanded. "Your wolf. Do you see her?"

River couldn't do more than nod.

"Is there a rope? Is she tethered to a rope?"

River nodded again. "It's red," she managed.

Cherry roared and pulled a gun from her back pocket. "He bit her! He bit her against her will!" She ran to where no less than a dozen pack members restrained the now bleeding and feral-looking male. "I'm gonna blow your f-ing head off, you son of a bitch." Cherry cocked the hammer of her gun, but as it went off, their Alpha pushed the gun out of the way. The bullet missed the male by less than an inch.

Cherry whirled on the Alpha and pointed the gun straight in his face. The Alpha told Cherry to drop the weapon.

"He bit my daughter. He tried to claim her without consent. He deserves death."

The Alpha remained calm. "Yes. But that's not our place to decide."

Cherry glared at the male and back at their Alpha. "He's a rogue. No one will miss him. He dies for the violation of my daughter." Cherry raised the gun and pulled the trigger a second time, but this time, their Alpha moved so fast River barely saw the blur. The bullet struck the male in the shoulder, but Cherry flew across the kitchen and smacked the wall with a crack. Strider growled and rushed to her.

"Enough," the Alpha roared. A wave of Alpha aura shot through the room, making everyone drop to one knee. Everyone except for River and her mother. Not that River could have gotten to her knees unless she fell off the counter.

The Alpha stared hard at Cherry, and Cherry knelt next to Strider.

The Alpha turned his attention to River and sniffed

the air. His eyes narrowed, and he called to her. "River, come here."

She sat up shakily but didn't experience the pull to obey everyone else did. Expressions of confusion surrounded her, and a murmur and several small gasps sounded around her.

"River," the Alpha commanded.

She'd never felt the compulsion everyone else did. Her mom had always told her to pretend, but in light of what had happened and that their Alpha wasn't willing to kill the Lycan who had bitten her, she decided not to pretend any longer. Her wolf snarled and fought the red rope. She didn't like the Lycan being allowed to live any more than River or Cherry did.

River walked to the Alpha, and he peered into her eyes for the first time in her life.

River never knew why her mom had told her to stay away from the pack Alpha and his Betas, but she hadn't argued. She'd always figured it had to do with being unable to compel River with their commands, but now, looking into his eyes, there was more to it.

The Alpha inspected her and sniffed again. His eyes narrowed and went Alpha golden. What was he looking at?

She moved her shredded sundress to the side, exposing the bite, which had already stopped bleeding but remained open and raw.

"You have two choices," he said. "You can allow his marking to stand and go with him or reject him."

Cherry stood, but Strider pulled her back down and whispered to her.

River's wolf strained against the rope.

Not. Him. Hurt. Forced. Not. Him.

River fixed her eyes on the still handsome but bloodied male and then at her Alpha. "Not him," she repeated.

The Alpha nodded and ushered River forward until her knees connected with the male's.

"Tell him," said the Alpha. "Reject him. It's the only way to break the bond and free your wolf."

River's mouth dried as the crazed look faded from the male's face, and instead, fear replaced it as he blinked at her. His eyes went from black to a beautiful blue. Gone was the beast who had come into the pantry. Gone was the man who had bitten her. Replaced by the face of a terrified, desperate man.

No! He'd bitten her. He'd taken from her one of the only things wolves never took. *Agency.*

She swallowed hard, but her throat stuck together like she'd drunk super glue.

A Lycan Alpha had tried to mate her. He'd called her his. His Omega.

Terror flooded River, and her body shook. Everyone knew about the Lycans. The elder pure-bloods of her race. The original werewolves. Bigger. Faster. Filthy rich and utter killing machines. But

Lycans didn't live in the States; they lived in Canada and Europe. So, what was a Lycan doing there? And why was an Alpha Lycan a rogue?

"Tell him," her mom commanded. "Tell him you reject him, River."

River regarded her mom and then the male. His scent invaded her again- sweet and musky.

"I..." Why did an Alpha Lycan want her?

He roared and pulled against the men holding him, and his gaze connected with hers again, but this time, there wasn't anger, only pain.

"Don't," he pleaded. "Please."

Those two words crashed down around her like the emotion in his eyes, and she paused.

Her wolf howled. *Not. This. One.*

The pain and pleading in her wolf's voice spurred River into action.

She let her grip on her wolf slip, and her claws extended and swiped straight across his handsome face, slicing it open from ear to cheekbone. "Not. You."

Anger seared in her bright as the red rope tethering her wolf. The bite in her neck burned like ice.

"I reject you," she whispered.

His eyes went wide, and they both stopped breathing as the rope unwound from her wolf, leaving behind a patch of missing fur where it had first snaked around her leg.

He sucked in a breath before roaring and breaking

free from the men. He lunged at River, but she held out the peeler again.

"I said, I reject you!"

She had no idea where the strength had come from, nor the command in her voice, but somehow it made the male stop.

His eyes flashed, and emotions played all over his face for a moment. He reached for her but stopped. His expression changed to one of pain and utter loneliness.

"I'm sorry, Omega. I'm so sorry," he whispered before fleeing out the door.

River shook from adrenaline, and everything stood still before she fell to the floor. Her mother rushed to her and grabbed onto River. Strider followed suit, and the whole room of shifters stared at them.

Cherry released her. "Are you okay? Is your wolf okay?"

River nodded. "Mom? Why did he call me Omega?"

"Yes, Cherry," said the Alpha. "I think you better tell all of us."

Dear Reader,

Thank you for taking the time to read *FOUND Because of the Moon.* I love writing this series. It's been a lot of fun writing a series about shifters in real-world situations. I love Wolfe and Opal because they've both been through a lot, but still manage to find who they were meant to be with and to heal each other's wounds.

If you enjoyed the book, please take a moment to leave a review on your favorite retailer. Your reviews make all the difference to an author and the success of books.

Feel free to take a moment and email me and let me know what you liked about the book or who your favorite character was and why. I love hearing from readers. It makes writing so much more fun when I hear from my readers.

VampWereZombie@Gmail.com

To find out more about me and my Upcoming Releases, Please Join my Street Team for Swag and Freebies.

I also love connecting with readers! Stalk me everywhere!

I look forward to hearing from you!

Rebekah R. Ganiere - BOOKS WITH A BITE

USA Today Bestselling Author

Rebekah R. Ganiere

Dead Awakenings

Kissed by the Reaper

Fairelle Series

Red the Were Hunter - Book One

Yanti's Choice - Free Fairelle Short Story

Snow the Vampire Slayer - Book Two

Jamen's Yuletide Bride - Book Three

Zelle and the Tower - Book Four

Cinder the Fae - Book Five

Belle and the Beast - Book Six

Gerall's Festivus Bride - Book Seven

Jak the Giant Healer - Book Eight

Olivia and the Giant - Book Nine (2026)

Eric's Wayward Bride - Book Ten (Coming Soon)

Wolf River

PROMISED at the Moon

CURSED by the Moon

RECLAIMED from the Moon

TAMED under the Moon

UNLEASHED with the Moon

FATED despite the Moon

FOUND because of the Moon

ROCKED (2027)

The Society Series

Reign of the Vampires

Rise of the Fae

Vengeance of the Demons

Lycan King Wars

Alpha Marked

Alpha Claimed

Alpha Queen

Alpha King (2026)

Alpha Rogue (2026)

Tharnaxian Chronicles

The First

The Many (2027)

The Last (2027)

The Otherworlder Series

Kidnapped at Christmas

Vigilante at Valentine

Massacre at Mardi Gras

Hoodwinked at Halloween

Nightmare at New Year (2026)

Of Gods and Monsters

Thor's Feiry Mate

Loki's Warrior Mate (2026)

Fenrir Innocent Mate(2026)

Tyr Celestial Mate (2026)

Freya's Eternal Mates (2027)

Nocturne Bloodlines

Queen of the Night (2026)

Protector of the Night (2026)

Son of the Night (2027)

Immortal Monsters

Dracula's Bride

Frankenstein's Bride (Coming Soon)

Happy Holiday Romances

Rekindling Christmas

Christmas Lodge

NEWSLETTER

To claim your Two FREE Books and find out more about Rebekah R. Ganiere and her other Upcoming Releases
You can Go Here:
www.RebekahGaniere.com/Newsletter

www.ingramcontent.com/pod-product-compliance
Lightning Source LLC
LaVergne TN
LVHW010559100826
845148LV00014B/2771

9781633000957